BROKEN PRIDE

ALSO BY ERIN HUNTER

WARRIORS

EXPLORE THE WARRIORS WORLD

FIELD GUIDES

Secrets of the Clans
Cats of the Clans
Code of the Clans
Battles of the Clans
Enter the Clans
The Ultimate Guide

NOVELLAS

Hollyleaf's Story
Mistystar's Omen
Cloudstar's Journey
Tigerclaw's Fury
Leafpool's Wish
Dovewing's Silence
Mapleshade's Vengeance
Goosefeather's Curse
Ravenpaw's Farewell
Spottedleaf's Heart
Pinestar's Choice
Thunderstar's Echo

NOVELLA COLLECTIONS

The Untold Stories
Tales from the Clans
Shadows of the Clans
Legends of the Clans

MANGA

The Lost Warrior
Warrior's Refuge
Warrior's Return
The Rise of Scourge
Tigerstar and Sasha #1: Into the Woods
Tigerstar and Sasha #2: Escape from the Forest
Tigerstar and Sasha #3: Return to the Clans
Ravenpaw's Path #1: Shattered Peace
Ravenpaw's Path #2: A Clan in Need
Ravenpaw's Path #3: The Heart of a Warrior
SkyClan and the Stranger #1: The Rescue
SkyClan and the Stranger #2: Beyond the Code
SkyClan and the Stranger #3: After the Flood

SEEKERS

Book One: The Quest Begins
Book Two: Great Bear Lake
Book Three: Smoke Mountain
Book Four: The Last Wilderness
Book Five: Fire in the Sky
Book Six: Spirits in the Stars

RETURN TO THE WILD

Book One: Island of Shadows
Book Two: The Melting Sea
Book Three: River of Lost Bears
Book Four: Forest of Wolves
Book Five: The Burning Horizon
Book Six: The Longest Day

MANGA

Toklo's Story
Kallik's Adventure

SURVIVORS

THE GATHERING DARKNESS

NOVELLAS

BROKEN PRIDE

Peachtree

ERIN
HUNTER

HARPER
An Imprint of HarperCollinsPublishers

Special thanks to Gillian Philip

Bravelands: Broken Pride
Copyright © 2017 by Working Partners Limited
Series created by Working Partners Limited
Endpaper map art © 2017 by Virginia Allyn
Interior art © 2017 by Owen Richardson

Library of Congress Control Number: 2016963712
ISBN 978-0-06-264202-8 (trade bdg.) — ISBN 978-0-06-264203-5 (lib. bdg.)
Typography by Ellice M. Lee
17 18 19 20 21   CG/LSCH   10 9 8 7 6 5 4 3 2 1
❖
First Edition

BROKEN PRIDE

PROLOGUE

The dazzling plains seemed to stretch forever. Even Windrider, a vulture soaring high above the savannah, struggled to see where Bravelands reached its end.

Narrowing her ancient eyes, she let her gaze trail over the great yellow-grass sea, and pinpointed at last where it met the endless blue sky in a shimmering line of light. A wingtip twitched, and she banked, riding the warm air downward in a broad, graceful spiral.

Her flock followed her lead, calling out to one another in harsh, guttural voices, but Windrider was silent, scanning the savannah. Far below, herds of animals as small as ants moved across the land, following the paths beaten by countless generations. A gash in the land marked the muddy, trickling river; a horde of wildebeests was teeming into the gully and galloping up and over the sheer bank. Zebras and gazelles, grazing

1

together on the far side, glanced up incuriously at the wilde-beests' approach. Then they dipped their heads to graze again, ambling and milling peacefully.

A dark spot on the landscape caught Windrider's keen eye—a creature separate from the others, and not moving. She flew lower, adjusting her path with great beats of her broad wings.

"There, my flock. There."

The others followed her down, in swooping circles. "May Windrider's eyes be forever sharp," cried Blackwing, as the others took up the chorus of gratitude. "She has found us flesh once again."

It was just as Windrider had hoped: the corpse of a gazelle. Its old and tired spirit had gone; its eyes were blank and dead. Perhaps a cheetah had brought it down. It lay half hidden between ocher rocks, barely visible to wingless rot-eaters; and though its killer had fed, much of its torn flesh remained on its bones. The gazelle had enjoyed its time and its life; now it would nourish the vultures—just as they, in their turn, would one day become food for others. All was as it should be . . . or at least, so Windrider hoped.

"We must test the flesh, brothers and sisters," she called. "Then we can feed in peace."

Windrider tilted her head, banking sharply in to land, the other vultures flapping and clamoring behind her. Her claws touched the gritty ground, and she hopped a couple of paces toward the gazelle. With a glance to the birds on her right and left, Windrider nodded once.

"A bad death will linger with the fallen."

"May the Great Spirit always grant good death," chorused the rest of the flock.

Each vulture tore a thin strip of meat from the carcass's flank, gulping it down. They all paused, looking to Windrider for the final judgment. She closed her eyes briefly.

"The kill is clean," she reassured them at last. "Feed, my flock."

When the carcass was picked bare, its bones stripped of the last tattered remnants of flesh, Windrider stepped back. Beating her wings, she launched herself skyward once more. Every vulture, sated, followed her in a chaos of feathers and rasping cries. It felt good to return to the air, to soar higher and higher into the fierce blue, knowing that the flock had eaten well and survived for another day.

When she was high enough to catch a broad current of warm air, Windrider let it take her, twitching her wings, gazing down once more. From the shimmering horizon to the dark sprawling forests, to the low range of mountains far beyond the plains, she surveyed the land. Ahead lay a cluster of slender, flat-topped acacia trees; at their edge, just within their shade, shifting golden-yellow shapes were visible against the dry earth.

Lions, she thought, *lounging in the heat of the day.*

"They will not hunt, for now," remarked Blackwing, following her gaze.

"No, not until dusk," Windrider agreed.

Then they will feast. And we will follow.

Windrider had mixed feelings about the great prides of Bravelands. Lions meant food, unsullied and copious; like all the creatures of the land, they followed the Code, killing only to survive. But she loathed their arrogance. They were among the few creatures who would not follow the Great Mother, leader of all the animals, and give respect to her wisdom.

Two cubs were romping and play-fighting, full of energy and mischief even in the heat of the high white sun. As her shadow passed over the smaller of the two, he started and looked up. His golden eyes met hers, and he opened his small jaws.

She was still high above him, but the sound of a roar buffeted the air around her. With astonishment, Windrider felt her wings tremble, and she was momentarily rocked off her course.

"Windrider?" came Blackwing's concerned voice.

Glancing back, Windrider realized none of her flock had felt the impact of that roar.

No. It was not the little lion's voice. That is not possible!

"It is nothing," she told Blackwing curtly.

Half angry, half fascinated, she forced her wings to readjust, balancing her flight once more. *No grown lion's roar could reach the heights of the sky, let alone a tiny cub's. There is more here to know.*

Windrider tilted in the air, seeking out the little lion once again. He still stood there, stiff-legged and defiant, his golden gaze fixed upward. At last, his tail whisking with triumph, he turned away. The other cub followed him as he bounded back to his pride.

Lost in thought, Windrider veered east. What she had just seen—it was an omen, she was sure of it; though she could not imagine what its message might be. *A tiny cub, with a roar to make the sky shudder. This is a vision, a portent!*

She led her flock higher and farther into the clear blue sky, until the small pride of lions and even the huge herds of the savannah were lost in the beautiful vastness of Bravelands.

CHAPTER 1

Swiftcub pounced after the vulture's shadow, but it flitted away too quickly to follow. Breathing hard, he pranced back to his pride. *I saw that bird off our territory,* he thought, delighted. *No rot-eater's going to come near Gallantpride while I'm around!*

The pride needed him to defend it, Swiftcub thought, picking up his paws and strutting around his family. Why, right now they were all half asleep, dozing and basking in the shade of the acacia trees. The most energetic thing the other lions were doing was lifting their heads to groom their nearest neighbors, or their own paws. They had no *idea* of the threat Swiftcub had just banished.

I might be only a few moons old, but my father is the strongest, bravest lion in Bravelands. And I'm going to be just like him!

"Swiftcub!"

The gentle but commanding voice snapped him out of his

dreams of glory. He came to a halt, turning and flicking his ears at the regal lioness who stood over him.

"Mother," he said, shifting on his paws.

"Why are you shouting at vultures?" Swift scolded him fondly, licking at his ears. "They're nothing but scavengers. Come on, you and your sister can play later. Right now you're supposed to be practicing hunting. And if you're going to catch anything, you'll need to keep your eyes on the prey, not on the sky!"

"Sorry, Mother." Guiltily he padded after her as she led him through the dry grass, her tail swishing. The ground rose gently, and Swiftcub had to trot to keep up. The grasses tickled his nose, and he was so focused on trying not to sneeze, he almost bumped into his mother's haunches as she crouched.

"Oops," he growled.

Valor shot him a glare. His older sister was hunched a little to the left of their mother, fully focused on their hunting practice. Valor's sleek body was low to the ground, her muscles tense; as she moved one paw forward with the utmost caution, Swiftcub tried to copy her, though it was hard to keep up on his much shorter legs. One creeping pace, then two. Then another.

I'm being very quiet, just like Valor. I'm going to be a great hunter. He slunk up alongside his mother, who remained quite still.

"There, Swiftcub," she murmured. "Do you see the burrows?"

He did, now. Ahead of the three lions, the ground rose up even higher, into a bare, sandy mound dotted with small shadowy holes. As Swiftcub watched, a small nose and whiskers poked out, testing the air. The meerkat emerged completely, stood up on its hind legs, and stared around. Satisfied, it stuck out a pink tongue and began to groom its chest, as more meerkats appeared beyond it. Growing in confidence, they scurried farther away from their burrows.

"Careful now," rumbled Swift. "They're very quick. Go!"

Swiftcub sprang forward, his little paws bounding over the ground. Still, he wasn't fast enough to outpace Valor, who was far ahead of him already. A stab of disappointment spoiled his excitement, and suddenly it was even harder to run fast, but he ran grimly after his sister.

The startled meerkats were already doubling back into their holes. Stubby tails flicked and vanished; the bigger leader, his round dark eyes glaring at the oncoming lions, was last to twist and dash underground. Valor's jaws snapped at his tail, just missing.

"Sky and stone!" the bigger cub swore, coming to a halt in a cloud of dust. She shook her head furiously and licked her jaws. "I nearly had it!"

A rumble of laughter made Swiftcub turn. His father, Gallant, stood watching them. Swiftcub couldn't help but feel the usual twinge of awe mixed in with his delight. Black-maned and huge, his sleek fur glowing golden in the sun, Gallant would have been intimidating if Swiftcub hadn't known and loved him so well. Swift rose to her paws and greeted the great lion affectionately, rubbing his maned neck with her head.

"It was a good attempt, Valor," Gallant reassured his

daughter. "What Swift said is true: meerkats are *very* hard to catch. You were so close—one day you'll be as fine a hunter as your mother." He nuzzled Swift and licked her neck.

"*I* wasn't anywhere near it," grumbled Swiftcub. "I'll never be as fast as Valor."

"Oh, you will," said Gallant. "Don't forget, Valor's a whole year older than you, my son. You're getting bigger and faster every day. Be patient!" He stepped closer, leaning in so his great tawny muzzle brushed Swiftcub's own. "That's the secret to stalking, too. Learn patience, and one day you will be a *very* fine hunter."

"I hope so," said Swiftcub meekly.

Gallant nuzzled him. "Don't doubt yourself, my cub. You're going to be a great lion and the best kind of leader: one who keeps his own pride safe and content, but puts fear into the heart of his strongest enemy!"

That does sound good! Feeling much better, Swiftcub nodded. Gallant nipped affectionately at the tufty fur on top of his head and padded toward Valor.

Swiftcub watched him proudly. *He's right, of course. Father knows everything! And I will be a great hunter, I will. And a brave, strong leader—*

A tiny movement caught his eye, a scuttling shadow in his father's path.

A scorpion!

Barely pausing to think, Swiftcub sprang, bowling between his father's paws and almost tripping him. He skidded to a halt right in front of Gallant, snarling at the small sand-yellow scorpion. It paused, curling up its barbed tail and raising its pincers in threat.

"No, Swiftcub!" cried his father.

Swiftcub swiped his paw sideways at the creature, catching its plated shell and sending it flying into the long grass.

All four lions watched the grass, holding their breath, waiting for a furious scorpion to reemerge. But there was no stir of movement. It must have fled. Swiftcub sat back, his heart suddenly banging against his ribs.

"Skies above!" Gallant laughed. Valor gaped, and Swift dragged her cub into her paws and began to lick him roughly.

"Mother . . ." he protested.

"Honestly, Swiftcub!" she scolded him as her tongue swept across his face. "Your father might have gotten a nasty sting from that creature—but *you* could have been killed!"

"You're such an idiot, little brother," sighed Valor, but there was admiration in her eyes.

Gallant and Swift exchanged proud looks. "Swift," growled Gallant, "I do believe the time has come to give our cub his true name."

Swift nodded, her eyes shining. "Now that we know what kind of lion he is, I think you're right."

Gallant turned toward the acacia trees, his tail lashing, and gave a resounding roar.

It always amazed Swiftcub that the pride could be lying half asleep one moment and alert the very next. Almost before Gallant had finished roaring his summons, there was a rustle of grass, a crunch of paws on dry earth, and the rest of Gallantpride appeared, ears pricked and eyes bright with curiosity. Gallant huffed in greeting, and the twenty lionesses and young lions of his pride spread out in a circle around him, watching and listening intently.

Gallant looked down again at Swiftcub, who blinked and glanced away, suddenly rather shy. "Crouch down," murmured the great lion.

When he obeyed, Swiftcub felt his father's huge paw rest on his head.

"Henceforth," declared Gallant, "this cub of mine will no longer be known as Swiftcub. He faced a dangerous foe without hesitation and protected his pride. His name, now and forever, is Fearless Gallantpride."

It was done so quickly, Swiftcub felt dizzy with astonishment. *I have my name! I'm Fearless. Fearless Gallantpride!*

All around him, his whole family echoed his name, roaring their approval. Their deep cries resonated across the grasslands.

"Fearless Gallantpride!"

"Welcome, Fearless, son of Gallant!"

His heart swelled inside him. Suddenly, he knew what it was to be a full member of the pride. He had to half close his eyes and flatten his ears, he felt so buffeted by their roars of approval.

"I'll—I promise I'll live up to my name!" he managed to growl. It came out a little squeakier than he'd intended, but no lion laughed at him. They bellowed their delight even more.

"Of course you will," murmured Swift. Both she and his

father nuzzled and butted his head. "You already have, after all!"

"You certainly—" Gallant fell suddenly silent. Fearless glanced up at his father, expecting him to finish, but the great lion was standing still, his head turned toward the west. A light breeze rippled his dark mane. His nostrils flared.

The pride continued to roar, but with a new strange undertone. Fearless wrinkled his muzzle and tried to work out what was different. He began to hear it: there were new voices. In the distance, other lions were roaring.

One by one, the Gallantpride lions fell silent, looking toward the sound. Gallant paced through them, sniffing at the wind, and his pride turned to accompany him. Swift walked closest to his flank.

Overcome with curiosity, Fearless sprang toward the meerkat hill, running to its top and staring out across the plain. His view was blurred by the haze of afternoon heat, but he could see three lions approaching.

They're not from our pride, thought Fearless with a thrill of nerves. He could not take his eyes off the strangers, but he was aware that other lions had joined him at the top of the slope: Gallant, Swift, and Valor. The rest of the pride was behind them, all quite still and alert. Swift's hackles rose. Gallant's whole body looked taut, his muscles coiled.

"Who are they?" asked Fearless, gaping at the three strange lions.

"That is Titan," replied his mother. "The biggest one, there, in the center. Do you see him? He's the cub of a lion your father once drove away, and he's always hated Gallant for that. Titan's grown a fine mane, I see." Her voice became a low, savage growl. "But he was always a brute."

The three lions drew closer; they paced on, relaxed but steady, toward Gallantpride. Fearless could make out the leader clearly now: he was a huge, powerful lion, his black mane magnificent. As he came nearer, Fearless found himself shuddering. His mother was right—there was a cold light of cruelty in Titan's dark eyes. His companions looked mighty and aggressive, too; the first had shoulders as broad as a wildebeest's, while the other had a ragged ear, half of it torn away.

"Why are they in our territory?" asked Fearless in a trembling voice. He didn't yet know whether to be furious or very afraid.

Gallant spoke at last. "There's only one reason Titan would show his face here," he rumbled. "He wants to challenge me for leadership of this pride."

"*What?*" Fearless stared at his father.

"Come." Gallant turned and began to pad back down the meerkat hill.

Fearless followed with the rest, staying close to his sister's flank. "Valor, what does Father mean?" he growled. "Titan can't do that, can he? He can't just take over Gallantpride. It's not possible!"

For a moment Valor said nothing; Fearless did not like the tension in her face. "I've heard of such things," she said at last, grimly. "It happened to Fiercepride, from beyond the forest. Fierce had been leader for ages, Mother told me, but he was challenged and defeated by a lion called Strong who'd recently grown his mane. And his family became Strongpride, and his pride had to live under Strong's rule. Fierce was forced to leave and live alone, and hunt by himself."

"That's horrible," breathed Fearless.

"Worse than that, Strong was a terrible leader. He was cruel and unfair and stupid; the pride fell apart in the end. He killed the cubs. Other lions died too."

Fearless gaped at his sister. "But that won't happen to Gallantpride," he insisted. "No lion can beat Father. He's the bravest fighter and the strongest lion in Bravelands!"

Valor didn't reply. Fearless looked around at the other lions of their pride, and a wave of cold rippled along his spine. None of them looked as confident as he'd hoped; they seemed nervous and edgy, as if an army of ants were marching across their paws.

Gallant was walking out onto the grassland now, toward Titan. When they were almost close enough to touch muzzles, both lions halted and stared into each other's eyes.

Titan was even more frightening up close, thought Fearless. His shoulders were broad and thickly muscled, and his paws were huge. There were deep, roughly healed scars drawn into his face and flanks, and when he opened his jaws to speak, his fangs were long, yellow, and deadly.

"Gallant of Gallantpride," he snarled in greeting.

"Titan, Prideless Lion," growled Gallant. "What is your business here?"

Titan drew himself up, his black mane rippling over his powerful neck and shoulders. He slapped the ground with a massive paw.

"By the laws of our ancestors," he roared, "I, Titan, come to claim this pride of Gallant."

Gallant's muzzle curled back from his own long, deadly fangs.

"By the laws of our ancestors," he snarled, "I, Gallant, fight to keep this pride."

For a long moment they stared at each other, the air seeming to quiver with anticipation. Both huge males half crouched, their muscles coiled.

Then, as one, they launched their attacks, colliding with a terrible grunting roar and an impact that shook the ground. Rearing up, Gallant sank his claws into Titan's shoulders; twisting, Titan shook his huge mane, gripped Gallant's flank with his claws, and raked his flesh in return. They broke apart, only to slam together once more, jaws wide and claws tearing.

Fearless could hardly bear to watch, but neither could he look away. His heart was in his throat. Now that they were gripped in close combat, and he could see them together, the two lions looked equally matched.

The pride stood watching, their tails lashing with anxiety—all except Swift, who was pacing back and forth on the edge of the fight. She was the only one who was silent; the others roared their encouragement to Gallant, and snarled in contempt whenever Titan landed a good blow. But Swift said nothing, only paced and looked afraid.

"Mother," pleaded Fearless, unable to watch her fretting anymore, "why don't we help Father? Together we can beat Titan, can't we? There's more of us!"

"We can't," said Swift, her voice choked with anxiety. "I'm sorry, my son. Those are the rules. The pride leader must win this fight alone."

There was a roar from the pride. Gallant had doubled abruptly and sprung for Titan, landing a mighty blow on the side of his skull. Titan reeled back, stumbled, then fell hard on his flank; Gallant pounced, slamming both his forepaws onto his fallen enemy.

"He's won!" shouted Fearless in excitement, as the pride roared its approval.

"Yes," cried Swift. "It looks like—" Then she gasped.

Titan's sidekicks, the two lions who had arrived with him, sprang suddenly forward, attacking Gallant from both flanks. They hung on him, claws digging in, dragging him down and away from Titan.

"Stop! No!" roared Swift, and the pride joined in her protest. "Cheats! Traitors—"

She leaped forward, but Titan was already back on his feet. He lunged, as fast as a snake, and sank his jaws into Gallant's exposed throat. Fearless saw his father stagger back, off balance, the two lions still fastened with their claws to his sides.

Swift and two other lionesses flew at Titan, but his companions released Gallant and turned on them, snarling and biting, holding them off. Swift gave panicked, roaring cries as she tried desperately to fight her way to Gallant, but the two big males were too strong.

As the rest of Gallant's pride joined the attack, the interlopers finally backed off, teeth bared and eyes defiant. With a crash and a grunting exhalation, Gallant collapsed to the earth, and every lion froze and stared. Titan stood over his fallen foe, his jaws still locked on Gallant's throat.

Fearless felt as if a cold night wind had swept through his body. Titan was not merely holding his father down. His fangs were buried in Gallant's flesh, and bright red blood was pooling under his great black mane. Gallant's paws, sprawled helplessly on the ground, twitched in a horrible spasm.

Swift gave a screaming roar. *"No!"*

"What— Mother, what—" Fearless's words dried in his throat, and he gulped hard. He had never seen a lion die, but he had encountered plenty of dead antelopes and zebras. That was how his father looked now: limp, blank-eyed, his lifeblood spilling into the dusty earth.

Father can't be dead! He is Gallant of Gallantpride!

The lions stood motionless, glaring at one another over Gallant's body. An awful silence hung over them. Fearless closed his eyes, desperately hoping it would all go away. But when he opened them again, his father was still lying on the ground.

A hawk screeched. Swift glanced up at it, then her face twisted in rage and grief and she stalked forward, snarling at Titan.

"You broke the rules, Titan Prideless! Worse, you broke the

Code! You may kill only to survive!"

Titan sneered. "What do I care for the Code? This pride is now *mine*—Swift Titanpride!"

With a roar, Swift leaped forward. Titan, shocked for a moment, staggered back, and the rest of Gallant's pride joined the attack. Fearless gaped, horrified, as great tawny bodies clashed, jaws snapped, and claws tore.

But Titan was fighting back hard, and so were his two side-kicks.

"Kill them!" bellowed Titan above the chaos. "Kill the ones who resist! Titanpride will not allow rebels!"

Fearless hopped and bounced frantically, trying to see a way into the fighting. But the lions looked so big, and so terrifying. He might be crushed by one of his own pride before he could even reach Titan. At least Valor was at his side. . . .

Titan flung off a young lioness and shook his huge mane. His head turned, and his dark eyes locked with Fearless's.

"The cubs!" he grunted, his face full of vengeful malevolence. "Kill the cubs, Cunning! Gallant's heirs must not live!"

The lion with the torn ear wrenched himself out of the battle. He paused for a moment, seeking out the cubs. Then his cruel eyes lit on Fearless.

He sprang.

For an instant Fearless thought he was already dead. His heart froze in his rib cage and he could only watch the huge lion flying at him. But a golden body slammed into Cunning, knocking him off his feet. It was Swift.

"Fearless! Valor!" their mother gasped. *"Run!"*

Fearless was still rigid with shock. What did she mean? *Run where?*

Valor nipped his rump hard. "Go, go!"

He scrabbled around, half stumbled, then forced his paws to move. He ran, lengthening his stride, but the savannah was so broad, so open and flat; there was nowhere to hide, and the dust stung his throat and blurred his vision. He could hear Valor right behind him, panting with terror.

Fearless's breath burned in his chest. He hadn't known he could run this hard. *Even Valor isn't catching up.* Terror drove him on, faster and faster across the dry red earth. *Even Valor—*

With a gasp he twisted and looked over his shoulder. And he realized why Valor wasn't with him: Titan's other companion had intercepted her, driving her back, roaring and swiping with his claws.

"Valor! Hold on!" Fearless squealed. He skidded to a halt and turned, ready to rush and save her.

"No!" she roared. She ducked another lash of her attacker's claws. "No, Fearless, run! I can take care of—" She dodged, stumbling. "*I can take care of myself! We all* have to!"

The one called Cunning appeared a few paces away, his mouth red with blood. Fearless's knees almost gave out beneath him. *Whose blood? Mother's?*

"Run, Fearless!" cried Valor.

Fearless spun around and fled. He did not know if the sound of great pounding paws behind him was a pursuer, or the echo of his own panicked running, or just his imagination; he could only keep racing on, until his paws were stinging with pain and his chest ached. A lizard darted out of his way and a flock of bright blue starlings scattered with shrill cries, but he didn't even pause. He sprinted on, desperate with terror, his eyes streaming from the dust so he could barely see where he was going.

And then, abruptly, his paws slid from under him. The ground sloped and rocks tumbled away, and he skidded helplessly. Tumbling head over tail, he crashed down, clutching frantically for a pawhold. The last thing he saw was the bright blue sky, somehow in the wrong place and at the wrong angle.

Then he was spinning in the air. A hard sudden impact, and one dazzling flash of light, and Fearless's world turned black.

CHAPTER 2

Fearless blinked. The light was too bright, and his head hurt. There was something odd about the sunlight; it flickered and dipped and sparkled. For a moment he dared to hope it had all been a dream—that he was lying under the flat branches of the acacia trees with his mother and Valor and . . .

No. He gasped and opened his eyes fully, wincing with pain. He was lying not on grass, but on a rough tangle of twigs and sticks and green leaves. And of course, there was no Swift and no Valor. No Gallantpride.

I'm alone.

A great wrench of grief twisted his stomach. *And Father is dead.*

Strange smells drifted into his nostrils. Sniffing at them helped take his mind off his misery. Fearless frowned and looked around; there was one scent he recognized. *Feathers.*

He remembered it from the time Valor caught a stork, pretty much by accident.

The instant of happy memory was drowned at once. *Valor's gone*, he remembered again. *Father's dead, and she and Mother probably are, too.* His chest heaved with grief. He tried to sit up, though every part of him ached. The twigs beneath him held steady: they appeared to be tangled together with deliberate care. *It's not just a pile of forest litter*, he thought. Something had made the twigs into a broad, secure circle.

Panic rose in his throat. *I'm in a nest*, he realized. *A really, really big nest . . .*

And the nest was in a colossal jackalberry tree. Through the leathery green leaves he could see gray branches spreading out, and, peering over the edge, the solid earth below looked hazy with distance. Heart thundering, he shuffled back from the edge of the nest and whimpered in terror. *How did I get up here?*

Not by myself. I can't do anything by myself. His grief was suddenly overwhelmed by terrible shame. *I'd just been given my name: Fearless. I swore to Father I'd live up to it. And what did I do? I ran away at the first sign of trouble.*

He had to do better, try harder. Hesitantly, Fearless got to his paws, being careful not to disturb the nest. It looked sturdy, but he didn't want to dislodge anything; the whole thing might collapse and send him plummeting down. As he stretched his aching muscles, his flanks stung, and he peered at them, shocked. There were deep puncture marks, crusted with dried blood. Fearless gave a small mewl of distress.

He gritted his jaws. *Mother isn't here. I have to help myself, like Valor said.*

Licking at the wounds, he made himself think. It was obvious, now, what had happened: a bird had brought him up here. It must have seen him lying where he fell. Swift had told him all about birds, and how some of them ate flesh or rot-meat: vultures, eagles, hawks. Whatever it was, it must have been huge. Maybe it was that vulture he'd seen and roared at. Fearless shuddered. *And it might come back any moment....*

I have to get down from here!

Fearless swallowed hard and crept back to the edge of the nest. Oh, it was a *very* tall tree. He could see the green crowns of surrounding trees, so he was high above even them. The mountains far in the distance had never been much more than a thin blue haze, but now he could clearly make out farther peaks beyond; there were grooves and gullies in the savannah that he hadn't noticed before, and he could see whole herds of grass-eaters, tiny and distant.

There was no way he could jump. He'd have to climb down backward, clinging on to the branches and the trunk with his claws. *I might fall to my death.*

It seemed a terrifying prospect, but what choice did he have? *Something built this nest. Something big, with sharp claws.*

If I don't try to climb down, I'm going to get eaten instead. Another whimper of terror escaped from Fearless's dry throat.

The nest had been built over a couple of thick branches; Fearless clambered over the edge and onto one of them. Just one paw at a time, he decided. *And don't panic.*

Crouching low, he pulled himself along the branch. The nest was not far from the enormous, thick trunk. He narrowed his eyes. *Come on, Fearless. Live up to your name!*

He reached out a paw, dug in his claws, and dragged himself a little farther. His heart thudding, he stretched out his other paw and did it again.

Not far now. He looked down.

Ohhhh . . . that was a mistake. The ground seemed farther away than ever, now that he was outside the relative safety of the nest, and his head swam. *The trunk, the trunk, I just have to get to the—*

He lurched forward, too fast, snatching with his claws at the branch. He missed and flailed even more wildly, trying to keep his balance. But his body shifted sideways, and Fearless felt himself slipping around the branch.

There was another, thinner bough, just below him and to the left. Panicking, he let himself slip and grabbed for it. His claws sank into the bark. He was dangling by his forepaws, his hind legs swinging in the air, but his grip was good, and he gave a shuddering cry of relief.

At that moment, the thinner branch creaked and gave a little.

No, no, no . . . .

It snapped.

Fearless tumbled down through the branches. He snatched hopelessly with his claws, but couldn't catch another hold. His rump thudded against a branch and he squealed, but it didn't matter, because he was still falling, faster now, and in a moment he would hit the ground hard and—

Something seized his scruff, yanking him up short and halting his fall so abruptly the breath was knocked out of him.

For long moments, he could only dangle there helplessly, panting in high-pitched, whistling breaths. Wide-eyed, he stared through the branches and leaves at the yellow earth, still far below. The thing that had caught him must have long toes with claws—he could feel them snagged in his fur—but he was unable to twist his head to see more. Only when he was lifted and dumped on a branch did he get a glimpse of the creature.

It dusted its slender brown paws together, tilted its head, and studied him.

Fearless stared back. He had never seen anything like it. It sat perfectly comfortably on the bough in front of him, peering at him with dark amber eyes fringed with brown fuzzy fur. Its snout was long and black, a thin white scar slashed above the nostrils, and when it grinned at him, Fearless could see long yellow fangs.

He didn't know what it was, but those teeth made it look very much like a flesh-eater. He backed onto his rump and lashed out at the thing with his claws.

He wobbled on the branch again and had to grab it with his forepaws. The creature tilted its head the other way.

"I wouldn't move too much if I were you," it said.

Fearless, panting and trembling, sat very still again.

"That's better," said his rescuer. "Shall we introduce ourselves? My name is Stinger." Whatever this creature was, it didn't seem about to eat him. If anything, there was a sparkle of humor in its eyes.

Though I can't see anything to smile about.

"Can you speak?" said the stranger. "This will be tricky if you can't."

"I'm Fearless," Fearless growled, with as much ferocity as he could manage.

"Fearless, eh?" The creature yelped with amusement. "I should say you are. Do you know who made that nest? I don't know many animals who would go visiting one of the biggest eagles in Bravelands."

"I wasn't visiting it, I—" Fearless stopped short when he saw the humor in the animal's expression. *Oh. He's joking.* He licked his jaws nervously. "What are *you*?"

"I'm a baboon, *obviously*." Stinger shook his head and tutted. "Why, what are *you*?" he mimicked.

"I'm a . . . a lion. I'm Fearless Gallantpride!"

He'd heard of baboons before. Flesh-eaters, sometimes. This one wasn't all that scary, though.

"Oh, you're a *lion*." Stinger grinned, and Fearless realized he was mocking him again. "Well, I've never seen a lion being carried away by an eagle before, so I came to investigate. And aren't you lucky I did!"

Fearless swallowed. He glanced down and back up at Stinger. The baboon seemed friendly enough, even though his teeth did look nasty. "I guess so," he muttered. "Thanks."

"That's better." Stinger sat up and held out his elegant paw. "Now, let's get you down from here."

"I'm not sure I—ow!"

Stinger was quicker than he looked. In an instant, he had Fearless tucked under his long foreleg and was swinging elegantly down through the branches, springing with ease to the most secure footholds. Fearless barely had time to be scared. In fact, he barely had time to draw a breath. When the branches ended and Stinger began to climb down the last long section of trunk, Fearless could see that he hadn't come alone: a big crowd of baboons was gathered at the base of the tree, and they were all staring up with curiosity.

The light beneath the trees was all green shadows, and the foliage grew dense and verdant, but everywhere Fearless looked he could see more baboons—they were perched on mossy branches, crouched on damp rocks, peering out from fern clumps, or simply staring at him from out in the open. The sheer numbers, combined with the strange, rich scents of the forest, made his head reel. Stinger's pride—or whatever baboons called their groups—was much bigger than Gallant's.

There must have been fifty baboons there, some even bigger than Stinger, some much smaller. All of them had the same long, clever paws, powerful forelegs, and vicious-looking fangs. When Stinger reached the bottom and set down Fearless in the middle of them, he decided the best thing he could do was stand very still, try to look tall, and let them stare.

I just hope I haven't escaped being eagle-food only to become baboon-food.

"Wow," said one of the baboons, stalking curiously forward. "It really is a lion cub."

"Indeed it is," said Stinger proudly. "And not just any lion cub, he'll have you know. This one calls itself *Fearless Gallantpride.*"

"Gallantpride, eh?" A small female baboon, clasping a baby to her chest, walked a circle around Fearless, examining him from nose to tail-tip. "So where is this pride of yours, youngster?"

Fearless flinched. "Titan stole my pride," he growled. "And I'm going to take it back!"

A terrible, earsplitting howl erupted from the baboons. Fearless took a startled pace back, but he realized after a moment that they weren't threatening him. It was worse than that: they were laughing.

The female slapped the ground, hooting with hilarity as the others whooped. "Titan must have been a terribly big lion to be able to steal *your* pride."

"Now, Mango, don't tease," said Stinger, but he was grinning.

Fearless hunched his shoulders, glowering and blinking. "It was my father's pride. My father, Gallant. Titan killed him and stole his pride."

The baboons' laughter faded into gasps and hiccupping coughs. Mango scratched her tail, looking a little remorseful. "Oh. You poor cub."

"I *will* get my father's pride back," Fearless growled. "I *will* beat Titan."

Stinger tapped his back with a paw. "I'm sure you will, Fearless Gallantpride, but not yet. All in good time, eh? For now, you'll have to stay with us. We're the Brightforest Troop, and we're very hospitable." He grinned, an unnerving sight given the size of his teeth, and gestured to the sky. "The Great Spirit sent you, that's what I think." He raised his head to include his fellow baboons: "This youngster fell from the sky! He's Fearless, Cub of the Stars, and he'll bring good fortune to the Brightforest Troop."

They all looked at one another. One baboon wrinkled his snout. "I don't know. What does the Starleaf say?"

Fearless snuffed in a breath, uneasy. He didn't know what a Starleaf was, but the baboon's voice had been filled with respect and anticipation. *This must be important, I guess.*

The crowd was parting, and through the gap walked a stately-looking baboon with a serious face, the fur on her forehead streaked with white. She stopped right in front of Fearless, but instead of looking him up and down as the others had, she gazed directly into his eyes. Her amber stare was so intense he felt dizzy, and his tail twitched with anxiety. The chatter of the other baboons died away, and Fearless could sense their anticipation as they waited for the Starleaf to speak.

At last she dropped her gaze from Fearless. She raised her forepaw, uncurling the long toes to reveal a small pale stone. She lifted it skyward, and as the stone caught the mottled light slanting through the trees, it burst into glowing white brightness. Fearless couldn't help gasping—it looked as if she were holding one of the stars.

Finally, with a twitch of her snout, the Starleaf lowered

the stone and spoke to the troop. "Stinger speaks wisely," she announced. "A cub, found where he should not be, and brought there by the greatest of the eagles? The Moonstone tells me that this is a good omen. The sky is home to the Great Spirit, and the sky gave us this cub."

There were mutters and murmuring from the troop. Some of them scratched at their fur; others picked their teeth.

"I don't know, Starleaf," growled a smaller male. "A lion in a tree? How can that suggest good luck and not great chaos? It's unnatural."

"There's another thing," put in a grizzled older baboon. "He's small now, your Cub of the Stars, but he won't stay that way. Do we want a fully grown lion hanging around our troop?"

"Far too dangerous," muttered another.

"I'm not lion-food," cried a baboon from the back. "I say we kill him now, before he's big and strong enough to do it to us."

"I agree, Grub," called a mother baboon, clutching two little ones. "He shouldn't be around our babies."

"He'll grow huge," complained another young male. "*Much* too risky. I know he's little, but kill him quickly and it won't be unkind."

"And think of the *future enormous lion* while you kill him," pointed out a sulky-looking senior. "Then you won't feel quite so bad. It's not as if we'd be breaking the Code—we'd be protecting the troop! Come on, Stinger, let's get this over with."

"I'll tell you another thing," said Grub, pushing past

Stinger. "There's good eating on a lion." He licked his jaws as other baboons gathered behind him. Fearless tried to return his yellow-eyed stare, but when Grub opened his jaws and displayed his enormous fangs, Fearless couldn't help but tremble.

They were crowding around him now, teeth bared and jaws gaping. He couldn't see Stinger anymore—and all the faces were hostile.

But I'm Fearless Gallantpride! I won't bring shame on my name again. I'll make my father proud!

He swallowed hard, closing his eyes briefly. He could feel the hot, rank breath of the baboons on his face, but he wouldn't flinch, not again.

I wanted to be with my family, didn't I? And they're gone forever. Soon I will be too. He gulped hard and fixed his jaws in a defiant snarl.

This time I'm not going to run. This time I'll face death bravely. . . .

CHAPTER 3
ONE YEAR LATER

"Stay quiet, Mud. And still!" Thorn placed a paw on his friend's foreleg.

"Don't worry, Thorn," whispered Mud. "I won't make a sound. We're going to do this!"

The two young baboons were crouched near the top of a fever tree, keeping as still as they could, well concealed by drooping leaves and yellow flowers. From this vantage point they had a clear view of the next tree, and the buzzard's nest near its crown. *If we can avoid being spotted as we run along the branch,* thought Thorn, *we'll be able to jump across quite easily.*

Then it would just be a matter of dodging the beak of an angry buzzard. . . .

The bird hadn't moved in ages. It was tawny-colored and small compared to some of the huge eagles Thorn had seen.

He was pretty sure it wasn't strong enough to carry one of them away—not even a baboon as small as Mud—but its hooked beak and curled talons meant he didn't want to take any chances.

He was determined to get himself one of its eggs, though. *And Mud has to have one too.* . . .

Mud tugged at Thorn's fur with his small paws. "Look!" he whispered. "It's Pebble!"

Following his pointed finger, Thorn scowled. Another young baboon was climbing the trunk of the buzzard's tree, climbing up quickly, paw over paw. "So we've got competition," he murmured to Mud. "But those eggs are *ours.*"

Every young baboon in the troop was hoping to filch one of the buzzard's clutch, of course. Steal the Egg of a Flesh-Eating Bird was the first task of the Three Feats—the challenges every young baboon faced in their sixth year, and their one and only opportunity to move up the troop hierarchy. Thorn wasn't going to waste his chance—or let some other baboon steal it from under his snout. He bared his teeth silently at the interloper.

"Pebble's got no chance," he muttered. "He's too impatient."

"I hope you're right." Mud clenched his paws, looking determined.

When Thorn's parents died several seasons ago they had still been Deeproots, happy to remain in the lowest rank and proud of the menial work they did for the Brightforest Troop. Thorn had loved them dearly, and he was glad they had been content with their lot—but it didn't mean he had to be. *If I can steal one of these eggs I'll be a Lowleaf. And after that, a Middleleaf. And finally . . . Thorn Highleaf!*

It sounded so good in his head. Highleaves were the senior baboons, the ones who ran the troop and fought to protect it, and Thorn could not imagine anything more challenging and exciting. *I'm not going to spend my life collecting bedding and cleaning up after the troop. No way!*

Besides, if he and Berry Highleaf were ever going to be together officially, he had to be of the same rank as her. And he did, more than anything else in the world, want to be with Berry Highleaf. . . .

Never mind Highleaf, Mud had joked, just this morning. *You want to be Thorn Crownleaf, don't you?*

Thorn had laughed at that. But on a day like today, even eventually becoming leader of the troop seemed possible. The sky above the fever tree was a startling blue, but massive clouds piled on the horizon; the rains had already begun to make the savannah green and fertile, and the rivers were running fuller. A bright future as a Highleaf, a life at Berry's side, seemed to open out before him.

His daydreams were interrupted by a growling rumble in his stomach. Thorn scowled, feeling his good mood rapidly fade. He and Mud had been watching the buzzard's nest for two days now, crawling a little closer every time the buzzard flew off, and they were both starving. And the rain might make the savannah look pretty, and the fruit grow plump and plentiful, but there was a dampness in his fur that he couldn't

get rid of. He could have sworn he smelled of mold. Thorn
fidgeted and scowled.

Beside him, Mud grunted. "That buzzard has to go feed
again soon, *surely.*"

"How long since it last hunted?"

Mud glanced knowingly at the sky. "Long enough. It's definitely due to go again, any moment. We're lucky—if its mate
was still around, this would have been a lot harder."

"But it never leaves the nest for long. What if it doesn't fly
far?"

"This one prefers hares or hyrax. There aren't any burrows
nearby, so it'll have to fly a little way at least. We can do it if
we're quick."

But we can't wait much longer, Thorn thought, glancing at the
sun. It seemed to be dropping through the sky much faster
than usual, like a gazelle with a hyena on its tail. The rules of
the First Feat gave them only until the moon was full to find
an egg—and that would be tonight. Over the last few days several baboons had returned to the troop's camp at Tall Trees,
clutching eggs and triumphant at becoming Lowleaves. If he
and Mud didn't do the same before sundown, they would have
blown the First Feat forever.

He glanced at Mud. His friend's eyes, huge in his small
face, were fixed patiently on the nest. Thorn forced himself
to stop worrying. Mud wasn't just his best friend—he was one
of the smartest baboons Thorn knew. His plan to watch and
wait would work in the end.

It has to!

Thorn twisted his head to eye their rival, who had chosen to climb directly up the tree. Thorn clicked his teeth in exasperation as Pebble continued his greedy scramble up the trunk. *He's going to spook the buzzard.* Sure enough, the buzzard spread its huge wings and shrieked in anger. It rose up in the air and swooped down on the rash thief, squealing threats in its strange bird language of Skytongue. *I could have told him that would happen,* thought Thorn.

Pebble whooped in alarm and scuttled back down the tree, dodging the buzzard's raking talons. The bird didn't continue its pursuit for long; huffing and grumbling, it flapped back to its nest, taking long moments to peer suspiciously around the trees below. Thorn and Mud kept still, and at last the buzzard seemed to relax, half closing its yellow eyes.

Was it going to settle again?

"We could be here a *long* time . . ." muttered Thorn.

He let his shoulders slump, but at the same moment, the buzzard stretched its wings and took off into the sky. The two young baboons watched, hearts thumping with excitement, as it flew away swiftly westward.

"Now's our chance!" exclaimed Thorn in delight.

"Wait until it's out of sight," Mud reminded him. "Just in case it finds some rot-flesh nearby and—"

Before he could finish, another young baboon flung himself from the opposite treetop, landing on a branch close to the nest. Blinking in surprise, Thorn recognized his heavy forehead and long limbs. He gave a groan of despair. "That's Nut!"

"Oh no," said Mud, staring miserably. "He's going to beat us to it."

Thorn spent half his life protecting his friend from Nut, the nasty-tempered young baboon who was now within reach of their eggs. He clenched his paws in frustration.

"No, wait!" Mud pointed at the sky. "The buzzard's coming back!"

Thorn grinned. That served Nut right! The buzzard must have spotted him, and was flying back with swift beats of its enormous wings. Diving at Nut, it screeched and clawed at him; Nut barked in anger, but he was forced to scamper back from the nest and down the tree. This time the buzzard didn't give up the chase; it swooped after Nut as he dodged and scurried through the scrub, buffeting him with its wings whenever he was exposed, and snatching at his back with its savage talons.

Thorn didn't wait to enjoy the show any longer. "Now's our chance!"

He raced along the branch and leaped for the nest. Glancing back, he saw Mud creeping carefully along, some way back, looking nervous. He sighed to himself. *If only Mud wasn't so scrawny*, he thought. *Everything frightens him, even that stupid bully Nut.*

"Wait there, Mud!" he hooted softly. "I'll get the eggs."

Scrambling into the nest, he spotted them at once—three big eggs, cream-colored and speckled with brown. Seizing one in each long-fingered paw, he raised his head and glanced around anxiously, half expecting the buzzard to dive at him, beak snapping and stabbing. But he could still hear it, distantly, harrying a squealing Nut through the scrub. Thorn allowed himself a grin.

But he wasn't going to make the mistake of hanging around. Cradling the eggs against his chest with a single paw, he made the jump to the next tree, then hurried back to Mud.

He passed his friend an egg. "We've done it!"

Mud's wide eyes shone with delight as he gazed at the treasure in his paws. "*You* did it! Thank you, Thorn!"

"We did it together," Thorn insisted. "You did all the thinking, and I only did that very last bit on my own. Now we're both Lowleaves!" Victory thrilled through his bones. *I'm not a Deeproot anymore! I'm really, truly on my way—straight to the top!*

Chattering happily, the two of them made their way carefully down the tree, handling their eggs with care. Mud couldn't stop gazing at his; he looked, thought Thorn affectionately, as if he might burst with pride.

It took a while, since both baboons were nervous of stumbling and breaking their eggs, but they had finally bounded a good way from the buzzard's nest, and slowed to a strutting walk. Mud grinned. "My mother is going to be so surprised."

"She's going to be *thrilled*—" began Thorn.

"Well," said a new and vicious voice. "What have we here?"

Thorn halted, bristling, and bared his teeth. "Hello, Nut."

Nut crashed aggressively out of the bushes ahead of them.

He looked ragged and out of breath after his escape from the buzzard, and there were bloody scratches on his back and neck, but Nut was still big and brutish, and Thorn wasn't about to let down his guard.

"How did you get those eggs?" Nut snapped, glaring at them.

"With patience," retorted Thorn. "And by waiting until the buzzard was gone."

"Until it had attacked me, you mean." Nut hissed through his teeth. "Those are *my* eggs."

"No," said Thorn. "They're not. It's not our fault you were too stupid to wait."

"Those scratches look nasty," put in Mud hastily.

Thorn sucked in a breath, wincing. His friend was trying to calm things down, Thorn realized, but offering sympathy was never a good strategy with Nut. Nut would think Mud was mocking him—or worse, he'd see it as a sign of weakness.

Sure enough, Nut turned on Mud, snarling. "Yes, they really hurt! Because *I* did all the work to get those eggs, and *you* stole them!"

"That's not true—" began Mud.

"I don't care. *I'm* the one who deserves to be a Lowleaf. Not you, Skinnylegs!"

Then, before Mud could catch his breath to reply, Nut lunged, snatched the egg from his paws, and fled.

Nut had vanished into the newly lush undergrowth before Thorn could stop him. Thorn gave a screech of fury, then jumped and slapped the ground; but although it relieved his feelings a little, there was no point. Nut wasn't coming back, and he certainly wasn't returning the egg.

Thorn turned to Mud. His small friend was staring at his empty paws as if he couldn't quite believe what had happened.

"Oh, Mud. I'm sorry, I should have grabbed Nut. Stopped him."

"It's not your fault," whispered Mud. "I didn't stand up to him."

Thorn sighed and sat back on his haunches. He looked down at his own egg. *Mud's got plenty of brains, but that doesn't mean he's cut out for the Three Feats. What if he fails all of them and stays a Deeproot forever?*

A horrible thought struck him. While he was exploring the forests of Bravelands, hunting and defending the troop from monkey attacks, Mud would be stuck at the camp. He'd spend his life being bossed around by all the other ranks, fetching food and bedding, cleaning up and scrubbing around for scraps. *It's not right*, thought Thorn fiercely. *Mud's far too smart for that. And anyway, what's the point of going on adventures if my best friend can't be there too?*

"Here," Thorn blurted, holding out his egg. "You take this one. I can get another."

Mud's eyes widened in gratitude, but he shook his head. "No. No, Thorn, I didn't get it out of the nest. I couldn't use your egg to make myself a Lowleaf—I wouldn't feel as if I'd earned it."

"I don't mind," insisted Thorn. "And if I go now, I can be back at the nest—"

"No," said Mud, catching his shoulder. "It took us long enough to get this egg. And anyway, look." He pointed at the sun, which was dipping ever lower through the trees. "It's too late, Thorn. I've failed this Feat."

Thorn knew he was right. It was bitterly disappointing. If it weren't for Nut, they would both be bounding back to Tall Trees as Lowleaves. But Mud's triumph had been snatched away, and the rules forbade the baboons from ever trying a Feat again.

"I'm not leaving you behind," said Thorn. "You're my best friend."

"That won't happen!" Mud put his paw on Thorn's shoulder and crooned reassuringly. "We've still got two more Feats to go, haven't we? If I pass them, at least I'll be a Middleleaf." *Poor Mud.* The Second and Third Feats were even more demanding, and he didn't sound any more convinced he'd manage than Thorn was. They both knew that stealing the bird's egg had been Mud's best chance of success. With a heavy sigh, Thorn hugged his friend. "Just wait, when I get hold of Nut—"

Mud shook his head again, more emphatically. "No, don't get yourself in any trouble. It won't help. And Nut won't get any satisfaction from this anyway. He *knows* he didn't really earn that egg."

I don't think that matters to Nut, thought Thorn, as the two friends made their way back toward Tall Trees. *But if believing it is any consolation to Mud, I'm not going to tell him differently.*

The two baboons padded back to the small forest that had been the troop's base for the last few seasons. It was a prized camp, cool and green and lush, the envy of the other baboons and monkeys of Bravelands; the high trees gave shelter and protection, and now that the rains had begun they were heavy with desert dates, figs, and jackfruit. The treasure of the Brightforest camp was the mango tree that had somehow seeded itself among the others; their leader, Bark Crownleaf, was strictly fair in sharing out its sweet-scented gold fruit.

The Brightforest Troop was busy relaxing as Thorn and Mud returned. Mothers nursed their new babies; youngsters chewed on figs; pairs of baboons groomed one another. Thorn felt some of his anger fade away as he watched his big family. It was hard to hold on to resentment when the troop looked so contented and at peace.

"I'd better say hello to Mother," Mud told him. There was trepidation in the small baboon's voice, and Thorn watched his friend anxiously as he bounded across to where she sat beneath the mango tree. As the Starleaf, Mud's mother was high-ranking in the troop, with vital skills in reading the stars, the clouds, and the flight path of birds—any sign, in fact, that was sent by the Great Spirit in the sky. Thorn knew she had ambitions for Mud to follow in her footsteps. *But he'd have to become a Highleaf first*, he thought sadly, *and now that's not going to happen. Poor Mud. Well, maybe the signs told the Starleaf that he'd return without an egg. She might be expecting it.*

Mud was speaking to the Starleaf quietly, but she wasn't saying much in return, just sitting very still and shaking her white-streaked head.

I wish she'd hide her disappointment better. All Mud needs is a bit of confidence.

Sighing, Thorn turned away and went in search of Stinger. The big baboon wasn't hard to spot; he was crouched in the center of a small clearing, surrounded by a fascinated cluster of little baboons. Best of all, Berry Highleaf was sitting nearby. The sunlight picked out golden strands among her fur, and her large brown eyes shone as she watched her father teach the youngsters.

"See how I've made a trap for it with these twigs?" Stinger was explaining. "That means it can't get at me."

He's showing them how to catch a scorpion, realized Thorn, spotting the scuttling brown shape between the twigs. He remembered fondly when Stinger had taught the same trick to him. *Every small baboon thinks he'll learn to do it even better than Stinger*, he thought with amusement. *And no baboon ever quite manages.*

Berry hadn't spotted him yet. She was following her father's every move, adoration on her kind, sweet-tempered face.

I'm going to surprise her, he decided. *Wait until she hears I've completed a Feat!* Holding his egg carefully behind his back, he padded over to her side.

"Thorn!" Her eyes lit up, sparkling in the filtered sunlight.

"Hello, Berry," he said, wishing he had the nerve to groom her shoulder. "Scorpions again?"

She laughed. "My father's quite determined that the troop's going to live on them one day. Just because *he* loves them. I'd sooner have a mango anytime!"

"He's a very good teacher, though," said Thorn, settling down on his haunches to watch.

Stinger brought down a twig, lightning fast, trapping the furious scorpion beneath it. "Like this. See?" He seized it by the tail, avoiding the sting, and squashed it with his other paw. "There. It never got a chance to sting me."

There were gasps of awe from the young baboons. "I want to try, Stinger!" squealed one.

"We'll have to find another scorpion first." Stinger laughed, the scar above his nose wrinkling.

"Aren't you scared?" asked a small female shyly.

"Course not. How do you think I got my name?" Stinger flicked the dead scorpion with a claw. "It's because I love scorpions so much!"

"Do they *really* taste good?" The littlest male made a slightly skeptical face.

"Delicious!" declared Stinger. "The fresher the better!" He pulled off the scorpion's tail and dropped it on the ground. "There, that's where its venom is, so you need to throw the tail away. You can eat the rest of it, though. Here." He pulled the scorpion into small pieces and handed them to the youngsters.

As they nibbled uncertainly, then gulped them down with exclamations of delight, Stinger turned to Thorn. "Hello, Thorn! How did it go?"

Now was his moment. Thorn returned Stinger's grin, but he couldn't help looking at Berry as he pulled the egg from behind him. She gasped in delight; then she touched his arm gently and smiled.

"Thorn!" she gasped, her wide brown eyes full of happiness. "Well done!"

"You've stolen yourself an egg!" exclaimed her father.

Thorn nodded, pleased. "Yes, Stinger."

"Congratulations, Thorn Lowleaf!"

"This is such good news," agreed Berry, gazing at him with joy. "Congratulations, Thorn!"

Thorn felt tongue-tied. Besides—especially in front of Stinger—what could he say? Baboons were forbidden to take a mate from outside their own rank. Thorn restricted himself to a nod and a shy smile.

Stinger took the egg from him and turned it in his paws, studying it. "This is very fine, Thorn. These buzzards are watchful and sharp-eyed! It took skill and patience to get its egg."

Thorn glowed with pride. Such praise from Stinger, the cleverest baboon in the troop, made his heart sing.

"Should I take it to show Beetle?" he asked. Beetle was a member of the Council of fourteen Highleaves who helped advise Bark Crownleaf on running the troop. He was responsible for overseeing the Three Feats.

Stinger waved an airy paw. "No need; I'm on the Council, so I can confirm to Beetle you're now a Lowleaf." He handed

Thorn back the egg. "Keep this up and you might even complete all Three Feats, as Berry did." He flashed an adoring grin at his daughter.

"I wish I was as talented as Berry," muttered Thorn, thrilled but embarrassed. As Stinger turned away to ask the little baboons how they liked their pieces of scorpion, Thorn shot a glance at her. His heart felt warm and huge inside him. Impulsively, he put the egg into Berry's paws. "I want you to have this," he whispered hoarsely.

"Why, thank you, Thorn!" The delight in her eyes was all the reward he needed. He was still smiling a little stupidly at her, speechless, when he felt a massive paw strike his back, knocking him onto the ground.

He rolled over, staring up into gaping jaws. Sunlight glinted on long fangs and cast over him the shadow of a powerfully muscled creature.

Thorn gave a shrill yelp as he scrambled back up.

"Fearless! Watch those clumsy great paws of yours!"

The big lion cub roared happily, right in his face.

"You got your egg!" he exclaimed, licking Thorn until he staggered. "I want to hear *all* about it!"

CHAPTER 4

Fearless gnawed desperately at the rotten log between his paws, sticking his tongue deep under the peeling bark. *I'm hungry. I know it's ungrateful but I can't help it. I'm always hungry.* He felt another few termites stick to it, so he lashed his tongue back into his jaws and chomped noisily, pretending they were a mouthful of antelope.

Oh, antelope . . . I still remember you, antelope. . . . You were so delicious and meaty and big. . . .

Mice and birds were tasty enough, but they were the most substantial prey he'd eaten in ages, and they didn't fill the belly of a growing lion. He thought with aching longing of zebra-flesh. *Mother and the other lionesses used to bring us zebra. And wildebeest. And bushbuck . . .*

He mustn't think too much about it, and not only because

he missed the taste of warm, chunky meat. Thinking of his family sent a wrench of pain through his gut.

I'm one of Brightforest Troop now. They are my family. He knew how lucky he was that Stinger had found him and rescued him, and how kind the other baboons had been to let him stay. That was down to Stinger, too: with his charm and tact and clever words—and the backup of the kindly Starleaf—Stinger had talked his whole troop around.

Some of them might have had second thoughts, but Fearless had been one of the troop ever since, and they could hardly kill him and eat him now. *I need to feel more thankful, I know. I might have had no family at all, now. I might have been dead.*

It's just . . . zebra . . .

Fearless gave a deep sigh.

"Hey, Fearless!" Berry, Stinger's gentle daughter, loped toward him. "I'll show you a better way. Look." Taking a twig, she sat down beside him and began to poke at the log. Her gold-speckled brow furrowed in concentration, then she brightened as she pulled the stick back out. Its whole length was clogged with termites. "There!"

"Thanks, Berry." Fearless dutifully licked the termites from the twig. "The trouble is, I don't have paws like yours." He raised one dolefully, showing the pads. "I can't pick up a stick myself."

"Maybe you could use your claws to grip it?" she suggested. "You do have very long claws. . . ."

That didn't sound like a bad idea, but before Fearless could try Berry's suggestion, Stinger bounded to his daughter's side and greeted him cheerfully. "Fearless! I need you to come to the Council meeting with me."

Fearless sat up on his haunches at once. "Of course, Stinger." The Council that advised the Crownleaf was made up of the fourteen eldest Highleaves of the troop, and each of them was allowed to choose a retinue—a small group of baboons, selected from any rank, who would help them carry out their Council duties. Highleaves usually picked out baboons they thought had a glowing future, so Fearless was proud to be one of Stinger's retinue; he knew it was a great privilege, especially since it let him attend Council meetings to watch and listen. More than almost anything else, it was this that made Fearless feel he belonged in Brightforest Troop.

Getting to his paws, he said good-bye to Berry and followed Stinger to the place where the Council sat: an almost circular clearing beneath the tallest acacia of the grove. Vines and ferns hung thickly from the surrounding trees, giving the glade privacy as well as an atmosphere of solemnity and shadow. Right in the center of the clearing was a huge, smooth-topped boulder: the Crown Stone. On it sat a big, grave-faced baboon, waiting in silence for the fourteen councilors to gather. Dappled sunlight played on her brown fur, shifting with the movement of the foliage above her. Her eyes were deep-set, solemn, and wise. Fearless dipped his head in respect to Bark Crownleaf, head of the troop.

Stinger and the other councilors settled in a circle around the Crown Stone, their retinues sitting behind them. Fearless crouched beside the two young baboons who also served

Stinger—Grass Middleleaf, who was tall and always chewing on a stalk, and Fly Lowleaf, who was slight but fast. An ant crawled up Fearless's leg, and Fly's front paw shot out to grab it. He swallowed it and grinned at Fearless, revealing chipped teeth.

The peaceful birdsong of the glade was interrupted abruptly by Grub Highleaf, the baboon with small yellow eyes and thin lips who had been keenest to kill Fearless when he was a cub.

"What's *he* doing here?" Grub complained. "Do you really have to bring your lion, Stinger? Do you think he'll get you your way in the Council?"

Stinger drew himself up onto his hind legs, curling his lip in offense. "This is Fearless, Cub of the Stars," he exclaimed. "He's one of our troop, Grub, as well as a member of my retinue, and don't you forget it."

"Council!" Bark Crownleaf stood up on the Crown Stone, and Stinger respectfully dropped back onto all fours. "We are not here to discuss Fearless's place in the troop." She stared at Grub until he lowered his eyes, grumbling. "And I am not interested in revisiting old arguments. We have come together to discuss moving Brightforest Troop to a new settlement."

The wizened figure of Beetle Highleaf rose. "It is a weighty question, Bark Crownleaf. We have kept our base here in Tall Trees for an unusually long time, but to move from here would be a drastic decision. The fruits are plentiful, the creek provides water, and the trees give us good shelter. There is room for all."

"Indeed," mused Bark. "But such abundance does not last

forever. The dry season will return as it always does; and it is not natural for baboons to stay in one place for so long. We are nomads and wanderers, Beetle Highleaf, and at some point we will have to leave here. Best to discuss it now, before it becomes urgent."

"Frankly," muttered Grub, "the movements of the troop are not the lion's concern."

"Grub, that's enough." Bark gave him a reproving glance.

"Well, Bark," murmured Mango, clearing her throat, "I think Grub has a point, actually."

Branch Highleaf pursed his thin lips. "Me too," he muttered. There were more sounds of agreement from around the Council Glade. Grass stopped chewing and shot Fearless a sympathetic glance.

Bark hesitated, seeming about to speak, then closed her mouth and gave a slow, regretful nod. Stinger coughed tactfully and turned to Fearless.

"Perhaps, then, the Cub of the Stars could leave us, this time," he said. He blinked apologetically at Fearless. "It might make our discussions run more smoothly. Would you mind, my friend?"

Fearless shot a quick look around the glade, but no baboon stood up in his defense. One of Grub's retinue, smirking, whispered something to his neighbor that made the other baboon snort with laughter.

Embarrassed, Fearless gave a rapid nod. "Of course, Stinger. No, I don't mind, not at all. I'll, er . . . leave you all to it."

"Bad luck," muttered Fly.

Fearless backed up a few paces, then turned and left the glade with as much dignity as he could muster.

He felt the stares of the councilors and their retinues on his rump, and was glad when he was out of sight among the trees. *The trouble is, I do mind*, he thought sadly. *I understand why Stinger said it. And I'm happy living here with Brightforest Troop.*

I just wish they all accepted me the way Stinger does.

He'd just have to prove himself, that was all. Fearless picked up his paws, trying to feel more confident. *I'm a good guard for the troop, Stinger said so. No animal dares to mess with Brightforest Troop while I'm around.*

Among Stinger's responsibilities as councilor was to keep the troop secure, and Fearless helped him with this. He patrolled the boundary, watched for threats, defended his friends, and deterred their enemies. "You're the troop's protector," Stinger had told him, and Fearless still remembered the glow of pride he'd felt at these words. It was an important job, and he did it well—better than any baboon could. Surely that made him indispensable?

As he padded toward the Tall Trees boundary, he heard a yelp of greeting.

"Hey, Fearless!"

He flicked his ears forward. Thorn was scampering toward him, Mud at his side as usual. At the sight of his best friends, Fearless's spirits lifted, the Council meeting forgotten.

When the troop had brought their Cub of the Stars back to Tall Trees, the kind Starleaf had introduced him straight away to her son. Mud had taken to Fearless immediately and had become the cub's staunch friend and defender—which might not have meant much practically, given Mud's size, but Mud had also introduced him to Thorn. And Thorn, completely loyal to Mud, had befriended Fearless wholeheartedly and without hesitation.

Fearless growled in cheerful greeting. "Thorn! Mud! I'm going to patrol the camp."

"Then we'll come with you. Right, Mud?"

Mud nodded eagerly, and Fearless crouched down to let his friends scramble up onto his back. His mood lightened instantly; it was hard to be gloomy in the young baboons' company. But he had to stay focused on the patrol too.

"The next Feat is coming up," chattered Mud. "Crossing the Crocodile River!"

"We've been wondering how we're going to do it," said Thorn, idly grooming Fearless's neck as he rode along. "You can help us work it out, Fearless."

"I will," Fearless promised. "We'll find a way, but . . ." An idea struck him. "Hey! Why don't I try the Three Feats too?"

He looked over his shoulder to see the two baboons exchange a surprised glance.

"I don't see why you shouldn't," said Mud, though he sounded doubtful. "The rules say you have to be six to take part, though."

Fearless tossed his head. "That's in five years' time! I can't wait that long—and anyway, I'm a lion. I'll be fully grown when I'm three. No, I'm going to do the Three Feats now."

He looked back at his friends once more. Thorn was study-ing him curiously. "What's brought this on?"

"Something Grub said." Fearless told them what had hap-pened at the Council meeting. "So if I do the Three Feats," he said, climbing carefully over a branch, "no baboon could say I wasn't a true member of the troop."

Thorn gave a snort. "Don't listen to Grub! He talks a lot of monkey dung. Of course you're one of us."

"You don't need to prove anything," agreed Mud. "Besides, the deadline for the First Feat has gone. I failed, remember? Even if you did get an egg, it wouldn't count."

Fearless picked up his paws, stepping around a crawling nest of termites. "It'll still show Grub and the others, won't it?"

Thorn laughed. "There's no point arguing once you've got an idea in your head, is there?" He ruffled the fur between Fearless's ears playfully. "It'll be hard for you, though. You don't have fingers like ours. How will you get hold of an egg?"

"I'll find a way," Fearless told them.

"I'm sure you will," Mud said, "and we'll help you. Hey, Thorn—this is a good place. Look at those logs. Let's practice here."

The two sprang down from Fearless's back, and he watched them wrestle two big logs into place so that they were posi-tioned across from each other, like the banks of a river. Thorn clambered onto the bigger log, squatting on his stocky haunches as he scratched his broad, gray-furred face thought-fully. On the opposite log, Mud was gesturing excitedly with his skinny forelegs, pointing out ways to dodge the imaginary crocodiles between him and his friend.

"It'll depend on the part of the river the Council chooses. See, if there are sandbanks, we should be able to swim to each one and take a break. Not for long, because the crocs won't just stay in the water, but see what happens if we change direction a few times. . . ."

Fearless's confidence waned a little. *Mud's so smart—and Thorn's so clever with his paws.* They hadn't seemed hugely convinced by his plan. And even if he did manage to complete all the Three Feats, would Grub and the others still say he didn't belong?

He shook himself. That kind of thinking wouldn't help. And anyway, he had more pressing things to think about at the moment—keeping the troop safe.

Solemnly he began to pad along the boundary of Tall Trees, where the lush, cool greenness of tree and palm and fern ended in an expanse of savannah that shimmered gold in the heat. He sniffed and narrowed his eyes. *When I'm a Highleaf warrior,* he thought, *this is how I'll protect my troop. Take that, Titan!* He swiped his paw at some rustling leaves, and saw a big furry spider scuttle away in panic. *That showed you. . . .*

Above him, starlings were jabbering in a thorn tree. He gave a grunting roar and slammed his paws against its trunk, sending the whole flock screeching skyward. *You won't ambush me from a tree, Titan!* He was feeling much more confident now, and far happier. *I'm good at this.*

Following the boundary, Fearless checked each tree

thoroughly. By the time he'd scared a snake back into its hole and scattered some lazy egrets in a panic of white wings, there was a swagger in his step.

He was so wrapped up in important defensive measures, he barely noticed the dimming of the sky. Only when Thorn hooted, "Fearless, where are you?" did he realize dusk was falling.

Surprised, he turned back to see his friends loping toward him. The sky above was a deeper, darker blue, and flat-topped acacia trees were silhouetted against a far orange horizon.

"Time to get back to camp, Fearless," called Mud. "We've been looking for you!"

"I didn't realize," he told them. He glanced back at the deep golden glow that lay along the horizon. Something was moving between two solitary acacias; Fearless narrowed his eyes.

"Wait a moment. . . ."

The figure was a lion, its stride easy and relaxed; a lone adult male with a crooked tail, silhouetted against the sunset. Fearless didn't often spot lions, now that he lived in Tall Trees, but whenever he did, a wistful feeling came over him. He watched the great beast as it padded unhurriedly over the line of the horizon many hundreds of paces away, and disappeared.

What would it be like, living like a real lion? Would I be going back to my pride now, like he is? Would I spend the night hunting, or leave it to the lionesses?

The savannah looked so open and inviting, stretching out to what seemed like infinity. The haze of twilight was deepening to dark blue as the horizon faded to bronze, and the vast web of stars had begun to twinkle into life. Behind Fearless, the forest lay dark and deep and damp, already echoing with the chirp and croak of insects and frogs. It was home, but it was not a place a lion could run forever, where he could leap and bound and stretch his muscles pursuing the herds.

He swallowed hard. He'd had his own pride once, a place where he truly belonged. The old guilt crept into his belly. *Maybe I should have stayed to fight Titan. I should have tried to protect my family, even if it was hopeless. But I fled.*

"Fearless, come *on!*" called Thorn impatiently. "If you don't hurry up, we'll be eating twigs tonight."

Fearless turned from the open savannah. It was useless gnawing over his regrets. *The baboons are my friends, and I care about them. That's what I do. I keep them safe.*

All the same, as he padded back to his friends and paused to let them climb on his back, he couldn't help a last, longing stare toward the sunset where the lion had vanished.

Fearless stood up on his hind legs, clawing in frustration at the bark of a kigelia tree. He peered up through its branches and its long, dangling fruit, some even larger than Mud, and stared longingly at the eagle's nest in the topmost branches. *It's not that far. It's not. I can do this.*

"What are you waiting for?" Nut slapped the ground impatiently with his big foreleg. "You're wasting your time, though. The Council will never let this count as a Feat."

Thorn frowned. "Why were you so keen to find him an eagle's nest, then?"

"Oh, it isn't a waste of *our* time," sneered Nut. "We're going to enjoy watching him make an idiot of himself." The small cluster of cronies around Nut yammered in agreement. "The eagle will come back soon," barked one. "Get on with it, Fearless!"

"Fearless, ha!" Scornfully, Nut peeled back his lips from his fangs. "What a ridiculous name, when you think about it. You can't even get up the nerve to climb a tree!"

His gang hooted with laughter. "That's right, Nut. You're right!"

"Maybe your name should be *Big Talk*," Nut went on, warming to his theme. "Because you say you're Fearless, but you're all Big Talk!"

This was almost too much for some of his gang. They shrieked hysterically, bouncing up and down, jaws gaping wide with hilarity. Only Mud and Thorn stayed quiet, glowering at Nut's accomplices.

At last Mud scratched his head and furrowed his brow. "I think it's odd the eagle's been gone for so long," he muttered. "Birds need to sit on their eggs to keep them warm, or they won't hatch. Why isn't it here?" He narrowed his eyes, scowling deeply as he watched the nest. "And anyway, surely all the flesh-eating birds around here will have realized by now that we're after their eggs?"

"You're such a know-it-all," mocked Nut, baring his teeth at Mud. "Pity that didn't help you get an egg of your own."

Thorn gave an angry growl. "You only got your egg by

cheating and stealing," he reminded Nut sharply. "You've got nothing to be so proud about."

Nut made a rude face. His gang sniggered, but the rest of the young baboons fell silent as Fearless dug his claws into the tree. He began to haul himself up, pushing with his strong hindquarters, dragging himself with his forepaws.

He gritted his jaws. *Thorn says the secret is not to look down. . . .*

Higher and higher he climbed, until he was in the fork of the first branches. He paused, panting. He was bigger and heavier than any of the baboons, but the tree was thick and sturdy. He was sure it would take his weight.

"Watch so the fruits don't fall and hit your great thick head!" yelled Nut.

Fearless heard Thorn screech and snap angrily at Nut: "Let him get on with it." But he didn't look down. Tensing his muscles, narrowing his eyes, he began to clamber up through the branches. There was one just above him that looked strong; he sprang for it, clutching with his claws, and hauled himself up. He lay along it, getting his breath back, feeling it sag a little under his weight.

Now the branches above him didn't look quite so big and thick. They were getting downright spindly.

Keep going, Fearless! Clenching his jaws, he balanced himself, wincing as a memory surfaced. *Not so long ago I was desperate to get down from an eagle's nest! And now I'm desperate to climb up to one. . . .*

He scrambled onto the next branch quite easily, but it bounced wildly and sagged beneath him. With a growling yelp, he felt himself slip around it, though his claws were dug deep. He clung to its underside, panting with fear.

"Just above you, Fearless!" cried Thorn from below. "There's a stronger branch. You can do it."

"What's wrong, Big Talk?" yelled Nut. "Given up already?"

Fearless gave a deep, angry growl, and hauled himself back on top of the branch. He could see the one Thorn meant; he grabbed it with the claws of one forepaw and lurched clumsily onto it. Before he could think any harder, he reached for the next, and then the next.

He wasn't held up by a single branch now—they were too thin to hold him. He was sprawled across a mesh of three or four skinny ones that seemed barely more than thick twigs. Fearless gulped. The boughs creaked and groaned.

"Fearless!" barked Thorn. "Come down! Forget the egg, the branches are going to snap!"

"No," he gasped, though he wasn't sure if Thorn could even hear him. "I'm nearly there!"

The sun was shining full on his back now, and the edge of the messy nest was only a paw stretch away. He was at the top! Fearless brightened, feeling his courage return. Taking a deep lungful of air, he scrambled across the treetop and lurched onto the side of the nest, squashing the rim of cracking twigs. He flattened himself on his belly, afraid the nest would topple right off the tree with him still clinging to it.

Blinking, he stared in horror. There were no eggs. The nest was empty, and now he could see it was dilapidated, with a hole in the base. The twigs were broken and falling away, and the lining of leaves was dry and crispy and brown.

"It's abandoned!" he roared in dismay.

The sound of cackles below sent birds scattering in alarm from the trees around him. The gang screeched and hooted, and Nut himself was hopping on the spot, slapping the ground and yelping with helpless laughter.

"Nut!" Thorn roared angrily. "That was mean and stupid!"

"You tricked me!" yelled Fearless, jumping to his paws.

"Fearless, no—stay still!"

Mud's shout of warning came too late. The broken nest collapsed around him; both it and Fearless tumbled down through the tree, cracking branches and dislodging long, heavy fruits that plummeted to the ground.

The crashing, thumping descent seemed to last forever. Fearless snatched desperately at branches, but none of them would hold his falling weight. Every time he clawed for a hold, the boughs splintered and collapsed. *And there's no Stinger to catch me this time. I'm going to die, I'm going to—* He slammed through the last branches and hit the ground hard.

It knocked the breath from his chest, and for a moment Fearless thought he really was dead; but Nut and his cronies were still screeching with helpless laughter. *Even Nut wouldn't laugh if I was dead . . . I think.* Fearless scrambled awkwardly to his paws and shook leaves and twigs from his coat. He was scratched and battered, but he was alive.

And he was *furious.*

"Nut!" he roared.

"You idiot, Nut!" barked Thorn. "Fearless could have been killed!"

"So what?" Nut sneered, in between gasps of amusement. "He shouldn't be pretending he can do the Three Feats. This'll teach him a lesson—he's no baboon!"

"That doesn't matter!" cried Mud angrily. "He's part of Brightforest Troop!"

"Hardly," scoffed Nut. "He can't even climb a tree without falling off it!"

Their squabble intensified, accusations and insults flying faster and louder, but Fearless was suddenly distracted. He frowned. There was an odd smell on the air, one that shouldn't be there. Falling quiet, he tilted his head and twitched his tail. He opened his jaws to taste the faint breeze, trying to ignore the screeching of the quarreling baboons.

"Thorn," he said, "something's coming."

"What's your problem, Nut?" Thorn was yelling. "You've always been a stupid bully and—"

"Thorn. There's a strange scent." Fearless lashed his tail faster. "I don't like it."

"—And all you do is cause trouble, and—"

"Thorn!"

Thorn finally swung his head toward Fearless, a quizzical, annoyed look on his face. But just at that moment, something huge leaped from the spiky undergrowth. It was bigger even than Fearless, with a long, sloping back, and greasy fur spotted in yellow and brown. Its jaws hung open, dripping saliva and displaying savage fangs. Its breath was rank and hot, and its wild black eyes glinted with ravenous greed.

"Hyena!" screeched Thorn. *"Run!"*

Fearless stiffened in shock, his hackles springing erect. The baboons bolted in several directions, and the chaos momentarily confused the hyena. It snapped wildly, trying to pounce on one baboon and then another.

But Mud was closest to it. Fixing on Mud, the hyena flung itself in pursuit. Eyes white-rimmed with terror, Mud scampered toward a tree—but the hyena was closing, looming over him, jaws wide for the kill. Fearless sucked in a shocked breath, his ears flattening and his muscles coiling.

He saw Thorn dart into the hyena's path, snatching his scrawny friend in the nick of time and yanking him into a hollow behind a thornbush. The hyena's jaws snapped shut on empty air, but it turned on both baboons with a snarl.

It'll kill them both!

The heat of fury rushed through Fearless's veins. Bunching his shoulders, he opened his jaws wide in a screaming roar of challenge, slaver flying from his bared fangs. Then he sprang at the hyena, forelegs stretched out and claws extended to slash and tear.

It spun on its haunches, astonished. Fearless landed on its back, clawing and snarling; as it gave a shriek of pain, he sank his jaws instinctively into the side of its neck.

Beneath him the creature wriggled and writhed, its wild struggles yanking at his fangs; the stench of its fear and shock filled Fearless's nostrils, and the hyena's hoarse, screeching yelps were all he could hear. It had tremendous strength, but Fearless was too enraged to let go easily. It kicked and fought and yelped, and at last it flung Fearless off and shot into the trees, still hollering.

Panting, Fearless stood for a moment, staring after it, chest heaving. A sense of exhilaration filled him to bursting. Opening his bloody jaws wide, he gave a great roar of triumph.

One by one, the baboons were creeping out from the undergrowth and swinging down from the trees where they had sought refuge. They were blinking, gaping; some looked awestruck, some unnerved, and some positively terrified. Only Thorn and Mud bounded up to him, whooping with delight.

"You were great, Fearless!" cried Thorn.

"Seeing off a hyena is a *lot* better than stealing an egg," hooted Mud with a grin of satisfaction.

"Hmph." Nut was creeping out from the hollow of a rotten log, picking bits of wood and bark out of his fur. "You're all overreacting. It was only a hyena. It wasn't *that* scary."

"You looked scared enough," mocked Thorn, contemptuously eyeing Nut's messy fur.

"I thought it was a young, strong one," snapped Nut. "It must have been old and sick if Big Talk there could beat it."

But for once, Fearless didn't care about Nut's malicious tongue. *I know I saved them all. And from their faces, Nut's cronies know it too!*

It made him feel good, better than he had in a long time.

The baboons clustered around him, bouncing with excitement and hooting their approval as they all made their way back to Tall Trees. Fearless picked up his paws, strutting proudly. He raised his head high, imagining his neck was already swathed in a flowing, golden mane.

The troop gathered to watch as the young baboons paraded into the glade around their new hero, Thorn and Mud riding on his back. As they jumped down and scampered off to share the story, Fearless caught sight of Bark Crownleaf. Their imposing leader sat on a fallen branch, studying him thoughtfully.

"Fearless," she called gently. "Come to me for a moment."

He trotted over to her, still warm with pride and pleasure. "What is it, Crownleaf?"

"Sit with me, Cub of the Stars." She laid a paw against his shoulder. "I was high in the fever tree when the hyena attacked. I saw what happened."

Fearless dropped his gaze, a little embarrassed at such attention from the Crownleaf herself. "It was nothing," he mumbled awkwardly. "I didn't really think about it."

"No, you did it instinctively. You knew what had to be done. And I'm very grateful to you. You saved Mud's life, and Thorn's, and probably more." Bark smiled at him.

Fearless's chest swelled. "I'm just glad I could help," he grunted. Hurriedly he added, "I was trying to get an egg to show everyone I could do the Three Feats. . . . I didn't manage, but maybe chasing off the hyena could count instead?"

She was gazing at him, her expression kind, and Fearless found he was holding his breath. His heart beat painfully. There was something about the look in Bark's eyes. . . .

"What you did," she said at last, "the way your instincts told you to attack and save your friends? That shows just how much of a lion you are, Fearless." She patted him gently. "What it tells me is that the Three Feats aren't for you. It's not that I don't think you could do it," she added, as he opened his jaws to protest. "It's just that . . . Fearless, you're a lion. A hunter. You shouldn't be seeking a permanent place with Brightforest Troop. You need to live with lions and lead a lion's life."

Fearless stared at his leader, speechless. Bark gave him a final consoling scratch and turned away, stalking off toward the rest of the troop. Fearless watched her go, his heart thudding painfully in his chest.

She's wrong, he decided.

Maybe he'd belonged with lions when he was little, but that life was over, and his home was here now. What pride would ever have him? His place was with his friends—Thorn, and Mud, and Stinger. He could even put up with Nut.

I'm glad I saved them all from the hyena, but I mustn't let my instincts take over again. That's what made Bark say what she did—I let my lion side take over.

He set his jaws.

I'll show her. I'll prove I'm more of a baboon than any of them.

CHAPTER 5

Sky Strider peered out between the legs of two grown elephants. It was hard to see anything through the dust clouds, but she could catch glimpses of zebras and wildebeests stampeding in panic, hordes of them. The herds jostled and shoved, but the protective circle of adults stood firm, stamping, bellowing, and flapping their ears. Red dust flew up in the whirlwind created by their great feet and their snorting, swinging trunks.

Angling her ears forward, Sky frowned. She too spoke Grasstongue, but the sheer clamor of frightened voices made it hard to pick out any words. Then an outlying zebra fled past, closer to the elephants, and she heard its bellow of warning.

"Lions! *Lions!*"

Sky gave a gasp and shambled back another step. *Lions.* All she knew of them was that they had killed her mother, bringing her down while she was still weak and ill after Sky's birth. *Lions!* A chill rippled down her spine.

"Sky, I'm frightened." Inside the defensive circle, the small voice was just audible.

At once Sky turned to her little cousin and stroked his trunk with hers. *I must pretend to be brave, for him.* "It's all right, Moon. They can't reach us here. The grown ones won't let them." Gently she rubbed the back of his bristly neck. "I'll keep you safe, and the family will protect both of us. There's nothing to be afraid of."

"But *lions* . . ."

"Think, Moon, Great Mother is with us! What lion would dare to attack her?"

Moon thought for a moment, then nodded, looking hugely reassured. He snuggled his head against Sky's flank and tried to hook his tiny trunk over her back. "You're right, Sky. I feel better now. Thanks."

"Remember, the Great Spirit lives in Great Mother," she whispered to her little cousin. "Sometimes lions frighten me too, but she won't let them touch us."

"I wish we didn't have to share Great Mother with all the animals," murmured Moon.

"Oh, it's a great honor, Moon—be proud of her!" Sky glanced adoringly at Great Mother, who was facing the stampede with her trunk raised. Her noble face was lined with age now, the edges of her ears torn, but her long tusks still gleamed as white as the stars. For as long as Sky could remember, and long before that, her grandmother had been far more than just the loving matriarch of the Strider Family. Lowering her voice, she whispered to Moon: "Our own grandmother is the leader of the whole of Bravelands!"

Great Mother, as the holder of the Great Spirit, gave advice and counsel to all the creatures of the savannah. She judged their disputes, interpreted their omens, and resolved their fights, all with wisdom and stern patience. Great Mother might be growing old and frail, but she could still face down stampeding herds and prowling predators.

Right now, she looked downright irritated.

"That is *quite* enough," Great Mother trumpeted. She stamped a foot, making the ground vibrate. "The pride have their prey, and it is *over!*"

Almost immediately, the chaos began to subside. The galloping hordes slowed, cantering and trotting and finally halting to mill around the elephants. Some even looked a little embarrassed about their panic. As the hubbub died down, one wildebeest brayed a sad call to a friend who would never answer again.

Great Mother strode forward, and the ring of elephants broke up, relaxing. Sky took the chance to peer across the savannah, nervously seeking out the lions. At last she caught a glimpse of them, a long way across the dry grassland, dragging their kill beneath the shade of a spreading acacia. She let herself breathe a sigh of relief, keeping it silent so that her little cousin wouldn't notice.

"You see, Moon?" Sky rubbed his small head gently. "We were safe the whole time."

The panic might be over, but some of the zebras and wildebeests were still barking and neighing furiously at one another, pawing the ground and peeling back their lips from their teeth. Great Mother paced closer until she was standing right over them, and they were forced to look up.

"What, by the Great Spirit, is going on here?" she demanded.

A wildebeest stepped forward, dipping its head respectfully. "The zebras didn't keep watch properly! And now the flesh-eaters have taken one of ours!"

"That's nonsense!" a zebra snapped at the wildebeest. But when he turned to Great Mother, he too lowered his head. "Great Mother, the wildebeest tried to direct the lions toward my herd. Self-preservation is all very well, but a deliberate attempt to sacrifice a zebra instead—"

"That's not true!" retorted another wildebeest. Yet again, she turned toward the huge elephant with respect. "There was chaos, Great Mother. You know how it is."

Great Mother swayed thoughtfully, then blew with her trunk into the ground, sending up a small flurry of dust. "Listen to me," she said patiently. "As grass-eaters, you must trust one another, and you must accept that other herds act in good faith. You rely on one another to keep watch and survive."

Not one of them argued; they simply dipped their heads and pawed lightly at the ground, looking faintly ashamed. "Yes, Great Mother."

"And remember," she added in a kind voice, "predators will follow you and they will hunt you. It is the Bravelands way.

Remember the Code? *Only kill to survive.* Lions too must survive, my friends, and they have a right to eat."

"And this time," admitted the zebra gruffly, "every zebra survived to run and graze again. We were lucky." He shook his stiff mane and turned back to the wildebeest. "May your herd-mate's spirit run free in the savannah of the stars," he said gravely.

Both wildebeests dipped their heads in acknowledgment. "May the Great Spirit repay his sacrifice," they intoned together, "with sweet grass that grows fresh forever."

Reconciled, the three grass-eaters walked away from the elephants and were soon lost once more in the milling multitudes of their herds. Great Mother nodded in satisfaction, then turned without a word and began to march on with her steady, ponderous stride. The other elephants fell in behind her, and the zebra and wildebeest herds moved alongside them, grazing and talking civilly once more.

Sky was glad it was over; she had hated the idea that lions were so close, and secretly she didn't blame the grass-eaters for being angry. *No wonder every beast is grumpy*, she thought. She was tired and thirsty; they all were. The herds of elephants, zebras, and wildebeests had been traveling through the dry season, after all, and though the rains had begun, there was still a way to go before they reached the watering hole where the Great Gathering would take place.

All the same, Sky was excited about the journey. Throughout the year it was the vultures who carried news from across Bravelands to Great Mother; even now, as she marched at the head of all the herds, the huge birds spiraled down from the sky to speak to her, bald heads gleaming, and she answered them in their own screeching Skytongue.

Moon was watching the vultures too. "If those birds bring all the news to Great Mother, why do we have the Great Gathering?"

"Because that's when all the animals know she'll be there, and they can come and talk to her," Sky told him patiently. "Hundreds and hundreds of them travel to see her and ask for her help with their problems." She blew dust at the little elephant with her trunk. "Besides, Moon, the Great Gathering is *fun!*"

"Oh. Well, I can't *wait.*" Moon darted in a circle at a floppy canter.

At least Moon isn't too thirsty, thought Sky. *He's full of energy.* But then he was still drinking his mother's milk, and while poor Star looked tired and much thinner after the dry season, she was still producing enough to sustain her little one.

Sky plucked a blade of grass as she walked and tickled Moon behind the ear. He giggled and dodged, so she picked another, enjoying the game.

It was when she reached for a third that her trunk brushed a bone fragment on the ground.

Something flashed, white and bright, inside her head. Sky gasped. It was a blur of images, and she could barely make sense of it; she knew only that a huge bird was swooping toward her out of the sun. Then, as fast as it had come, the vision was gone.

Sky paused and shook her head, her breath rasping, her heart thudding hard. *What was that?*

She squinted back at the bone. It was small, thin, and splintered; maybe it had broken from the leg of a small gazelle? *It was certainly no elephant bone!* All elephants could read the bones of their ancestors—but Sky knew that only Great Mother herself had the power to read those of other creatures.

I was mistaken. I'm tired and thirsty and I imagined it. Sky glanced above her. *The sun's high and my eyes got tricked, that's all. There are lots of birds around. . . .* She started, anxiously. *Oh! Now I've lost Moon!*

But he had only drifted to the edge of the herd, capering around the grown ones' legs. "Moon, are you all right?" she called.

"Yes," he trumpeted squeakily. "Just playing!"

"Well, be sure to keep up with the herd," she warned him. "And don't wander off!"

"I won't!"

At least the distraction of Moon had taken her mind off that silly bird-illusion, she realized. Feeling better, Sky trotted to catch up with Star and Rain, who were chatting together, reminiscing about previous treks to Great Gatherings. They turned as she approached, greeting her with caresses of their trunks.

"Sky," murmured Star in a singsong voice. "Are you tired?"

"Not too bad," Sky told her cheerfully. "But it's a long way yet and I want to listen to your stories, if you don't mind?"

"Of course we don't mind." Rain laughed, her mottled

trunk swaying. "I was just reminding Star about the year of the Three-Legged Cheetah. . . ."

Sky listened happily, glad to while away the time. She loved all the grown ones; they'd raised her together after the death of her mother. *I still miss her,* she thought, *but having Star and Rain and the others is like having a whole herd of mothers.*

"Go on, Sky," said Star, nudging her. "It's time for you to tell us a story. What's your favorite memory?"

Sky dipped her head shyly. "I'm not really old enough to have a story," she murmured. "But my favorite memory is . . . Oh! My mother, spraying me with water at the end of a hot day."

The two older elephants laughed. "Well, now that's a lovely memory!" rumbled Rain. "What I wouldn't give for a trunkful of water right now!"

"Is my son all right?" asked Star, glancing over at him. "It's time he had more milk."

"Moon's fine," Sky told her happily, nodding at her little cousin as he stirred up a miniature dust storm with his trunk. "Look, he's still playing. I'll go and get him if you like."

She ambled over to where he had wandered a little way from the herd. "Moon!" she called, raising her trunk. "Your mother wants you!"

"Sky, look what I found! A *huge* blue beetle!" he squealed happily. "Come and see!"

Sighing patiently, Sky trotted over. "Where is it, Moon? Listen, I told you not to wander away from the—"

She gasped as a massive, pale shape lumbered out of the

scrub, broad horn pointing accusingly at the two young elephants.

Rhinoceros! Oh no. Sky's heart sank in trepidation.

"Hey, this is *my* territory!" grunted the rhino. "Keep out! Hooligans!"

Swallowing hard, Sky lowered and swung her head in apology. "I'm sorry, Moon's little and didn't realize. I'll just—"

"I said go on! Be off with you!" The rhino pawed the ground and dipped its massive head in a clear threat.

"Sorry!" squealed Sky again. Hustling Moon with her trunk, she hurried back to her family.

Great Mother turned her huge head as the two youngsters trotted toward her, and blew a soft rumble of greeting. "Don't mind him, young Sky," she called. "Some of the rhinos in Bravelands are bad-tempered, that's all."

Letting Moon scurry back to Star, Sky fell in beside Great Mother as she strode along. "Why are they so angry?" she asked. "I thought he was going to charge us!"

"Oh, the rhinoceroses are envious," sighed Great Mother. "As long as any creature alive can remember, and further back even than that, the Great Mother or Father has been an elephant. The Great Spirit passes from one Great Parent to the next when we die. You know that, Sky, don't you?"

Sky nodded.

"Well, it has never passed to a rhino!" Great Mother told her with a dry, rumbling laugh. "And they've thought for a *long* time that it should be their turn."

"A rhino wouldn't be nearly as good and kind as you," said

Sky loyally. "And that's silly anyway. The Great Spirit chooses where it wants to go, so it's not our fault it's never picked a rhino."

"That's right, Sky." Great Mother stroked Sky's neck with her trunk, but the gesture meant she'd had to turn her head a little. Her foot knocked against a small rocky outcrop, and she stumbled, only just righting herself.

"Great Mother!" cried Sky in alarm. "Are you all right? Do you need to stop and rest?"

The old elephant rumbled a deep laugh. "No, Sky. Don't you worry about me." She lifted her head and walked on, scanning the horizon ahead. "I may be very old, but I have a long way to go yet. I'll know when the time has come for the Great Spirit to leave me."

Sky was silent for a moment. "How will you know?" she asked in a small voice. The thought of being without Great Mother was unbearable.

"I just will, my dear. And when the time comes, the Great Spirit will tell me where to find the next Great Mother or Father, so that it can pass to them. That is how it has always been, and how it always will be."

"Well," muttered Sky, "please don't pass the Spirit to that horrible rhino."

Great Mother laughed. "If that's what the Spirit wishes, that's what will be. Ah!" She pointed ahead with her trunk. "Water, look!"

Peering, Sky could see it now: a shimmer on the horizon,

fringed with lush greenness, dark against the paleness of the plains. A murmur of delight and relief went around the herd, and they picked up their speed.

Sky gave a trumpet of excitement as the small lake came properly into view, brownish-green, still, and cool. It looked delicious.

"We can have a water fight!" cried Moon.

"Good idea!" Sky trotted to the muddy bank and dipped her trunk toward the water's surface.

"Wait!" commanded Great Mother.

Sky hesitated, glancing over her shoulder as the matriarch approached the pool.

"No." The old elephant shook her great head and pointed with her trunk. "The water is tainted, my dears. I'm sorry."

Sky followed her gesture, and could barely repress a cry of dismay.

"You see it, Sky?" Great Mother shook her head slowly. "A dead impala. And it has lain there for some time."

It floated just below the stagnant surface, half eaten and horribly bloated. Now that they were so close, Sky could indeed smell the rank rottenness that permeated the water; she blew it from her trunk with a shudder. Great Mother was right. There were soft cries of disappointment from the rest of the herd, but no elephant argued with her.

Sighing, Sky drew back. "Come on, Moon. Don't touch it."

Moon looked miserable, but he plodded back to her side.

The others looked no happier; Star in particular gave the pool a wistful, longing stare.

"Now," said Great Mother encouragingly, swinging her trunk. "There's nothing else for it. Come along, my dears." She set off once more, resolute and stoic. "We must simply keep walking. . . ."

CHAPTER 6

The surface of the river was muddy and churned, but Thorn could quite clearly see the long, horny backs of the crocodiles that lurked in the water. He scratched his chin. Some of the reptiles looked dozy, basking in the dappled sunlight on the far bank, but the ones in the river were open-eyed and alert. And he didn't even trust the sleepy ones to stay that way.

A little way off, two Highleaves from the Council relaxed at the top of a shady tree, yawning as they waited for the young baboons to embark on their challenge. One of the watchers was Mango; she picked a tick from Branch's fur and popped it idly into her mouth. They did not seem very concerned or even particularly watchful, but Thorn knew that their half-shut eyes would register everything.

Behind Thorn and Mud, Fearless shifted restlessly on his paws. Thorn could see how anxious his lion friend was. *We have until sunset*, Thorn remembered. *If we don't complete the Feat by then, we fail forever.*

"Whose idea was this?" muttered Mud at his side. "Cross the Crocodile River, indeed."

"It proves we're fast," Thorn reminded him. "And it proves we have courage."

"It proves we're out of our minds," grumbled Mud.

"Well, I believe in you both!" declared Fearless.

Thorn was touched by the lion's faith. He knew Fearless was disappointed that his plan to attempt the Feats himself had come to nothing, and it was kind of him to be so supportive. The young lion crouched down, licking his jaws as he gazed at the sluggish flow of the river.

A flock of storks prodded the shallows with their great yellow bills, occasionally stirring the water with their feet. The crocodiles ignored them; some had already turned in the water and were eyeing the baboons.

In their tree, Mango and Branch became suddenly alert. Thorn followed their gaze to where Fang, one of Nut's friends, was hopping into the water. He swam quickly past the crocodiles, driven more by panic, Thorn suspected, than determination. His head bobbed like a shiny wet fruit until he reached the far bank, where he scrambled up and leaped around, hooting and hollering his victory. The Highleaves gave nods of approval.

Thorn sighed, wishing he'd been the first to go. The crocodiles were ready for them now. One of them crawled from the water, chasing Notch, who had ventured close, but she scampered out of reach with a shriek of fear. The crocodile subsided back into the river and muttered something to its neighbor in harsh Sandtongue. Both reptiles rasped something that sounded horribly like a laugh; a chill went through Thorn's bones at the sound.

"Be careful," whispered Mud shakily. "Mother says crocodiles don't follow the Code. They don't hunt only when they're hungry. They kill when they like and they answer to no creature—not even Great Mother."

Thorn took a deep breath. *If I want to be with Berry, I have to do this. I don't have a choice.*

A sharp movement caught his eye, and he turned to see Nut springing into the water, cheered on by his gang watching on the shore. With one eye on the looming crocodiles, Nut paddled a little distance, then scrambled up onto some tangled, floating debris.

That raft won't save him if he doesn't move, thought Thorn, his heart in his mouth. *The crocodiles will just knock him off!* He disliked Nut, but he did *not* want to see him get eaten.

But Nut was already leaping nimbly from log to stone to fallen branch, darting away from snapping jaws. His final leap took him right onto the ridged back of an enormous crocodile. Before it could twist in the water and dislodge him, he was off again, leaping and splashing for the bank. When he reached it, scurrying easily clear of the pursuing jaws, he gave a whoop of triumph.

"I'm a Middleleaf! Chew on that, crocs!"

Mango and Branch, eyeing him from their shady vantage

point, exchanged a nod of agreement. Nut's friends whooped and slapped the sand.

"Nut's done it." Thorn couldn't help but be impressed, but a glance at Mud told him his friend was more frightened than ever.

"Come on, Mud," he said, trying to sound confident. "It's now or never." Thorn gently nudged his little friend toward the water's edge.

"Good luck!" growled Fearless. "Remember, just keep *moving*."

Thorn's paws were in the water now; crocodiles drifted lazily around to watch him. They clearly knew there was no hurry. "Stay close to me, Mud," he whispered. *Maybe I can just drag Mud with me if we get into difficulties. . . .*

With a gasp of determination he plunged into the river, Mud right behind him. One of the floating branch-rafts Nut had used was not far ahead, and Thorn headed for it, swimming furiously.

"We can do this!" he panted to Mud.

There was a sudden, wild thrashing in the water of rolling bodies and crashing tails. Startled, Thorn raised his head to see what was happening.

"It's Nut," exclaimed Mud, spitting out green water. "He's throwing stones at the crocs!"

Thorn looked over to the far bank and saw Mud was right. The vicious young baboon bent to grab another stone.

"Let's make this interesting!" Nut hooted. Grinning in malice, he stretched back a long foreleg and hurled his stone at the scaly spine of a crocodile. The huge reptile erupted from the river in a fountain of white foam, jaws gaping.

"*Oh,*" moaned Mud. "Its *teeth.*"

"Sky and stone," breathed Thorn, shuddering. The jagged teeth were savage, brutally big, and they lined the crocodile's entire mouth from front to back.

More stones pattered down as Nut flung one after another; they rattled on tough crocodile hide and splashed into the water, driving the reptiles into a frenzy of fury. The surface churned and a wave swamped Mud's face; he came up spluttering.

"Nut! Stop it, you idiot!" yelled Thorn.

Ignoring him, Nut grabbed and threw more stones. Storks flapped out of reach with a noisy beating of white wings, and incensed crocodiles were speeding through the water toward any baboon they could see. A huge one submerged, and Thorn could see ripples rising and arrowing from the spot where it had vanished. The pointed wake moved swiftly toward him and Mud.

It's swimming straight at us!

"Get out, get out!" he hooted in alarm, and turned, splashing back toward shore. Even as he and Mud reached dry land, he heard the crocodile break the surface of the water behind them, muttering angrily in Sandtongue. On all fours, the two young baboons raced back toward Fearless, who was waiting among the trees; the crocodile gave up, grunting, and slid back into the river.

"That selfish, mean little—*monkey!*" spat Thorn, using the

worst insult he could think of. "Nut just wants to stop anyone else completing the Feat!"

"And it looks as if he's succeeded," remarked Mud dolefully, gazing back at the now wide-awake crocodiles.

"Mango! Branch!" Thorn yelled at the two Highleaves. "See what Nut's doing?"

Branch gave a regretful shrug. "We're only here to report on the successful baboons. Mango, what do you think? Is this against the rules?"

"I don't know." Mango scratched her armpit. "Not sure. Never heard it's been done before, but there isn't a rule about it. Not as far as I know."

Infuriated, Thorn cursed the two Highleaves under his breath, then padded back to Mud. "I'm not giving up," he growled. "Not because of *Nut*. There's got to be something we can do." He glanced around, thinking hard. "Logs, Mud— remember we practiced with logs? Maybe we could lay a log over the river?"

"That's a great idea," said Mud.

Together, they picked their way through the trees, peering at the ground, pawing at the forest litter, and dragging supple boughs aside. Spiders scuttled away as they turned over stones and broken wood. There was a deep layer of rotting leaves and moss, and plenty of overhanging ferns and foliage, but a distinct absence of broken branches.

"There isn't anything long enough to use," sighed Mud at last. "On the other hand, there's one up there. . . ."

Thorn and Fearless followed his pointing paw. Mud was

staring up at a thick kigelia branch that dipped over their heads.

"No fruits on it," mused Fearless. "It could be dead. Might snap quite easily."

"How would we do that, though?" wondered Thorn.

"Oh, that's easy enough," Mud told him. He nodded at Fearless. "He's broken branches before!"

"Exactly!" Fearless opened his jaws to give them both a grin. "For once a big heavy lion might be useful in a tree."

"It's worth a try." Thorn slapped the ground with excitement. "Go on, then, Baboon-Lion!"

He watched, biting his paws as Fearless circled the tree, studying it. At last the young lion jumped up, grabbing and hugging the trunk with all four limbs. Paw over paw he dragged his weight up, claws raking the bark.

Thorn swallowed, his heart in his mouth. "I hope this works, Mud. I hope he doesn't hurt himself."

Fearless's tail lashed as he hauled himself up to the big, low-hanging branch. Then, taking a deep breath, he edged out onto it. Thorn could hardly watch as, digging in his claws, Fearless pulled himself farther along. Beneath him, the bough dipped and creaked.

"It's working!" cried Mud.

Fearless bounced the branch a little, making it sag farther. "I think it's pretty rotten," he called.

"Can you go a bit farther?" asked Thorn shakily.

Fearless crept out along the branch. It sagged wildly, and there was a hollow cracking noise.

"Yes!" he roared, just as the branch snapped off. Together he and it crashed onto the ground, but this time the fall wasn't nearly so far. The young lion bounced up and off the broken bough, unhurt.

"You're a hero, Fearless!" exclaimed Thorn, rubbing his paws.

"Now," said Mud with satisfaction, "let's get it to the river!"

Together, the three friends began to shove the log toward the bank, the baboons using their paws and Fearless his teeth. It was hard, awkward work, since the branch caught on every rock and hummock and jutting twig, and they were panting with exhaustion by the time they rolled it to the water's muddy edge. The other young baboons still waiting to attempt the crossing, their efforts frustrated by Nut, watched them with a mixture of skepticism and envy. At last, they managed to maneuver the log into position, jammed between two stones and thrusting out over the lazy river. Crocodiles surged through the water, lurking and watching.

"It doesn't quite reach the other side," grunted Mud in disappointment.

"It's all we've got," said Thorn grimly. "We have to give it a go."

"I'll sit on this end," offered Fearless. "That'll help keep it steady." He slumped over the splintered end of the branch, his weight anchoring it to the riverbank.

"Now." Thorn rubbed his paws together and climbed up onto the branch. Mud scrambled up behind him, and the two young baboons began to creep out over the water.

"Ow," yelped Mud, as one of Nut's stones smacked his flank. Nut's gleeful hoot carried across the water.

"So he's still at it," growled Thorn. "And it's still winding up the crocs."

Some of the crocodiles had clearly figured out where the rocks were coming from, and they were lunging out of the water after Nut. But he was quick and agile, and he danced easily away until they gave up. Then the huge reptiles would return to take out their irritation on the other baboons, and Nut would resume his stone-pelting.

The vast, open jaws of a crocodile surged out of the water and snapped together far too close to Thorn's paw. "Ahhh! It's going to knock us off. Go back, go back!"

"I hate Nut," muttered Mud, skittering quickly back toward shore once again.

"I know," agreed Thorn grimly, retreating with him. "But we'll show him."

Back at the bank, Nut's friends cackled mockingly as he and Mud scrambled up the sand. Thorn ignored them and cast around desperately in search of an idea. "Ah!"

The storks had settled a little upriver and they were probing the water once more, stirring up the riverbed with their long feet and taking no notice of the crocodiles or the baboons.

Thorn grinned at Mud. "I've got an idea."

He turned and loped along the bank toward the storks, Mango and Branch watching him curiously. When he was within easy reach of them he took a deep breath and bolted straight into the middle of the flock.

It was a lot more fun than trying to cross a lethal river. Thorn plunged in among the birds, screeching and yelling, "Out of my way, monkey brains! Sludge sitters!" From their angry stabbing beaks and shrieks in Skytongue, they clearly recognized insults even in a strange language. Thorn waved his paws and hooted and whooped, ducking as the storks flapped in alarm. One by one, the birds took to the air on white-and-gray wings, their red faces indignant. The whole flock was soon airborne, a flurry of feathers and long legs, soaring away from the leaping, screeching baboon.

Surrounded by a cloud of storks, Thorn bounded back toward the branch-bridge. White wings slapped his face as he ran but he didn't care; he dashed whooping toward Mud.

"Now!"

Under the cover of the mob of milling storks, Thorn sprang up onto the branch and began to run across. Mud gasped, catching on to his plan, and raced behind him.

It was hard to see more than glimpses of the end of the branch, through the chaos of feathers and legs and yellow beaks, but Thorn kept his eyes fixed ahead of him. He was aware of snapping jaws and the crashing showers of spray as crocodiles snapped wildly at the storks and fell back into the water, but he ignored them. The tip of the branch was in sight now, and he sped faster. Reaching the very end, he launched himself into the air.

His paws thudded down, splashing in shallow water, and they kept moving until he felt the gritty dry sand of the bank between his toes: *I made it! I'm a Middleleaf!*

Hooting with delight, he dodged and sprinted away from a land-bound crocodile, outpacing it easily and springing up onto a low overhanging branch.

"I did it, Mud, I did it!" he whooped. "You're nearly there! Run!"

Mud was almost at the end of the branch, but the cloud of storks was clearing now, the birds calming down and skidding in to land, fluffing their wings and preening their ruffled feathers.

"Hurry up!" Thorn yelled in sudden panic.

But Mud had frozen, terrified. The storks had settled completely; they were already beginning to dip their beaks in the shallows again, and Mud was completely exposed on the branch. Crocodiles shot toward him through the murky water, jaws widening to show those huge, jagged teeth; more of them lurched in from the bank. One of them rolled, exposing a pale, leathery belly, and its mighty tail lashed.

The tip caught Mud, and for a moment he wobbled on the branch, eyes wide with panic. With a scream of terror, he plunged beneath the foaming surface.

CHAPTER 7

Mud vanished in a mob of thrashing crocodiles, swallowed up by the green river. The two Highleaves and the watching young baboons shrieked and pounded the ground, aghast.

Fearless leaped to his paws, horrified.

"Mud!"

His small head came up once, spluttering, his face twisted in terror; then he sank under again.

"No! *No!*" Fearless sprang toward the river and launched himself in, the muddy water turning silver as it showered up around him. For a few paces his paws sank into the soft river-bed, and it was hard going—and then abruptly there was no bottom at all, and Fearless was afloat.

Instinctively he thrashed his limbs. Discovering that he didn't sink, he paddled and swam forward to the place where he'd last seen Mud. The river was a boiling riot of crocodiles, snapping at one another as much as at their prey, and Fearless tried not to imagine unseen jaws, closing suddenly around his legs. He had to find his friend.

Then a sodden head rose out of the water once more, lips peeled back in a screech of fright. Fearless powered through the water, ignoring the lashing tails of crocodiles and the screeching of baboons from the bank, and grabbed Mud's scruff gently in his jaws.

The baboon was fighting, and Fearless's head was yanked underwater with him. When he came back up, he saw why Mud was struggling—and why he couldn't move him.

Mud's leg was caught in a crocodile's jaws.

Horror shot through Fearless. Letting go of Mud, he swiped at the reptile's head, snarling and clawing. The crocodile only glared at him, its savage pointed teeth still buried in Mud's flesh. Fearless realized there was no way he could shift those massive, powerful jaws, or drag Mud away without leaving his leg behind. Gasping for breath, he lunged again, this time scratching wildly at the crocodile's eye.

The crocodile shook its head violently, making Mud yelp and splutter with pain. *Its eye. That worked!*

Finding purchase for his hind paws against the reptile's scaly flank, Fearless lashed out again, roaring. He felt a claw catch in the beast's eyelid; it grunted and snapped back its head, releasing Mud.

Fearless had no intention of hanging around for a fight, and he certainly didn't have time to make sure that Mud was alive. He seized the baboon once more in his jaws and paddled as hard as he could for the muddy bank. He'd been swept down-stream, out of sight of the other baboons, but he didn't dare try to swim back to them. *I have to get out of the water!*

Dripping, Fearless scrambled ashore and sprinted away from the excited crocodiles. They were still in pursuit, running surprisingly fast on their stumpy legs, and when he glanced over his shoulder he felt his heart lurch. He bolted for the forest, trying to veer as far from the riverbank as he could.

I can't wait for Thorn. He'll have to head for the narrow crossing farther downstream, where there aren't any crocodiles.

Fearless bounded on, Mud hanging limply in his jaws. He didn't dare look back until he was certain the sounds of pursuit had faded. At last he risked another glance over his shoulder, and realized the crocodiles were no longer behind him. His lungs aching, his muscles burning, Fearless slowed to a trot. Not until the narrow crossing came in sight, and he felt it was safe to halt, did he lay Mud's limp body gently on the ground.

Sure enough, Thorn was racing across the smooth river-rocks toward him, leaping from one to another until he was back on the bank. His eyes were wide and white-rimmed with fear, and he threw himself on Mud, rocking him gently. "Mud! *Mud!*"

"A croc had him," gasped Fearless, panting. "It bit his leg."

Carefully, his paws trembling, Thorn turned his friend over, and they both took a horrified breath. Mud's leg was bleeding from a bad tear, fur ripped.

"Is he . . . is he . . ." Fearless couldn't say the word.

"I don't think so. Oh, Great Spirit, I hope he's—" Thorn gave his friend a cautious shake. "Breathe, Mud!"

Mud gave a sharp, rasping cough, and his eyes blinked open.

"Mud!" they chorused together.

"You're alive," huffed Fearless, weak with relief.

"Thank you," mumbled Mud, spitting out river water. "Thank you, thank you."

"Yes, *thank you.*" Hugging Mud close, Thorn turned toward Fearless. "If it hadn't been for you, Mud would have died!"

Fearless wasn't calm enough even to nod in acknowledgment. "If it hadn't been for *Nut*," he snarled, "this would never have happened!"

"You're right," agreed Thorn. The expression on his gray-furred face was grim. "But all that can wait. Let's get Mud home."

Fearless crouched low, and as carefully as he could, Thorn heaved his friend up onto the young lion's back, then scrambled up after him. Fearless set off, trying to keep his stride as level as possible so that he wouldn't jolt poor Mud. As hard as he tried, though, he heard Mud stifling cries of pain every time his paws hit the ground.

As they came in sight of Tall Trees, the first baboon Fearless saw was Stinger. He came bounding toward them, his expression turning from expectation to anxiety to sudden alarm.

"What happened?" he barked. "Thorn, what's wrong with Mud?"

"He got bitten," Thorn said tersely as he jumped off

Fearless's back. "A croc knocked him off a branch we were using, and he fell in among them. He would have died if it hadn't been for Fearless." Thorn stroked his friend's neck. "Fearless jumped in and attacked the crocodile."

"Fearless," gasped Stinger as other baboons began to gather, hooting softly with horror and concern. "I'm so proud of you. Thank you for this."

Mud's mother was wriggling and pushing through the crowd; the baboons parted respectfully when they saw it was the Starleaf. She rushed to Fearless's side and stroked Mud's sodden head, chittering reassurance in his ear. He was awake, his eyes slitted open, but he lay limp across Fearless's spine.

"Fearless," she urged him, "bring Mud to the Goodleaves, quickly!"

The Goodleaf baboons must have heard the news already, because by the time Fearless carried Mud into their glade, they had already drenched many leaves in honey and were waiting. They set to work at once, bathing Mud's leg and wrapping his wounds in a leaf poultice.

Berry had joined them and was looking at Thorn, her brown eyes filled with concern. "He'll be all right," she murmured, touching his arm. "Mud might be small, but he's tough." Thorn nodded gratefully.

"The jackalberry leaves will stop the bleeding," the oldest of the Goodleaves reassured Mud's mother. "And the honey will help his wounds heal and stop them from turning bad. Don't worry, Starleaf. The bite is messy, but not too deep. He'll keep his leg."

"Thank the Great Spirit." The Starleaf sighed, closing her eyes in gratitude.

Fearless was suddenly weak with relief, the exhaustion of the day catching up with him. Beside him he heard Thorn let out a long sigh, and knew that his friend was feeling exactly the same. Berry squeezed Thorn's paw briefly and slipped away.

Some of the troop had followed them into the Goodleaves' peaceful glade and were observing quietly, but a little way away, echoing from beyond a clump of thorn trees, Fearless could hear whoops and hoots of unrestrained celebration.

"I'm a Middleleaf, I'm a Middleleaf!"

"You are, you are!"

"Monkey nuts to crocodiles, they don't scare *you*!"

Fearless recognized at least one of the raucous voices, and rage burned in his throat. Leaving Mud in the capable paws of the healers, he bounded toward the sounds of celebration. Thorn sprang to his side, and he could hear other baboons following inquisitively, but he didn't look back. He could focus only on the screeching laughter and cheering, and his muzzle peeled back from his teeth as he ran.

"Nut!" Fearless skidded to a halt in a shower of leaves, roaring. The cheering baboons fell silent with shock, staring at him.

"Why are you celebrating?" he snarled at Nut and his gang. "This was all your fault!"

Nut's eyes widened. Recovering quickly, he drew back his lips to show his fangs. "My fault? How do you reckon that, Big Talk?"

Fearless stalked forward. "You threw stones at the croco-diles. You drove them wild deliberately! You tried to stop any other baboon from crossing the river—and because of what you did, Mud almost died!"

"*Mud?*" Nut screeched in scorn. "Mud shouldn't have tried that Feat in the first place! It's not *my* fault if he's too scrawny and pathetic." He scratched his snout, then grinned mali-ciously. "Almost as pathetic as a lion who thinks he's one of us."

A familiar tide of rage flooded through Fearless; he could almost detect the stench of terrified hyena in his head. But he barely had time to recognize the thrill of furious power in his sinews before his forepaws slammed into Nut.

The baboon hit the earth hard. Fearless crouched over him, opening his jaws in a violent roar that made Nut shut his eyes tight. Fearless could feel him wriggling and squirming—could even hear his pleading whimpers—but he pinned him down tightly with his full weight. His claws pricked Nut's skin.

"Stop!" a voice cried desperately in his ear, and he felt fin-gers tugging at his fur. "Fearless, stop!"

His ears were ringing, and blood pounded in his skull, but he finally registered Thorn's pleas. He gave one last roar, his slaver dripping onto Nut's terrified face, and then he pulled away. Turning his rump on Nut, he flicked his tail across the young baboon's face in disgust.

The rage was subsiding now, and he could see more clearly—and what he saw was his own troop, shivering and terrified. A couple of smaller baboons crept backward, hiding behind their friends. One scuttled into a clump of ferns and did not emerge. Thorn and Stinger were watching him with shock in their eyes. Fearless blinked.

Oh, Great Spirit! What have I done?

Grub Highleaf was first to recover. He shambled forward and pointed at Fearless, his fangs bared. "See! I tried to tell you all. I knew what would happen if we let a lion into the troop!"

"I . . . I'm sorry," said Fearless.

"He'll kill us all!" screeched Grub.

"He wouldn't—" began Thorn.

"Yes! Yes, he would!" Grub snarled. "It's not natural for a lion to live with baboons. It isn't *right!*"

Stinger pushed himself between Thorn and the furious Grub. "Fearless is our friend," he said firmly. "He only attacked Nut because he was defending Mud!"

"Defending him?" shrieked Grub. "Mud is back there with the Goodleaves! This beast tried to kill Nut!"

As the argument raged around him, Fearless could only stand there, motionless with shock. Grub's harsh words didn't hurt at all; what really stung him was his own behavior.

Grub's right—I did nearly kill Nut. And just for a moment, I wanted to.

"The lion can't control himself." Nut, trembling still, was speaking to Stinger.

"Yes, he can!" snapped Thorn, fangs bared. "If he hadn't, you'd be dead now!"

Fearless swallowed hard. *You don't know how close I came, my friend. . . .*

"He's a danger to the whole troop," said Splinter, a young

female. "We can't let him stay."

The argument looked horribly likely to rage all night; Fearless wanted nothing more than to curl up and put his paws over his ears. It was a relief when Berry Highleaf ran out of the trees, barking an alert.

"Stop, all of you! Stop!"

A few of them turned, inquisitive and irritated, though Grub had opened his jaws to shout at Thorn again.

"All of you!" Berry cried. *"Listen to me!"*

The yells and screeches faded as every baboon turned to her. Silence fell.

She was panting, shaking, her brown eyes huge. "Stop, stop. You have to come with me."

Stinger ran to his daughter, stretching out a paw. "Berry, what—"

She sucked in a breath, and her words came out on a sob.

"Bark Crownleaf is *dead.*"

CHAPTER 8

Fearless raced alongside the baboons through the trees, following Berry's lead. She leaped a trickle of gray water, scrambled over a mossy log, and darted nimbly through a tangle of branches; the other baboons followed, light-footed and agile. Fearless crashed after them, determined not to be left behind by his troop. No one spoke, Fearless noticed as his paws thudded desperately; every baboon was fully focused on Berry's shocking words.

Bark Crownleaf is dead.

Bark Crownleaf is dead.

Berry led them to the edge of Tall Trees, to a deep ditch that filled with water in the wet season; now, at its beginning, there was little more than swampy mud. In it lay Bark Crownleaf, eyes glazed and half open, sprawled in death. Near her body lay another: the ragged, matted corpse of a hyena.

Brightforest Troop was silent as they crept closer. There was fear and distress in every baboon's eyes; a baby began to whimper.

As Stinger and some others jumped down to Bark's side, touching her gently and chittering sadly, Fearless slid down after them on his haunches. He sniffed at the dead hyena.

Oh no, he realized with a sick lurch. *It's the same one I scared away.*

He turned to stare at Bark's body. The smell of the hyena was all over her, and in a deep wound on her side, a long claw was embedded. Her jaws were open; one of her long teeth was snapped off. Stinger touched the broken stump, frowning.

Thorn crouched by the limp corpse of the hyena. Using his long fingers, he parted the coarse hair on its neck.

"Look," Thorn whispered.

Fearless's eyes widened: a broken fang was half buried in the hyena's neck. Thorn tugged it out and held it up for all to see.

Silently, Stinger took it from him, turning it over in his paws and studying it for a long time. "Bark's," he said at last in a choked voice. He rubbed his scarred snout. "She and the hyena must have battled. And somehow neither of them triumphed. Each one killed the other."

Every baboon watched Stinger as he carried the broken fang back to the top of the ditch. He rose up on his hind paws, displaying it reverently.

"Hear me, Brightforest Troop," he cried. "This is a sign of Bark Crownleaf's bravery and spirit. She killed the attacker who intended to kill us. She was a great and wise Crownleaf to this troop, and she will be missed."

The baboons hooted sadly, some of them pounding the ground with their forepaws. Fearless huffed along with them in agreement.

"Soon, we shall decide who will be our new Crownleaf," declared Stinger, stroking the tooth gently. "But for now, let us mourn Bark Crownleaf: finest of leaders."

Fearless watched as, one by one, the baboons jumped down into the ditch. Lovingly they touched and stroked Bark's lifeless body, before turning away and padding back in silence into the shadows of Tall Trees. Bark's body they left where it lay; it was the custom of all Bravelands creatures to leave their dead for the vultures. It made Fearless a little sad, but he knew it made good sense: Bark Crownleaf's body would nourish the life of Bravelands, just as every Crownleaf's had before her.

Just as my father's did, too.

Guilt wrenched Fearless's gut. *And I failed Bark Crownleaf, just like I failed Father.*

He waited until the last baboon had visited the body before he padded across and touched a paw to Bark's cold fur. *Goodbye, Bark. I may not be a baboon, but I was part of your troop. You were my leader.*

Thorn and Mud were waiting for him. "Bark died defending Brightforest Troop," Thorn said gently, patting his shoulder. "There's no more honorable way to go. Don't be too sad, Fearless."

"It's not that," he muttered. "Thorn, I had that hyena in my jaws. It's the same one. If I'd killed it instead of just scaring it, Bark wouldn't have died."

"You couldn't know what was going to happen," Mud comforted him.

"Mud's right," said Thorn. "Who could have imagined the brute would come back, after the fright you gave it? This isn't your fault, Fearless."

They're just being kind, thought Fearless miserably. *I know I'm to blame.*

The glade of the Council was crowded. For once it was not just the Highleaves of the Council in attendance; the whole troop had massed beneath the spreading trees. Baboons sat on the ground, grooming one another, and more balanced in the low branches, cradling their young or simply watching. One or two chewed morosely on figs. The amber glow of the sky had faded, and the silver orb of the moon hung above the high treetops; crickets and frogs were beginning to chirp the first notes of their nightly chorus. Right in the center of the clearing, the Crown Stone stood, desolate and empty.

Fearless lay with his forepaws outstretched, his head raised, waiting. He had never seen a leaderless Council, and despite his sadness he was curious to find out what would happen now. Thorn, Mud, and Berry sat with him; their anxious excitement was so contagious, he could feel it prickling his hide.

Old Beetle Highleaf padded slowly forward to stand in front of the Crown Stone, facing the troop. The low chatter grew hushed, until only the song of the crickets and tree frogs disturbed the silence.

Beetle cleared his throat. "The vote for our new Crownleaf will take place under the full moon, as tradition demands. I remind the troop that only Highleaf-ranking baboons may put themselves forward; any of you who wish to do so, please speak now, and address Brightforest Troop from the Crown Stone."

His part finished, the old baboon returned with dignity to his Highleaf comrades and sat back to watch.

Fearless half expected a delay, with baboons only reluctantly putting themselves forward. It would have seemed more respectful to Bark, he thought. But Grub Highleaf loped instantly to the Crown Stone and sprang up onto it. He peered down at them with small yellow eyes.

"Beetle speaks the truth," he declared, letting his gaze roam around the troop. "Traditions are important! I am a baboon who respects our customs, and the Way of the Troop. You can rely on me to safeguard Brightforest's best interests at all times. Our family, our troop: we come first, and no leader should ever forget it. Choose me, and I will protect you from *every outsider* who would harm us."

Fearless blinked in shock. Grub was staring straight at him as he uttered his final words.

To a chorus of approving murmurs—and some whoops of support from his own retinue—Grub leaped back down from the Crown Stone. If he had expected to become leader that instant, though, he was quickly disappointed; Fearless was relieved to see more baboons stalk forward to stake their claim.

As Twig Highleaf bounded up onto the Crown Stone to begin her speech, Fearless noticed that Stinger had come to sit beside Berry. An idea struck him.

"Stinger!" he growled. "You should put yourself forward for Crownleaf. You'd be great."

"Yes!" Thorn agreed eagerly. An older baboon turned to frown, shushing him, and he lowered his voice. "Stinger, you really should."

"I agree," whispered Mud.

"Oh no," murmured Stinger, shaking his head. "I don't think so. I'm not cut out for leadership."

"That's not true, Father!" Berry told him severely.

"I'm with Berry," murmured Thorn, with a glare across the glade at the first contender. "Grub's far too sure of himself."

"And that's never good in a leader," added Mud. "Honestly, Stinger, you'd be much better."

Stinger gave an uncertain shrug. "I'm not sure." He turned his bright eyes on his daughter. "Do you think I should, Berry?"

She touched his arm with her paw. "Father, you'd make a wonderful leader. I know it. And the fact you're so unsure about it—well, that just makes you even more suitable. It's like Thorn and Mud say—a leader who's too sure of himself will never be a good one. The Crownleaf has to be wise as well as strong, and he has to listen to his Council. Grub would be bad at that."

"Grub may not win," pointed out Stinger.

"But he *might*. Go on, Father," urged Berry. "At least stand."

The last speaker was just finishing, and Beetle was looking around to make sure there were no more contenders. With a reluctant sigh, Stinger got to his paws.

"I will speak," he announced.

"Very well, Stinger Highleaf." Beetle withdrew with a respectful nod and gestured for him to come forward.

Stinger dipped his head to Beetle, ambled to the Crown Stone, and leaped onto its smooth surface. He glanced down and touched it, looking a little overwhelmed, but when he began to speak, his voice was strong.

"Brightforest Troop," he announced. "Our leader, Bark Crownleaf, has left us a fine legacy. She respected our traditions, but when she heard the song of change in the air, she was not afraid to listen to it. She combined humility with strength, and that made our troop strong—stronger than ever. *That* is a legacy I would honor. The world is an uncertain place. It's true Bravelands is eternal, but it is ever changing. A leader needs to think quickly. A leader must think new thoughts, be able to adapt." His gaze roamed over the troop, meeting the eyes of individual baboons. "I think you all know me; you know that fast and flexible thinking is a quality of mine. I will never be hidebound by custom when I make decisions—but I will respect our troop's traditions, the ones that have served us so well. I will keep Brightforest Troop safe and secure in our shifting world, and I am clever and cunning enough—I think you would agree—to keep us fed and watered in the driest of dry seasons." He lifted his head proudly. "I, Stinger Highleaf, would lead this troop beyond survival—I would raise it to greatness."

As Stinger sprang down from the Crown Stone, Fearless's heart swelled with hope, and he opened his jaws to pant with the excitement. Grass and Fly were whooping. Thorn was jumping up and down with delight, and Mud's eyes shone with awe. Berry wrung her hands together, then nervously scratched at her neck. There was a mixture of adoration and anxiety in her face.

"That was brilliant!" whispered Mud.

"I know. And straight from the heart," growled Thorn, "unlike Grub's speech. That sneaky baboon had obviously been planning what he was going to say for a *long* time."

The clamor of approving hoots was louder than it had been for the other candidates, and Fearless could make out a rumbling murmur of appreciation from many baboons.

"That was great, Berry," he growled. "You father always speaks so well."

She nodded. "He does. But when it comes to voting . . . we'll see." There were creases of nervousness on her face as her father sat down at the end of the row of candidates.

"And now that we have our prospective leaders," announced Beetle in his reedy but clear voice, "we will cast our votes."

One by one, the baboons moved forward into a line, waiting patiently to collect a smooth pebble each from Beetle. And one by one, they moved forward to the line of hopeful Highleaves, placing their smooth stones before their preferred choice. A little shyly, and feeling very new to it all, Fearless joined the line for Beetle's pebbles.

He couldn't help his gaze sliding to the piles of stones before each candidate. They were growing larger—and the biggest piles were before Grub and Stinger. His heart in his mouth, Fearless crept forward in the line, eager to cast his own vote.

He realized he had reached the front. Beetle stood there staring at him with some puzzlement, a pebble in his wrinkled paw.

"Fearless, Cub of the Stars," he said, startled. "What are you doing here?"

Fearless bowed his head. "I'm waiting to vote, Beetle Highleaf."

"Sky and stone, Fearless!" The old baboon blinked and shook his head vigorously. "Only baboons may vote for the Crownleaf. I'm sorry."

"But . . ." Taken aback, Fearless licked his jaws. "I'm a member of Brightforest Troop. . . ."

"You're a lion!" Beetle peered at him, disapproval in his eyes. "I'm sorry, Fearless, but this is how it has always been and always will be. You are not a baboon, and you may not vote for our Crownleaf."

"But Beetle Highleaf, he's one of us!" objected Thorn.

Beetle shook his head. "Rules are rules, young Thorn. Now take your pebble, please. Your friend must step aside. *Thank you*, Fearless."

Crestfallen, and more than a little embarrassed, Fearless dropped his gaze from Beetle's and slunk aside. Padding away on heavy paws, his hide hot from mocking stares, he lay down in the shadows to watch the voting go on without him.

Why am I surprised? Bark Crownleaf herself told me. I'm too much of a lion.

But it still hurt.

The last baboon cast her vote, and Beetle stalked in front of the candidates. He glanced down at the separate piles of pebbles, then raised his head.

"It's clear that the two most popular are Grub and Stinger," he announced. "Therefore the Council thanks the other contenders for their loyalty and their willingness to serve. Let us count the stones for Grub and Stinger."

As the disappointed Highleaves padded back to their places in the troop, Fearless found his claws were digging into the earth with the tension. He watched in silence as Beetle and the other Council members began to count out the two piles of pebbles. His chest felt tight, and his skin prickled with nerves.

Oh, Great Spirit, if you're there? Let Stinger win. I don't think I'll have a happy future in Brightforest Troop if Grub is Crownleaf. . . .

When Beetle cleared his throat and turned to the troop, Fearless stiffened and gulped hard. Beside him, Thorn patted his shoulder.

"Here's hoping," Thorn whispered.

Mud and Berry edged closer to Fearless, pressing themselves against his flanks. He knew they were reassuring themselves as well as him. All four friends held their breath.

"The result is narrow," announced Beetle solemnly, "but

the votes have been counted three times, and the tally is agreed by all the Council. Brightforest Troop, greet and salute your new leader . . ."

He puffed out his chest with the importance of the moment. "Grub Crownleaf!"

Fearless's head swam with disappointment. His stomach was a stone-weight inside him. *Oh no. Not Grub.*

Stinger was dipping his head, congratulating Grub on his victory, but Fearless could tell from the slump of his shoulders how disappointed he was beneath his charm and dignity.

And Grub's winning speech had been all about Fearless's outsider status. *That was how it sounded to me, anyway.* It hurt not only that Grub had said it, but that so many of the baboons must have agreed with him. Fearless felt a wrench within his rib cage. *If Stinger's been rejected, that goes double for me.*

Grub was clambering back onto the Crown Stone, barely able to hide his eagerness and delight. He patted its smooth top and sat down, thin lips spread in a wide grin.

"I, Grub Crownleaf"—his voice rolled over the words as if he found them delicious—"will defend and guide this troop always, until my death; this I will do with the help of the Great Spirit."

The baboons yammered and jumped, chorusing their approval. Older baboons began to dart off and return with gifts; in a short time Grub was surrounded by small heaps of roots, berries, nuts, and the tenderest of edible leaves. He looked as if he might burst with pride and pleasure.

The younger baboons were following suit now—Thorn

and Berry had bounded off to find gifts, with Mud following slowly after them, still limping from the injury he got from the crocodile. Fearless knew very well that he had to join in; it was his only option and his only fading chance for acceptance. He padded off to retrieve a plump dead bird he had caught earlier; but when he laid it on the ground at Grub's paws, the baboon's smirk turned to a scowl.

It's looking every bit as bad as I feared, Fearless told himself as he backed off, head lowered. *This is a bad time for me. It's going to be so difficult with Grub in charge. I'm going to have to fight hard to prove him wrong.*

He clenched his jaws. *And the only way to do that is to prove myself, to all of them. But how? I wasn't allowed to try the Three Feats—even Thorn and Mud thought I shouldn't.*

An idea sparked suddenly in his mind, kindling into a flame of righteous determination. *Wait. There is a way to prove I am truly Baboon. I know what I can do!*

"Thorn. Mud." He trotted over to his friends, lowering his head to accept their friendly, comforting scratches.

"I'm sorry about this, Fearless," murmured Mud. "Grub's the last leader we wanted, too."

"I know." He nuzzled the little baboon. "But I know what I'm going to do."

"You're not leaving?" asked Thorn, alarmed.

"No," Fearless told him. "I'm going to avenge Bark's death. That will prove to Brightforest Troop that I belong here with them, that I'm loyal."

Thorn gaped at him. "But how will—"

"I'm going to find that hyena's troop. Or its pride—whatever hyenas call it." Fearless lifted his head proudly. "I'm going to drive them far away from here so that they'll never hurt another Brightforest baboon."

He gazed expectantly at his friends. They didn't look nearly as enthusiastic as he'd hoped. Indeed, they shared a glance of concern.

"Oh, Fearless," muttered Mud. "I don't think that's a good idea."

"I think it's a *terrible* idea," declared Thorn.

Stinger came bounding over, his expression horrified. "Did I hear right, Fearless? You're going to go chasing hyenas?"

"Yes," said Fearless, indignant at their less-than-confident reaction. "That's exactly what I'm going to do."

"Thorn and Mud are right," said Stinger firmly. He drew himself up to his full height, his gaze level with Fearless's. "It's a dreadful idea, and it's far too dangerous. You may be a lion, but you're one lion—and you're talking about a whole pack of hyenas. We need you here!"

Fearless gave a defiant roar and pawed the ground, wishing he had a mane to shake.

"I beat one hyena," he growled. He glared at his friends. "I can certainly scare off the rest of its stupid pack." Turning away, he began to stride from the glade, but he stopped to look over his shoulder.

"I'll be back soon, and those hyenas won't be," he told them with a low snarl. "I'll prove my worth in Brightforest Troop. To *all* of you!"

CHAPTER 9

A *cloud of dust hung low* over the savannah, raised by thousands of hooves as the elephants and the other grazers made their way across the parched Bravelands. Sky struggled to see through the hordes of traveling animals, but in the glimpses she caught of the far horizon, it was blurred by a shimmering yellow haze of heat. She trudged behind her family in a kind of trance, her aching thirst so familiar by now that she could hardly remember the taste of water.

Then, like a miracle, a single patch of green caught her eye; she was so deep in her daze, it was behind her before she realized. Sky's eyes widened as she glanced back, trying to catch sight of it again, but already it was lost in the dust.

It didn't matter, though, because there was more! Her heart swelled as swathes of grass began to appear underfoot, their fresh greenness shocking against the dry, ocher earth. Sky picked up her feet. She brushed her trunk across a rippling tussock of leaves, and as the pace of the great march slowed, she snatched at some blades with the tip of her trunk, plucking them free. Closing her eyes, she brought the grass to her mouth and chewed on it. It was sweet and fragrant, rich with the promise of water.

My first fresh grass of the season!

The mass of grazers had almost come to a halt, she realized, as all around her animals bent their heads to tear eagerly at the green shoots. Sky's family had slowed, too, pulling and tugging at bushes that were vibrant with new growth. Sky wrapped her trunk around a supple young branch and snapped it off, chewing enthusiastically. Around her she could hear cries of delight as the elephants ate their fill.

"Have you ever tasted such tender grass?"

"Try these shoots—they're amazing!"

As Sky ate, she noticed the air suddenly cool, but it wasn't until the first fat drop of rain spattered her flank that she looked up and saw the sky had darkened under a tower of billowing cloud. Its front was sweeping across the savannah, blotting out the sun.

"Rain, Moon!" she cried.

The drops quickly became a torrential downpour, washing the red dust from the elephants' hides and turning them a gleaming dark gray. Moon knelt down, then tipped over to roll, squealing, in a patch of new mud. Sky tickled him with her trunk, enjoying the cool mud he splashed against her legs.

A zebra neighed happily nearby. "Great Mother has brought us to the living lands!"

"She never fails us," responded another.

It was as if the shadow of the rain clouds had driven away a heavier darkness lurking in their hearts. Sky could sense every creature's spirits lifting as they ambled on, snatching at rich mouthfuls of grass, their hides drenched. Her trunk tingled with the warm, rich scent of rain soaking into the earth.

"Do you smell that, Moon?" she whispered to her cousin. "That's the best scent in the world!"

He waved his little trunk in the air, sniffing delightedly. "It is!"

Ahead of Sky, Great Mother had halted beside a huge boulder, steep-sided like a miniature mountain. Its smooth, dark gray sides, gleaming in the rain, were etched with crisscrossing grooves in an elaborate pattern. Sky recognized the place they had reached: those marks had been scored in the rock by the tusks of her forebears, over too many years to count.

Great Mother caressed the rock once with her trunk before lifting her head to call to the herds.

"Zebras, gazelles, wildebeests—noble herds of Bravelands—follow the green shoots, and keep walking toward the forest. We will be with you soon. But there is something we elephants must do before we join you."

Sky heard the message being passed across the plains. With neighs and whickers and bellows of agreement, the groups of animals moved on, slow but relentless, a seething mass of gray and brown and white-and-black stripes. Sky watched them go, content to wait with Great Mother. She knew why they had stopped; what the family had to do was something they did every year. Even before her own first trek, Sky had listened in awe to the reminiscences of the grown ones.

Great Mother nodded once to the other elephants, then turned to lead them off the trail. Sky followed behind Star and Rain, her heart thumping slowly with the solemnity of the occasion.

"Sky! Sky! Where are we going?" Moon was trotting at her side. "What are we doing? Why can't we follow the herds any-more? Why can't we go to the Gathering? What's wrong?"

"Nothing's wrong, Moon." She glanced down at him, amused at his breathless questions, but rather proud that she could be the one to explain it to him. "We're going to the Plain of Our Ancestors."

"Ohhh." He fell silent at once, but his eyes shone with excitement. He trotted faster, eager to keep up with Sky.

The detour was a long one, taking the elephants far from the trail, but with leaves and water plentiful now they strode on energetically. The gritty, well-trodden path became rocky, and then rose up steeply through a narrow pass between sheer crags, but the herd barely slowed.

Mist gathered as they climbed higher, settling in thick tendrils of cloud between stunted trees and craggy outcrops. The way grew narrower, until the elephants were climbing the slope in single file.

The rocky pass reached a crest, then dipped and opened up very suddenly. As if Great Mother had lifted her trunk and blown the mist away, it disappeared, and the herd halted to gaze at the high, smooth landscape.

The looming walls of stone swept out wide on either side, encircling a vast, sunken plateau that was green with grass and flowers. Scattered in the undergrowth were strange shapes, stark gray and white against the greenness.

Sky stood speechless. Even though she had known what awaited them, the vista took her breath away.

The elephants fell quiet as they walked forward. Bleached bones and creamy tusks jutted skyward; Great Mother moved among them, gently touching the skeletons with her trunk, and the rest of the family followed her, hushed and reverent.

Sky's heart swelled within her. Somehow, the great grave-yard was not a sad place—it was awe-inspiring. Her hide prickled as she gazed around at the bones of her ancestors. Beside her, even Moon was quiet, his eyes huge. Above them, the sun broke suddenly through a rift in the dark rain clouds, its light gleaming on the mighty skeletons.

"Why are they here?" whispered Moon shakily.

Sky stroked his bristly neck with her trunk. "When an elephant knows it's time to die, they will make their way to this place. If they die somewhere else, their family brings the bones of the dead one here," she murmured. "I don't know why. Maybe Great Mother knows. But it's a very special place for all the elephants of Bravelands."

Moon bobbed his head, then sidled away without another word to huddle close to his mother. Sky understood. She remembered how overwhelmed she had been on her first visit to the Plain of Our Ancestors.

And there's someone I need to be with, too. . . .

She picked her way between the bones, careful not to disturb them. Some were so huge, the rib cages were like an eerie, white forest, but Sky did not feel intimidated. *These are my ancestors: my family who lived and died long before I was born. I can almost hear them whispering to me. . . .*

The herd of living elephants had dispersed now, each of them making their own way to particular remains. Sky edged past Twilight, who was running her trunk across a magnificent tusk and murmuring to it, and Rain, gently caressing a far smaller skeleton, her eyes closed in grief.

Sky herself moved toward the edge of the plateau. She knew where she would find the skeleton she was looking for, and it was exactly where she remembered. Dipping her head, she reached out with her trunk to part the grass that had grown up around the remains. The skull and rib cage still rose clear of the undergrowth, gleaming pale gold in the light of the late sun's rays.

Oh, Mother, she told the bones silently. *I love my herd, and I know they love me, but I still miss you so much.*

She wondered if Boulder ever came here. Her older brother was somewhere out on the savannah, she knew, roaming with his own herd of bulls, but it had been a long time since he had come of age and left the Strider herd. She could hardly remember what he looked like. His tusks must be huge by now; he'd been so much older than her. *Does he visit Mother's bones? Will I ever meet him here? Or somewhere else, out there in Bravelands?*

If I could see him, we could talk about Mother. We could remember her together.

Sky gave a deep sigh and gathered herself. Her trunk trembled a little as she reached it toward her mother's bones. *What will you show me this time, Mother?*

The tip of her trunk brushed a rib bone, and the Plain of Our Ancestors blurred and receded into a hazy, silvered glow.

The scene cleared, and the land was visible again, but Sky no longer stood on the plain among the bones of her ancestors. Around her, Bravelands stretched to the horizon, dotted with flat-topped acacias. The rain-heavy sky was deep gray, and she could feel the close, oppressive heat of the oncoming storm. Nearby, a frail elephant stood with her baby at a watering hole.

It's me! And Mother!

But this Sky was so small, barely more than a newborn calf.

Almost twelve years ago. I hadn't even been alive for a full season.

Glancing up, baby Sky gazed adoringly at her mother above her; a huge trunk caressed her bumpy head. Before them, the broad lake glittered and sparkled despite the clouds. Sky's mother dipped her trunk into the cool water and sprayed it playfully over her baby's hot hide.

It's the memory I told to Star and Rain!

Sky stood quite still and watched the scene, enchanted, but aching with wistful longing.

The tiny elephant shook herself in delight and trotted a

circle around her mother, then capered between her legs. The grown one swayed slightly, still weak from the birth but happy to watch her newborn play. Occasionally she would dart out her trunk, trying to grab Sky, laughing as her baby dodged.

I wish I could watch this forever....

But the scene was changing. Suns rose and set in flashes, rains came and passed, and the baby was growing, thriving. But her mother weakened, grew thinner, and in a flash of teeth and long, horrible claws, she was brought down by roaring, tawny predators. Other grown ones shielded the little elephant, urging her away; the killing was swiftly over, and then the rot-eaters descended. The lonely bones dried and bleached in the heat.

The sun raced across the earth, over and over again, from horizon to horizon. Hundreds of herds swept across the land; days and years flew across her vision. Sky caught a glimpse of Great Mother calming a group of grass-eaters, and she blinked in recognition.

That was only a few days ago! When Great Mother resolved the quarrel between the zebras and the wildebeests.

Yet still the sky darkened and lightened, the whirling sun a blur, and as the colors of Bravelands became lurid and unnatural, Sky realized she was no longer seeing the past.

This is the future!

The land burned fiery red; the sky was a distorted, melting mass of vivid orange. The watering hole was still there, motionless and menacing, as if every hint of breeze had died. Pacing toward it was a huge lion, its dark mane rippling with every earthshaking step. It was powerful, splendid, almost radiant. But the most extraordinary thing about the great beast was the creature that rode on its back.

A baboon?

Sky could barely breathe. The sight was so unnatural, so bizarre and threatening, she could feel herself trembling.

Suddenly, the great lion staggered under the weight of the creature on its back. It gave a roar of pain, and the baboon slowly turned its head. Now Sky could see its face. It was hideous, a twisted mask of evil; the eyes glittered with an intelligence that was sharp and wicked. As the lion stumbled and fell, the baboon's jaws stretched wide, exposing long, malicious fangs, and it gave a bone-rattling scream.

The watering hole was suddenly a startling red, the surface churning and foaming. Water rose and spilled onto the land, and Sky reeled in horror. It wasn't water at all.

It was thick, bright blood.

Sky tore her trunk away from her mother's bones, gasping, her breath whistling in terror from her trunk. Her whole body shook.

Twisting around, she hunted desperately for her herd. She could hear their deep, resounding rumbles as they called to one another; there they were, making their slow way back to the narrow pass, coming together, exchanging gentle touches with their trunks. With a cry of fright, Sky bolted toward her family.

"We mustn't go!" she called after them. "We mustn't go to the watering hole!"

Her shout of terror echoed eerily across the field of bones. Elephants turned, shocked, to watch her, their ears flapping forward as she hurtled across the plain.

"I'm telling you, we can't go! We have to turn back!" Sky stumbled into the midst of the herd, panting. "That lake, it's dangerous!"

"Night and morning, young one!" exclaimed Rain. "Whatever do you mean?"

"What are you talking about, Sky?" Star patted her kindly with her trunk. "The watering hole isn't dangerous!"

"No, it is, it is!" Sky spoke so fast, she tripped over her words. "I saw it—my mother's bones, they showed me terrible things. Something awful is going to happen there!"

"Oh, Sky," murmured Great Mother. The others drew back to let her through, and she bent her wise, wrinkled head to butt Sky gently. "It's been upsetting for you. The bones can be disturbing, especially to a young one. Try not to worry."

"Communing with your mother is distressing, of course it is," murmured Twilight. "But you mustn't be afraid, Sky. There's nothing to fear."

"Indeed," agreed Great Mother, stroking Sky's head. "No elephant can see the future, little one. You saw something that frightened you, but it wasn't something that is to come; we can see only our past. Your grief is stronger than ever in this place, and it gave you horrible imaginings, that's all."

Sky was still shivering, but Great Mother turned and gestured with her trunk to the pass that would take them out of the plain. "Come, now. It's not far to the watering hole, and you'll see that there's nothing to fear. There will be food, and water, and peace, and the company of many animals. You'll feel better soon."

The other elephants fell in behind Great Mother, keen to get started on the last part of their journey. All around, Sky heard them exchanging tales of what the bones had shown them: happy memories and sad ones, recollections of good rainy seasons in the company of beloved family, visions of treks of the past. None spoke of watering holes overflowing with blood.

"You must listen to Great Mother," murmured Star, tweaking Sky's ear. "She knows so much more than all of us, and she protects us—even against our own fears. Come along, young one. Moon wants to play." She glanced meaningfully at her son, and Sky understood that Star didn't want her to make Moon afraid.

She picked up her feet, trotting alongside her family. Star and her aunts were surely right; she must have imagined the horrible vision.

And Great Mother is never wrong, she told herself firmly. *What do I know, compared to her?*

Yet as the herd trudged on, rejoining the trail of the grazers, Sky could not shake the chill along her spine.

CHAPTER 10

Thorn huddled behind a thick, verdant patch of ferns, holding his breath. *This is wrong,* he thought guiltily. *If anyone catches me, I'm going to get thoroughly nipped.*

The Highleaf Council didn't approve of eavesdroppers. But he couldn't bear to wait for the official announcement; the Council, Berry had told him, was discussing whether the Third Feat should go ahead that season at all. The notion that they might postpone it was awful, and his heart was pounding with nerves. *I've waited for moons and moons to be with Berry! All I need to do is win my fight, and we'll both be Highleaves. We're bound to be caught sneaking around before long, and then we'll be kept apart forever. . . .*

"Bark's death changes things," Twig Highleaf was saying as she shot a look of appeal around at her fellow Council members. "It would be—well, disrespectful to carry on after what's happened."

"I agree with Twig," declared Mango. She scratched at her shoulder. "The troop needs time to grieve. The Feats are an unnecessary distraction right now."

"Of course, the ranks would have to stay as they are," remarked Grub, rubbing his chin thoughtfully.

Thorn stiffened. *They can't* . . . He craned forward, desperate, parting the ferns a little more with trembling paws.

"It's unfortunate," said Mango, "but it cannot be helped. The Feats always take place during the spring of a baboon's sixth year. It's tradition. This year's youngsters will have to settle for whatever rank they achieved after the Crocodile River Feat."

Thorn tried to control his panicked breathing. Stinger was peeling the bark thoughtfully from a small branch, picking out ants and popping them into his mouth. "It's true that the troop needs to grieve," he murmured, "but I don't agree that continuing the Feats shows a lack of respect. How better to honor Bark's memory? If we stop the Three Feats now, it will be the first time we've broken a fine tradition."

"Hmm," growled Grub Crownleaf. "Stinger makes a reasonable point, but I believe Twig and Mango speak sense. They combine respect both for our traditions *and* for Bark Crownleaf's memory." He scratched his chin. "What does our Starleaf say?" He turned to Mud's mother, and every baboon in the clearing turned with him.

With a sigh, the Starleaf tilted her head back, closing her eyes. Then she opened them, gazing up through the crisscross of leaf and branch to the blue sky. Sunlight danced across her motionless features. She remained like that for a very long time, studying the patterns of the air.

At last she inclined her head forward once more. "The rain drifts eastward, toward the sunrise, and the birds fly with it. And I saw a weaver bird this morning, one as yellow as the sun, after the violent cloudburst." The Starleaf gave a murmuring sigh. "After turmoil and disruption, the troop needs stability and calm."

Behind his bush, Thorn squeezed his eyes tight shut. *Please, please, please . . .*

"But it also needs new strength, more than ever: just as the land needs sunlight to follow the rainstorm." The Starleaf bowed her head gravely. "The signs tell me the Three Feats should go ahead."

Thorn didn't realize he'd been holding his breath until it rushed out of his lungs. He clapped his paw over his muzzle, hoping no one had heard his sigh of relief. It was all he could do not to whoop with happiness.

"That settles the matter," said Grub, scowling a little. He didn't look happy, but he could hardly go against the Starleaf's interpretations, now that he'd asked for her opinion. "The Third Feat will take place at sundown today."

The debate over and the decision made, the Council members sprang down from their places on the branches around the glade, and one by one, or in small groups, drifted away into other parts of the forest. Thorn crouched low, waiting for the rustle of leaves and the pad of paws to fade. Any moment now, he could slink away.

"Well, young Thorn," said a voice above him. "Are you pleased with the result?"

Jumping up with a gasp, Thorn blinked up into Stinger's amber eyes, which glinted with a combination of disapproval and amusement. Stinger had parted the fern fronds with his long paws and was gazing down at the young baboon.

"Stinger! I'm sorry, I . . ." Thorn chittered his teeth. "I didn't mean to listen—I know I'm not supposed to, but—"

"It's all right." Stinger laughed. "Nobody else saw you. I know how ambitious you are, and I know how much it means to you that the Three Feats go ahead. I won't tell Grub, don't worry."

Thorn felt weak with relief. "Thanks, Stinger. I really am sorry. Are you sure nobody else on the Council saw me?"

"Ah, Thorn. Not many baboons in the troop have eyes as sharp as mine. It'll stay our secret; after all, it didn't do any harm, did it? And I'm pleased with the outcome too. I want you to win your fight!"

Thorn felt his face grow hot with pleasure. *I wish he knew the real reason I want to win—but soon Berry and I will be able to tell him!* "Thanks, Stinger. I'll try my best."

"I know you will." Stinger patted his shoulder and turned to pad away. "Good luck!"

Now that the issue had been settled, the preparations were going ahead with surprising speed. When Thorn rejoined the rest of the young baboons, Beetle was already gathering them to announce the pairings for their fights. Thorn scampered to join them, pushing through furry bodies until he found Mud.

"Have you heard which baboon you're fighting?" he whispered to his small friend.

"Beetle's just announced it!" Mud turned to him, his eyes wide with excitement. "I'm fighting Bug!"

Thorn was thrilled for him. "That's great news!" he whispered, hugging Mud. "You've got a really good chance of beating him; he's not much bigger than you. The Council must be trying to make the pairings really fair, then!"

Mud nodded. "My leg still hurts, but I do think I've got a chance. Let's find out who your opponent will be!" He turned back to listen to Beetle as he announced the rest of the pairings.

". . . will fight against Bird Lowleaf," Beetle was saying in his raspy voice. "And finally: Thorn Middleleaf will face—"

Thorn and Mud both went rigid, holding their breath.

"Nut Middleleaf!"

"Nut," whispered Mud in horror. "Oh, bad luck, Thorn."

Thorn swallowed hard. "Don't worry, Mud," he murmured. "Nut's big and vicious, but he's no stronger than I am. It's not a problem."

"The fights will commence at sundown!" declared Beetle, slapping the ground with an air of finality. "Until then, the rules say you must all separate. I suggest you all get some practice in before you come to the Glade of Duels." With a final grunt, he trudged away to rejoin the other Council members.

The young baboons began to disperse immediately; there was a new crackle of excited tension in the air. "I guess that's it, then," said Thorn. "I'll see you at sundown, Mud! Good luck."

"Be careful when you're fighting Nut," warned Mud. "He's not above cheating."

"Don't we know it," muttered Thorn.

"Hey!" Nut was bounding past with two of his cronies, Fang and Shard, but he paused to smirk. "You and me, Thorn Middleleaf! This is excellent news. Especially since you won't have Big Talk to do your fighting for you this time!"

Thorn growled. "*Fearless* is my friend, not my bodyguard. I can beat you myself, Nut." He turned his rump on Nut and stalked away, ignoring the taunts of Nut's gang.

"You told him, Thorn!" said Mud, loping to his side. "You'll beat him, don't worry."

Thorn said nothing; for all his defiance, he wasn't so sure Mud was right. Nut wasn't just a dirty fighter, he was strong and heavy. It was going to be a hard fight, Thorn knew.

Still, he thought, *I have to win. It's as simple as that. I have to be a Highleaf! And I'll enjoy beating Nut, much more than I'd like beating any other baboon.*

"We'd better split up now and start practicing, Mud," he said, trying to sound confident. "See you at the Glade of Duels!"

Mud gave him a quick hug and trotted away, his tail high.

Thorn was glad his friend was in good spirits; now he just needed to find some of his own. He loped through the forest to find a clear space where he could go through his moves. *I'll have to be quick and on guard*, he told himself. *But I can do this.*

In the clear space he found, there was nothing to attack but a few fallen branches and an anthill, but by the time he had rehearsed every dodge, lunge, and feint he could think of, Thorn felt strong and lithe and almost confident. Flexing and stretching his muscles, he paused at last, taking deep breaths of the cool woodland air and trying to calm himself.

Nut's a bully, but he isn't so tough. I have to win; it's as simple as that.

"Thorn?" Berry edged out of a gap between two date palms, glancing over her shoulder.

"Berry!" He couldn't help it; he bounded up and nuzzled her. She drew back, her eyes sparkling. "I know I'm not supposed to see you," she murmured, "but I wanted to give you a present. To wish you luck." From behind her she drew a ripe, golden, perfect mango. Gently she placed it in his paws.

Thorn stared at it, his heart in his throat. "Thank you," he whispered hoarsely.

"You're going to win." She pressed her forehead to his. "I know you are."

"Yes." His face split in a broad grin. "For you, for us—I'm going to be a Highleaf, Berry!"

The low sun glowed golden through the branches, and the sky high above them was turning a musky gray-blue. "It's time," Berry told him softly. "I'll see you in the glade." She scampered away.

Thorn blew out a nervous breath. He hid his precious mango carefully, in the foliage beneath the date palms. Later, if all went well, he and Berry would eat it in celebration. Then, with a last, silent plea to the Great Spirit, he headed for the Glade of Duels.

Already most of the troop was gathered around the edge of the broad, ferny space, and their excited chatter was deafening. Just as in the Council Glade, there was a wide boulder right in the center, but this one was much flatter and broader than the Crown Stone—the Duel Stone.

Thorn eyed it with trepidation as Beetle paced forward once more. The old baboon nodded to the five Council members who would witness the fights and cleared his throat pompously.

"Our first contest in the Third Feat," declared Beetle, "is between Kernel Middleleaf and Fang Middleleaf. Come forward, both of you, and let the strongest baboon win!"

Barely able to contain his nerves, Thorn watched the two baboons clamber onto the boulder. No blood was spilled in these battles—at least not on purpose. All Kernel had to do was wrestle Fang, trying to find the moment of weakness when he could shove his opponent off the rock. Once a baboon's paws touched the ground, the battle was over.

Thorn had been hoping for a win for Kernel, but now he could hardly think past his anxiety about his own bout. The yells and hoots of the watchers were a meaningless noise in his ears. When Fang twisted sharply, unbalancing Kernel and then lunging fast to send him flying from the rock, Thorn felt nothing more than a small twinge of disappointment.

Beetle murmured for a moment with the Council witnesses,

then nodded and turned to address the troop. "The winner: Fang Highleaf!" he cried as Kernel limped gloomily away, a Middleleaf forever. "The second contest in the Third Feat: Thorn Middleleaf against Mud Deeproot."

Thorn was still watching Fang caper in triumph. He barely heard Beetle's words.

"*Thorn Middleleaf!*" shouted Beetle impatiently. "Come forward, and let the strongest baboon win!"

In disbelief, Thorn finally registered what he was saying. He stared at Beetle, certain he had misheard. The old baboon so rarely made a mistake.

But sure enough, there was Mud—his best friend—edging hesitantly toward the boulder in the center of the glade. As Beetle nodded at him, and Mud turned to lock his eyes pleadingly on Thorn's, the little baboon's face was a picture of shock and bewilderment.

Thorn shook himself. *I have to fix this!*

"No," he stammered, embarrassed at having to correct an elder. "No, Beetle, I'm supposed to fight Nut."

Silence fell among the troop as Beetle glared at him. "Kindly don't contradict me, young Thorn. Come *forward!*"

Still confused, Thorn felt a tug on his forearm fur. "Thorn!" whispered Stinger in his ear. "Look! I had the order changed to make sure you win. This will be easy!"

"No," gasped Thorn in horror. *What has Stinger done?* "I can't!"

Stinger frowned. "Aren't you pleased?"

"I'm—I'm grateful, Stinger, but I can't fight Mud. He's my

best friend!" Thorn stared into Mud's anxious eyes. Baboons all around them were beginning to mutter disapprovingly.

"Listen, Thorn," hissed Stinger. "Be realistic. Mud's going to lose no matter who he fights. Bug would have thrashed him! He might as well lose to you—and you're much less likely to hurt him than Bug is. You want to be a Highleaf, don't you?"

I don't have a choice, realized Thorn in despair. Slowly he approached the boulder, climbing onto it to join Mud. *I do want to be a Highleaf. I want it so much.*

"It's all right, Thorn," whispered Mud. "This isn't your fault. Don't worry."

Thorn stared at him, breathing hard. Mud's legs were so skinny, his muscles scrawny and underdeveloped. His huge eyes were soft, dark, and gentle, without a scrap of killer instinct.

Maybe Stinger's right, thought Thorn glumly. *Mud did fail both the other tests. He wasn't made to rise through the ranks. Some baboons are Deeproots all their lives. He hasn't got the drive to make it to the top of a tree, never mind the troop.*

But all the reasoning in the world didn't make Thorn feel any better about what he was about to do.

The troop was crowding closer around the rock, hooting in impatience. They all knew Thorn would have a quick and easy victory; they just wanted him to get on with it.

All except Berry. He caught sight of her at the front; she was gazing up at him, her eyes wide and full of horrified sympathy.

She understands. Of course she does.

He shut his eyes, feeling a weight like stone in his belly. Thorn wanted to run away, but that was impossible too.

"Come along, come along," hooted Beetle, punching the ground with both fists. "Let the combat commence!"

I'm out of time, Thorn realized with a heavy heart. He looked at Mud's sorrowful face, and for a moment, he felt a flash of anger at his old friend. *I know what I have to do.*

I just have to get on and do it.

"Good luck," he told Mud brightly, and sprang at him.

Mud flinched, but Thorn's blow never landed. His paws slashed the air wildly, missing Mud's face and chest. Mud gave a squeak of alarm and ducked, butting Thorn almost accidentally in the belly. Thorn reeled back, staggering.

He jumped to his paws and flung himself at Mud again, gripping him in a strong hug and wrestling him toward the edge of the rock. Mud fought back bravely, his hind paws scrabbling at the smooth surface, and Thorn gave way, falling so suddenly that Mud landed on top of him. Again they both struggled upright and grappled together, swaying.

The troop was bouncing and yelling with excitement now, slapping the ground and hooting encouragement at both of them. Thorn peeled back his lips and growled, making a great show of lunging forward, seizing Mud's arms. With another squeal, Mud wriggled free, looking panicked, and flailed his paws wildly at Thorn.

Now.

Thorn ducked, but clumsily. One of Mud's little paws caught him square in the shoulder, and he toppled sideways.

With a despairing yelp, Thorn staggered and crashed down from the rock.

The fall was harder than he'd expected. He lay on his back on the gritty ground, panting. A weight of misery settled inside him.

It's over. I'm Thorn Middleleaf. Forever.

For long moments, he couldn't move. He didn't want to. Around him the troop shrieked and whooped, jumping and hammering the earth in their shock and delight.

It's not that they wanted me to lose, he consoled himself. *A lot of them are just happy to see Mud winning for a change.*

Mud had leaped down from the boulder; he seized Thorn's paws anxiously, dragging him up. "Thorn! Thorn, are you all right?"

Get over it, Thorn Middleleaf, he scolded himself. *You made your choice.*

Scrambling to his paws, Thorn congratulated his friend with a hug. "Well done, Mud. That was some move. You were too quick for me!"

"I can't believe it!" babbled Mud. "I'm a Lowleaf! Oh, I'm sorry, Thorn, I don't know how I did it!"

"With a clever bit of strategy," Thorn assured him, grinning broadly at Mud to hide the wrenching misery in his gut. "And you deserve to be a Lowleaf, so stop apologizing!"

"I still can't believe—I'm so happy—I'm a Lowleaf!"

"You are indeed, and I'm happy for you." Thorn hugged his friend tightly again.

But Mud's face fell, and he whispered, "Oh, Thorn—I'm sorry—Berry and you—"

"Never mind that," Thorn told him briskly. He forced another grin. "Hey, Mud, while Fearless is away, maybe you should take over protecting the troop!"

Mud giggled, still looking dazed and elated. His mother, the Starleaf, was the first of the troop to bound to his side, her face a picture of stunned pride. As the rest of the troop gathered around to congratulate Mud on his achievement, Thorn drew quietly away. A paw touched his shoulder, and he turned to see Berry.

"Meet me in the ravine," she whispered. She looked desolate as she squeezed his arm lightly. "We need to talk."

"I'm sorry, Berry." Picking up a handful of small stones, Thorn flung them furiously into the grass, one after the other.

"Don't, Thorn," she murmured. "Don't be angry with yourself."

He couldn't help it. His heart ached in his chest. *I did the right thing . . . didn't I? It seemed right at the time. But I feel like a fool. I've thrown away any chance we ever had of being mates.*

Night had fallen, but the great river of stars cast a pale silvery light across the grass and trees. Thorn loved to watch the glittering stream as it flowed from horizon to horizon, and he loved it best when he could watch it with Berry. They cuddled close together, gazing up at the night sky. *These stolen moments with Berry: they're the best thing in my life.*

And it had never felt like breaking the rules, not really. It had been exciting. Thorn had always known that one day they'd be the same rank, that he and Berry would be paired officially.

But now . . . everything's changed. We'd be in so much trouble if we were discovered.

Nearby a herd of gazelles slumbered in the darkness, some dozing on their feet as their sentries moved languidly around the fringes, chewing mouthfuls of cud, ears constantly swiveling. The ravine was a secluded haven, a grassy cleft in the plain that was hardly visible from more than a few strides away. Its protective walls were sheer and craggy, dotted with scrubby, prickly trees; Thorn had found the narrow path by chance one day, and he still felt a little guilty for keeping it a secret from most of Brightforest Troop. But the ravine was his own special, private retreat, and the gazelle herd did not seem to mind his presence. They must feel so safe here, Thorn realized: just as he and Berry always had.

Until now. Now, this is dangerous for both of us.

"All I wanted was for us to be together. But I've ruined everything." Thorn pressed himself closer to Berry, desperate to feel the comfort of her warmth.

"It wasn't your fault," she consoled him. "If anyone's to blame, it's my father—but he only tried to do what was best, Thorn. You letting Mud win was a good thing."

"Are you sure about that?" Thorn heaved a miserable sigh.

Berry groomed his shoulder gently. "You had to make a choice, Thorn, and it was an impossible one. I'd have hated to see Mud stuck as a Deeproot, cleaning and waiting on bullies like Nut for the rest of his days."

"I know." He rubbed his skull with his paws, defeated. "I just couldn't do it to him." He paused. "Are you angry with me, Berry?"

"Of course I'm not," she murmured. "I'm proud of you."

He swallowed hard. "Even though we can never be together?"

"Oh, Thorn. I wish we could, with all my heart. But you did the right thing." She stroked his forearm, then touched his face. "And you know what? I'm glad you didn't have to fight Nut. Did you see him winning? He was savage—he bit and scratched and drew blood. Poor River was in a bad way afterward."

"All the same," murmured Thorn, "I wish I could have faced him. I wish I'd had the chance to beat him. To give him a hard time, at least. Now he's a Highleaf, and he'll always be above me."

"He will *never* be above you," she told him, with a flash of anger. "You are ten times the baboon he is. I'll never forget that, and I am not going to let you go. We'll be together, Thorn. Maybe it has to stay a secret, but I will *always* be true to you."

He stared at her, a spark of hope flickering in his chest. "You mean that, Berry? Really?"

"I mean it. We'll have to be careful, but we're meant to be together. We're not exactly Sunrise and Moonlight, are we?"

Thorn shook his head, smiling. Every baboon knew the tale of how Sunrise Crownleaf and Moonlight Deeproot had fallen in love and become mates. Jealousy and resentment festered within the troop until war broke about between the different ranks; Sunrise was killed by her Council and Moonlight died of a broken heart. Since then, pairings between ranks had been forbidden. *Moon and sun*, the tale concluded, *shall never be one.*

"It's not as if either of us is Crownleaf," said Berry. She flung her arms around his neck. "No stupid legend is going to keep us apart. I will never take another mate."

"Neither will I. I don't want anyone who isn't you."

"Then that's all that matters," she told him softly.

He hugged her close, and they clung tightly to each other.

In the silence between them, the song of the crickets and cicadas grew louder. "Do you think they've noticed we're gone?" he murmured at last. "There'll be trouble if so."

"I know." Berry nuzzled him, then drew away. "I mean it, Thorn: I'm not letting you go. But we should go back to the troop now."

Distantly, Thorn heard the shivering yelps of jackals, and then the grunting call of a leopard. The alert gazelle sentries tensed, turning their heads. The nighttime bush was wide awake, and Berry was right: they had to leave.

With a last few murmured words of reassurance, they parted. As always, Thorn turned and padded back through the pitch-dark shadows of the narrow, steep, and stony path; Berry set off for the opposite end of the gully, and the sunrise side of Tall Trees. It was more vital than ever that they shouldn't be seen arriving back together.

Lost in regret, Thorn plodded along the path through the undergrowth, barely noticing the hanging fronds and creepers that batted his face. For once he didn't even listen for predators; wrapped in his misery, he ignored the rustle and skitter of creatures in the darkness.

Still, when a dark shape barged out in front of him and he glimpsed the flash of fangs, he almost yelped out loud. Nut stood in his way, grinning unpleasantly.

"What a nice time of night for romancing," he barked. "What's Stinger going to say when he finds out you've been sneaking around with his Highleaf daughter?"

Panic stirred in Thorn's rib cage. Rising up on his hind paws, he bared his teeth in a snarl. "What are you talking about?"

"Don't try to deny it," sneered Nut. "I saw you both leave the forest!"

Thorn's heart thudded so hard, he thought it might break out of his chest. "You don't know what you're talking about! And even if you did, it'd be none of your business!"

"Oh, yes it is. We *Highleaves* have to make sure we *all* maintain our dignity." Nut wrinkled his muzzle contemptuously. "It's not good for any of us to play the fool with *Middleleaves*."

The fear was receding now, and Thorn could feel his neck fur bristling with fury; he had to struggle to keep his temper. "You're only a Highleaf because you know how to cheat. What would Stinger think of *that*?"

Nut drew himself up. "You know the rule, Middleleaf. '*Only the Crownleaf can authorize pairings.*' Especially ones that defy the troop's traditions." He sniffed scornfully. "Grub will never allow a pairing between a Highleaf and a Middleleaf, and you know it. Our Crownleaf respects the law of the troop!"

Oh, how Thorn wished he'd had a chance to thrash Nut in a fight. He peeled back his lips and snarled. "We're not paired. We're *friends*. Berry doesn't care that I'm a Middleleaf—and that's all that matters to me!"

"We'll see." With a parting hoot of contempt, Nut bounded away into the darkness.

Nasty spy that he is. Thorn shook himself. His fur was still on end, and his heart thumped with rage, but he couldn't help the cold creep of fear in his blood. After all, Nut was right about Grub: the new Crownleaf would never allow a pairing across two ranks. No Crownleaf ever would! *And the troop . . .* Thorn's heart plummeted. He couldn't bear to contemplate Brightforest Troop's reaction if they found out. *They'll scream the tale of Sunrise and Moonlight in my ears as they throw me out forever.*

Or, possibly, while they tear me into furry scraps of baboon.

What if Nut told Grub what he'd seen? Even worse, what if he told Stinger? *Stinger likes me—or he does at the moment. But what will he say if he knows Berry and I have been courting?*

It was with huge trepidation that Thorn padded across the boundary of Tall Trees, and he almost jumped out of his skin at the sound of Stinger's call.

"Thorn!"

Does he know already? Thorn's heart turned over and he

gulped. *Is this when Stinger tells me to stay away from his daughter? Is this when he summons the whole troop to kill me?*

"Hey, Thorn!" Stinger bounded over. "Don't look so worried." He sat down in front of Thorn and eyed him critically. "I'm disappointed you threw away your chance today—the chance I gave you—but that's that. There's nothing either of us can do about it now. And however stupid you were"—he gave Thorn a sharp glare—"I kind of understand."

Thorn nodded, his nerves too shredded to speak.

"Anyway," Stinger went on with a sigh, "you've impressed me with the way you tackled the Three Feats. Well, except the last one, but we'll say no more about that. You've put on a good show. How would you like to join my retinue?"

Thorn blinked at him, startled. "Your retinue? Really?"

Stinger gave a nod. Behind him, Thorn could see Nut, still lurking in the deeper darkness at the foot of a tree. There was a sour glint in the young baboon's eyes.

Thorn felt a sudden surge of pleasure. *This is my chance to prove my worth to Stinger!*

He dipped his head gratefully, feeling excitement building inside him.

"I'd be honored to serve you, Stinger Highleaf!" he said. "Thank you—and yes, I'd like that very much!"

Traditions can change—Fearless is proof of that! One day Berry and I will be together. . . .

CHAPTER 11

The call of an eagle woke Fearless before dawn; the haunting cry drifted eerily across the savannah, scattering the remnants of his vague dream of hunting. Stretching his limbs, then clawing the ground, Fearless shook himself fully alert.

I think in my dream I caught that zebra. I wish the hyenas were as easy to hunt.

He began to pace across the plain, lowering his muzzle to the ground. The grass was verdant and young, the earth soft beneath his paws, and there were so many fresh, strong scents it was hard to pick out the trail of the hyena pack. He had spent the night curled awkwardly in the hollow of a tree, constantly disturbed by the grunting roars of faraway lions and the shrieks of other creatures he couldn't name. When he had finally fallen into a doze, a night bird had swooped close to his tree, uttering a scream that had jolted him straight back out of it. Now, despite the freshness of the morning, his head throbbed from lack of sleep.

At Tall Trees, he had known the voice and scent of every baboon; he had recognized the calls of friends and enemies in his sleep—the grunting snores of Stinger, the dream-squeaks of Mud, the terse barks and whoops of each sentry. But out here, on the unfamiliar grasslands, he had no idea who or what might be a danger. He had no clue when it was safe to move, or rest, or sleep.

And he was so *hungry*. He had caught only a few rodents and a single plump bird since he'd left the troop. Fearless knew he had to find more food soon, or he'd be too weak to do anything.

Ignoring his grumbling stomach, he followed the rank hyena smell; it was patchy and intermittent, but led him into a dense clump of fever trees. Flaring his nostrils, he pushed his nose into the damp undergrowth. *Wait. That's a different scent. Earthier, grassier.*

Something lives here. Not hyenas. But what? Hairs rose on the nape of his neck, and a low growl began in his throat.

He lifted his head a little. The trees were quite widely spaced and their crowns were far above him; dappled early sunshine danced and flashed through their high branches, making the leaves glow brightest green.

Not far ahead, there was an oddly patterned sapling of a kind he hadn't seen before. Fearless crept toward it, paw after suspicious paw. Stretching out his muzzle, he sniffed. The sapling had that strong, grassy smell of the unseen creatures, and the bark was a strange texture. *Almost like . . . fur . . .*

He jumped back with a grunt of astonishment as the sapling lifted, shifted, and settled down in another spot.

"Is it a *lion*?" boomed a shocked voice, high above him.

Fearless snapped up his head and gasped. He backed away, hide prickling in alarm, gaping at the animals above him.

There were five of them, and they were gigantic, almost impossibly tall; he wasn't surprised he had mistaken a leg for a slender sapling. The creatures' necks were even longer, ending in small horned heads, and their hides were a splatter of yellow and brown.

One of those horned heads ducked toward him and he flinched back, hackles springing erect, claws extending. *If I turn and run, can that huge thing just snatch me?*

But the creature simply peered at Fearless, then blinked at a low branch next to him. It stuck out a long purple tongue, wrapped it around a couple of green leaves, and yanked them back into its jaws. It chewed, thoughtfully.

Grass-eaters, then. But so are hippos, and everyone knows how dangerous they are.

"Yes, it's a lion," the creature told its friends, swallowing the leaves. Its enormous neck rippled as the leaves went down. "Ever such a small one, though."

"A youngster," said a female, dipping her head curiously. She blinked long black lashes. "What's happened to your pride, young one? Are you lost?"

Fearless's jaws hung open as he panted nervously. The animals' teeth were barely visible, and those he could see were flat and blunt. He risked a glance downward. At the end of those long legs, they didn't have paws and claws; they had split hooves, just as gazelles and wildebeests did. Fearless gulped and swelled up his chest, trying to regain his dignity.

"I don't have a pride," he told them. "I live with a baboon troop. I'm a baboon, really."

All five of them lowered their heads now, gaping at him, their dark eyes wide and astonished.

"I thought you smelled funny," said one.

"A *baboon*?" repeated another.

"Well, not *really*, obviously." Fearless coughed to clear his throat, making the creatures flinch back just a little. "But I've lived with Brightforest Troop forever, and I'm one of them."

One of the creatures chewed doubtfully on a mouthful of leaves. "So why aren't you with them now?"

"A hyena killed our leader, and *I'm* searching for its pack," growled Fearless. He eyed the tall creatures again, narrowing his eyes. "What *are* you?"

"We're giraffes," said one. "But that's quite enough about us. Hyenas, you say? Why would you follow *them*?"

"I'm going to make sure they don't hurt my troop anymore," he told them grandly.

"Well," harrumphed the female. "That's an *extremely* bad idea."

"I'll say," agreed her friend. "Hyenas are very dangerous."

"With respect," pointed out Fearless, "you would say that. You're grass-eaters."

"And you, apparently, are a baboon." The giraffes began to laugh, a snorting, grunting sound.

"I'm not going back home until I've driven the hyenas away," said Fearless indignantly. "It's important to protect the troop. And it's my job. It's what I do!"

"Well." The tallest giraffe shared a skeptical look with its neighbor. "I suppose if you insist, there's nothing we can do to stop you. If you *really* want to find hyenas—"

"I do," insisted Fearless.

"Oh well. Follow the line of trees there, toward where the sun sets." The giraffe nodded toward it, in a rather slow, extended gesture. "That's where the pack went."

"Thank you." Fearless dipped his head and turned to pad away.

"Hey!" one of the giraffes called. "Whatever you do, don't let the hyenas see you."

"In fact, you really should go home," brayed another.

Fearless shook his head irritably and paced faster. *Those . . . giraffes are overreacting. Grass-eaters!*

But they'd been right about where to find the hyenas; their distinctive scent, rank and musty, became much stronger as he followed the line of the trees. There were several trails running in the same direction, and Fearless's heart quickened. *How many are there? A whole pack?*

Soon the hyenas' pawprints became obvious. The line of trees had come to an end, but the trail was clear across a stretch of grass and then around some yellow-barked acacias. Beyond those the savannah stretched out, open and bright, toward hazy blue hills in the distance. Fearless padded on, determined.

A smear on the landscape—some kind of misshapen shadow—shimmered distantly in the afternoon heat. Hope rising, Fearless broke into a lope. A few rot-eater birds took off as he approached, cawing and flapping in annoyance; the shadow was a gazelle carcass, half eaten and already stinking. Fat flies hummed busily around its tattered flesh.

It's lain here for a while, and the hyenas certainly ate from it, thought Fearless, huffing in their pungent stench. *They'd usually strip the bones bare, but they're gone.*

He glanced up and around, frowning. The birds circling above him were black-and-white crows; a single ugly stork with a huge, fat bill had retreated to a safe distance and was glowering at him. But there was no sign of the vultures that would usually crowd around a feast like this. *What's keeping them away?*

His stomach growled again, and something his mother had once said came back to him. The lionesses, desperate after a long dry season, had brought back a dead tortoise. It hadn't tasted nearly as good as zebra.

Starving Swiftcubs can't be picky.

He sniffed at the gazelle carcass again. Well, he had to eat. And if crows could choke down something that smelled so foul, there was no reason a lion couldn't.

He crouched and tore off chunks and strips of rotten flesh, gulping them down as fast as he could. Flies buzzed up in angry clouds, but Fearless shut his eyes and ate, ignoring them. A taste of foulness and decay caught in the back of his throat, but it certainly filled his empty belly better than lizards and rodents.

Satisfied, Fearless rolled over and basked for a moment, licking his paws and rubbing the sticky blood from his face. But he didn't get long to relax. Something moved against the rippling horizon, and he blinked and sat up, trying to focus.

The sun was lowering in the sky, and its golden intensity made the shapes hard to see clearly across the vast stretch of grassland. Still, he could make out that there were three of them, and they were definitely getting closer. Fearless propped himself up on his forepaws. Some instinct told him to glance behind him, and he saw two more creatures, bulky and heavy-footed, coming from the opposite direction. At last they were close enough to see clearly, and Fearless could only stand up and stare.

A cubhood memory sparked in his head. He knew he'd seen these thickset, stocky creatures before. Their heads were wide and square, with a thick horn on the nose; their creased hides were gray, leathery, and furless. Billowing yellow dust rose in thick clouds as they trotted toward him. *Rhinoceroses, Swiftcub.* His mother's voice drifted back to him across the long seasons. *Don't get too close.*

"I'm looking for hyenas," he yelled as soon as he judged they were in earshot. "Have you seen them? Do you know where the hyenas live?"

No answer came; instead the rhinos broke from a brisk trot into a run. Lowering those fearsome horns, they galloped toward him, their great hooves pounding up clouds of sunlit dust. On the still air, he heard the low rumble of menace from their throats.

Fearless ducked and bolted to the side, then sprinted as fast as he could away from both groups. They hadn't looked fast, but appearances had been deceptive. He could still hear their heavy feet thundering as they swerved after him, and the ground shook.

The long grass. If I can reach that—

Fearless put on another burst of speed. His breath rasped in his throat and a sudden pang of fear struck painfully in his chest. *I can't keep up this pace for long!* The long grass was still too far away. He glanced back and saw that the rhinos were closing in. He could make out their tiny, black, malevolent eyes.

His lungs stung as he dragged in desperate breaths and his muscles burned with effort. *I can't outrun them!*

Now Fearless understood why the vultures had stayed away, and why the hyenas had abandoned the carcass. *The rhinos must have driven them off. Wait—did they actually kill the whole hyena pack?* His blood ran cold with fear. *They're going to catch me. They're going to kill me!*

There seemed to be only one thing left to do. Fearless skidded to a halt in a flurry of dust, spun around, and faced the charging creatures. Bunching his shoulders, he gave the loudest roar he could.

The animals skidded to an abrupt halt, so close their hot clouds of breath billowed over him. It didn't smell of flesh, which was reassuring; it smelled of smashed grass and leaves.

But they looked angry—really angry.

"Who do you think you are?" bellowed the biggest of them, pawing at the ground. "This is our land! This is rhinoceros territory!"

Fearless held his ground, baring his teeth. "I didn't know," he growled.

"A lone lion who doesn't know rhino territory? You've got a nerve." The leader raked her massive, three-toed hoof across the sand again. "The hyenas had the sense to run from us. So should you!"

There was a small bush beside her; she tore at it with her fearsome horn, scattering leaves and scraps of twigs. Turning back to Fearless, she narrowed her small eyes.

"Why," she rumbled, "are you still here?"

She lowered her horn again, this time in his direction. Fearless tensed, waiting for her to make her next move—but it was a horrible shock when she did. She lunged into a brutal, direct charge.

Twisting and leaping, Fearless bolted again, only to glimpse another rhinoceros, cutting across to intercept him. He dodged and ducked, fleeing back the way he'd come—and had to swerve again, out of the path of another. They were forcing him back, he realized, driving him toward the edge of a sharp slope. He slithered to a halt. Backing away from the rhinos, snarling, he sensed the empty air at his rump where the ground fell away.

They're heavy. They've got huge shoulders. Maybe they can't run downhill well?

I hope not, anyway.

Spinning, he sprang down the slope. His paws hit the incline and didn't stop, slithering wildly beneath him, and he only just stopped himself tumbling head over tail to the bottom. Grit and dust flew up, burning his mouth and nostrils with the hot scent of sand and stone. The clouds settled as he reached flat ground again; recovering, he spun back to face the rhinos, opening his jaws aggressively.

But the rhinoceroses hadn't followed. They stood on the crest of the slope, glaring down at him, grunting in frustration.

"Don't let us see you around here again!" bellowed the leader. "We'll stomp you to bits of cat-flesh if you come back!"

"Don't worry," muttered Fearless, shaking himself briskly. "I've no intention of coming near *you* again."

Fearless strutted along the grassland, heading toward a line of dark forest. The hyena scent was back in his nostrils and the trail was clear; even better, there was no more sign of strange-looking, oversize enemies. He was nearly there when he found another carcass in a shallow dip: a kudu this time, recognizable only by its huge spiraling horns and a few scraps of brindled hide—the bones were stripped quite clean. Finally, it seemed, the hyenas had found a kill where they could eat undisturbed by the rhinoceroses.

Picking the scent up again on the other side of the carcass, Fearless determinedly followed the trail, skirting the edge of the forest. Beyond the trees, where the plains swept out once more, he saw the darkness of a broad, rocky escarpment, clearly silhouetted against the low sun. He tightened his jaws and padded toward the steep bank.

Pausing, one paw raised, Fearless narrowed his eyes. Now he could make out details: low on the slope, half hidden by scrubby bushes, there was a darker smear of shadow. He took another few cautious paces and saw it was a hollow cavern—one that penetrated deep into the bank, farther than he could see.

As the sun melted below the horizon in an amber glow, Fearless crept stealthily closer to the rocks, his belly low to the ground. The shadowed hole was right ahead of him, and it wasn't just any tunnel; it stank strongly of hyenas. Fearless felt his excitement rising. *This must be where they live!*

Crouching low, he crawled inside, dragging and squeezing his haunches after him. The coldness within was almost shocking. Twisting his head awkwardly, he could still make out the sky, a round, dark blue patch behind him.

I'm a lion, he told himself. *And a lion hunts by night.* All the same, he had to shake off a tremor in his spine.

Fearless knew he must smell like a hyena himself now; their rank odor clung unpleasantly to his fur. But he'd found them, and he was soon deep enough into the tunnel to be in pitch darkness. Pausing, taking slow breaths, and summoning his confidence, he let his eyes adjust.

Shapes formed clearly in his vision; he could see the tunnel walls in shades of sludgy blue and green. Not much, but enough. He made out blacker blobs of shadow, too, where more tunnels branched off.

From deep inside one of them came the sound of a high-pitched, echoing squabble. The noise raised the hair on Fearless's spine, but he clenched his jaws and crept toward it, his belly low.

Far too close by, claws scrabbled on stone. Fearless stopped, his heart racing. Somewhere there was the click of rapid, running paws, but the echoes made it hard to pinpoint their source.

Are they behind me?

Uneasiness prickled his spine, but he couldn't stop now. He picked his way along in the darkness. He could make out only the occasional ridge of jutting rock, outlined by a pallid glow. It was his nose and his hide that told him when the tunnel opened out into a broad cave; the air simply seemed emptier. Fearless came to a halt, breathing as silently as he could.

Starlight must have leaked in from somewhere high above; several pairs of eyes glowed as they turned in his direction. His own eyes began to adjust, showing him the outlines of five hyenas, their hackles raised.

The hyenas were first to recover. One of them sprang to confront him with a squealing growl and showed its vicious fangs.

"What are you doing here?"

It was *huge*. Its fangs, bared and dripping saliva, were sharp and lethal, and its eyes burned a hideous yellow. Its fur was spotted, greasy tufts standing up from its long legs and broad, sloping back. Yet its vicious head looked almost small, hunched in front of its massive, thickly muscled shoulders.

Nut was right after all, Fearless realized with a plummeting heart. *The one that attacked our troop was a sickly weakling.*

These ones, quite clearly, were not.

His courage deserted him. Baring his teeth, trying not to tremble, Fearless backed away, one paw at a time. Then he heard a sniggering voice behind him:

"Not so fast, baby lion."

One hyena had indeed been sneaking up behind him; now it emerged from the tunnel, grinning in vicious glee.

No escape. Panic rose in his chest.

"Straight into our den, brothers and sisters," snarled the big hyena facing him. "Straight into our den he crawls."

"Lions," spat another. "So full of themselves."

The one behind him giggled again. "Not usually quite so *stupid*, though."

Fearless swung around to eye him fearfully, then spun back to face forward again. *How am I going to fight when I'm surrounded?*

"I never ate lion before," whined another from the cave. "I wonder how it tastes?"

"This one might be a little bitter," sniggered the leader. "So much regret. For being so stupid."

Fearless tried to ignore their taunts. His heart thundered in his chest as he glanced desperately around for a way out. However good his eyesight was, it was hard to distinguish one pool of shadow from another. He pressed his flank to the wall, widening his eyes as he tried to peer beyond the cave.

"Stand aside, brothers and sisters. The first bite of lion is mine." The leader bunched her haunches and sprang.

Fearless flung himself away from the wall, rolling and scrabbling in a desperate effort to escape the snapping jaws. He felt sharp fangs graze his flank, but as he dodged those, another hyena pounced, sinking its teeth into his shoulder. He gave a roar of pain and flung it off. More teeth stabbed into his hind leg; he twisted sharply and had the satisfaction of feeling his own fangs bite into hyena-flesh.

But there were too many of them. Lashing, roaring, snapping, Fearless spun and struck out as hard as he could, but he was tiring already, and the hyenas were smart, ducking away from his jaws and letting the ones at his rump spring in to bite.

Under their relentless assaults, Fearless staggered back, and he and the hyenas tumbled into the larger chamber. He shook off the beast that was fastened to his neck and rolled again, lashing out with his claws. His breath rasping, he glanced wildly around. In the chaos, he'd struck a single moment of luck—the hyenas were suddenly all on one side of him, next to the tunnel. Scrambling to his paws, he bolted away from them, deeper into the cavern, heading instinctively for the darkest patch of shadow he could see.

It's another tunnel! He leaped and clawed his way into it, kicking hyenas away from his rump. They howled and screeched with rage, biting at his hindquarters; they were right behind

him, but his way forward was clear for now. Trying to ignore
the pain of their snapping teeth, Fearless dragged himself on.

As the passage widened, he picked up speed, the pounding of his paws echoing from the rock that enclosed him. The
hyenas were still in pursuit, yammering and barking, but he
could hear something up ahead, too—another set of paws.
He caught the glow of eyes turning toward him, and his heart
missed a beat.

I can't turn back. Clenching his jaws, charging on, he sprang at
the new hyena. Taken by surprise, it squealed as it fell under
his pounding paws. Fearless bounded over it and kept running.

The tunnel was rising now, and more light filtered in. He
could see details again: rough sandstone walls, and an empty
circular gap, and the glitter of distinct starlight. *Oh please,
please . . .*

He burst into the open, gasping a lungful of fresh night air.
The vast sky was filled with stars, and the sight of them gave
him a new surge of energy.

He was out of the awful tunnels and still running, but the
hyenas hadn't given up the chase. He could hear their harsh-
throated cries of greed as they gained on him. Fearless's breath
rasped. He knew he was tiring, and when they caught him—

I don't want to think about that. I don't want to think!

Even the night air was overwhelmed by the stench of hyena
now. But as his nostrils flared, Fearless smelled something
else, something familiar: a rich, deep scent that was nothing
like the rankness of hyena.

Lions!

Hope surged in his aching chest. Summoning the last of his reserves, Fearless opened his jaws and gave a grunting, desperate roar for help. It echoed back from the rocks around him, and Fearless couldn't help but think the land itself was mocking him. When he curled back his muzzle to try again, he was slammed to the ground, and the roar stuck in his throat.

A hyena clung to his hindquarters, biting and tearing. The others were quickly on him too, piling on with snapping jaws. Terror rushed through Fearless's blood as he twisted and writhed on his back. He tried to rake at his attackers with his hind claws, but they were too fast, too agile. The leader lunged for his throat with a snarl of triumph—

The hyena was knocked flying as a great tawny force slammed into it. Gasping, half blinded by fear, Fearless could only gape as a huge, sleek lioness fought and grappled with his attacker. The rest of the hyena pack was under attack, too: more lionesses had charged into the fray and were fighting savagely.

Fearless rolled and staggered to his paws, just in time to see the first lioness deliver a brutal swipe of her claws to the hyena leader's flank. It gave a screeching yelp of pain, scrabbled out from under her, and fled, tail between its legs.

In moments, it was all over. Seeing their leader put to flight, the other hyenas yammered and bolted after him, leaving two of their number lifeless and bloody in the dust. As the sound of their racing paws and their whimpering yelps faded, silence fell.

Fearless staggered toward the first lioness. "Thank you. I didn't—I couldn't—*thank you.*"

She turned, her body lithe and elegant, and paced toward him. The bright river of stars picked out her pale gold muzzle and reflected in her dark liquid eyes, and as he looked at her properly for the first time, Fearless gasped.

She halted as he did, her eyes widening in astonishment. "Fearless!"

All the terror of the tunnels drained from him, replaced by the shock of joy.

"Valor!"

CHAPTER 12

The two lions bounded to each other, colliding in an ecstasy of happy greeting. The hyenas forgotten, Fearless rumbled with joy, licking his sister's ears, rubbing her face with his.

"I can't believe it!" he gabbled. She was fully grown now, strong and still bigger than him, but her eager caresses were gentle and loving. "Valor, you're alive!"

"And so are you, Fearless!" She laughed. "Sisters," she called to the other lionesses, "come over here! Do you remember Fearless, my little Swiftbrother?"

"The one we thought was dead?" A dark-furred lioness trotted up in surprise.

"Yes!" growled Valor happily. "But here he is!"

Fearless blinked, recognizing the other lioness. "Honor, it's you!"

All five of them bustled around him, licking and nuzzling, and Fearless growled in sheer happiness, reveling in their affectionate greetings.

"Agile! Sly! Regal!" he rumbled. "It's so good to see you again."

"And it's wonderful to see you," growled Regal, swishing her tail. "But we'll let you and Valor talk—you were both Swiftcubs, after all. You must have a lot to tell each other." She nuzzled him fondly, then padded away with her three friends to inspect the two battered hyena corpses.

Fearless turned back to Valor, who was gazing at him with shining eyes. "I can hardly believe it's you," he murmured, touching her nose gently with his own. "I thought you and Mother were dead. Did you get away from Titan?"

"I wish we had," she rumbled, pressing her light gold face to his. "No, Titan and his cronies forced us to stay. I think they would have killed us, but Mother convinced Titan to let her live for her hunting skills."

"And you?" He rubbed her neck.

"Mother told Titan she'd teach me to be a fine hunter too. So he spared my life, and now I hunt with the other lionesses." Valor laughed softly. "Though we didn't expect to catch a lion!"

"Where is Mother?" asked Fearless suddenly, glancing at the other lionesses. "Why isn't she hunting with you?"

Valor closed her eyes. "Life in Titanpride is . . . difficult, Fearless." She licked her jaws, as if what she had to say was hard. "Titan has a favorite mate, Artful. Artful isn't a great hunter; she's too lazy. She was jealous of Mother's skills—so she attacked her one evening. And . . ."

Fearless felt a sick, plummeting sensation in his gut. "And what?"

"She blinded her," said Valor sadly. "Mother can't hunt anymore. And Titan has threatened to drive her out of the pride unless I catch enough prey for both of us."

"If he casts her out now, she'd die!" exclaimed Fearless.

"Yes." Valor sounded tired and miserable; Fearless realized belatedly how exhausted she looked. Her muscles were still lean and strong, but her coat had lost its luster and her eyes were hollowed.

"I have to see Mother!" he growled.

Valor's eyes widened with horror. "No, Fearless, you mustn't."

"What's that you're saying?" Honor padded over to them, the other lionesses behind her. "Go back to the pride? Don't even think about it, Fearless!"

"Titan will kill you," growled Sly.

"Yes," said Valor urgently. "He won't let a son of Gallant live."

"But the way he's treated Mother!" snarled Fearless. "He can't get away with it!"

Valor shook her head. "What could you do about it? You're not nearly fully grown! You must stay away from the pride, Fearless—at least for now."

She's right, he realized, as the surge of righteous rage drained out of him and hopelessness seeped in. *Valor is still bigger and stronger than me—if she can't confront Titan, what could I do?* After all, he'd been confident that he could tackle the hyenas. Rushing in to fight Titan would be the last thing he ever did. His mood dark, he slumped into a crouch.

Valor licked his head gently. "Don't think about it just now, Fearless. It'll drive you mad. Now, tell me how you survived! What happened; where did you go?"

Rolling onto his side, he gazed wryly up at her. "You won't believe this—I was carried away by an eagle and left in its nest."

"What?" Valor's jaw fell.

"Which is where a troop of baboons found me. And I've been living with them ever since."

All the lionesses were staring at him now, their eyes huge and astonished. "You have baboon friends?" gasped Regal.

"Do you live in the trees?" asked Agile, gaping.

Fearless shook his head, amused. "No, but I live in the forest with them, and I protect the troop. The Brightforest Troop; they've been—they're like family. It works really well."

"That's"—Valor licked her jaws—"amazing. But wherever you live, you should go back there for now, Fearless. And you should eat before you go. There's no sense letting those two hyenas go to waste. There's not a lot of prey around right now, and they won't taste very good, but . . ."

"Starving Swiftcubs can't be picky." Fearless joined in to say it in unison with his sister, and they both gave rumbling laughs. Then he hesitated, licking his jaws uncertainly. "But if prey is scarce, shouldn't you take these back to Titan?"

Valor shook her head. "We'll take one of them, but we'll have time to hunt for more tonight. Go ahead, Fearless."

Fearless needed no second invitation; he padded over to the hyenas and began to eat hungrily. The flesh tasted bitter and strange, but he didn't care. The lionesses joined him, tearing off an occasional strip for themselves. They were very curious about his new life with the baboons, and he told them what he could between mouthfuls.

There were the Starleaf's stories of the Great Spirit, always told in the twilight as the troop settled for the night. There was the fun and excitement of sentry duty, when he would make sure his scent clung all around Tall Trees to deter hostile flesh-eaters. He explained how the baby baboons would cling to his belly, mistaking him for a grown baboon. He described Stinger and his passion for scorpions; he told them about the plants the Goodleaves found for the troop, to rub on their fur to keep the biting flies away.

"And of course I can't rub the leaves on myself," he added, "so Thorn and Mud do it for me. They're my best friends. Almost like brothers."

"It sounds as if you've found a home," said Valor softly, with a hint of sadness. "I'm glad."

"Valor," said Agile at last, standing and stretching, "we do still need to hunt. Titan won't be pleased if we come back too late."

"Yes, I know," sighed Valor. Rising to her paws, she gazed at Fearless. "We should go."

"It'll be good when the grass-eaters come back to the

watering hole," remarked Sly. "Finding food will be so much easier."

"I can't wait," agreed Honor. "Good-bye, Fearless, and *don't* go back to those hyenas!"

Fearless stood up, blinking at them. "Where should I go, then?"

"Back home to your baboon family." Valor laughed gently, shaking her head again as if hardly able to believe it. But his sister's voice held kindness, and she still lingered, giving him another farewell lick. "This troop obviously takes good care of you. You're lucky they found you."

It was what he'd always believed, but somehow, the words sounded hollow for the first time.

"Come on, Valor," urged Regal.

Valor sighed and turned. In single file the lionesses padded away, and as Fearless watched them vanish into the night, he wished with all his heart that he was going with them.

Bark Crownleaf had told him he needed to be a lion. Now, for the first time, he was beginning to think she was right.

Fearless's heart lifted a little as the dark green lushness of Tall Trees came into view, but that seemed mostly relief at the end of his adventure; the sight of his home didn't give him the spring in his step that he would have expected only a day ago. As he padded closer, he could hear the chatter and whoop of the baboons as they caught sight of him; the noise increased as the news spread through the troop, and by the time he was among the trees, every baboon seemed to know he had returned. Thorn and Mud emerged from a date palm thicket; they exchanged an oddly apprehensive glance before brightening and bounding toward him.

"You're back!" hooted Thorn, flinging his arms around Fearless's neck, then swinging up onto his back. "Oh my, Fearless," he gasped. "Are you all right?"

"What do you mean?" Fearless asked.

Thorn had hopped off and was tracing his forepaws across Fearless's flanks. "You're covered in cuts and your fur is torn."

"What happened?" asked Mud. "Did you find the hyenas?"

Fearless glanced at them sheepishly. "I did," he said. "It was a fierce fight."

"And did you beat them?" Thorn bounced at his side. "Come on, we want to hear everything!"

"They . . ." Fearless licked his jaws. He was ashamed to tell Thorn and Mud about his humiliating failure, but he had to tell them *something.* "I don't think they'll be a problem anymore," he said at last, with as much swagger as he could manage.

"Ah, I knew you could do it!" Thorn slapped the lion's neck with his paws, and Fearless tried not to grunt in pain. He padded on, head low. He was glad the two baboons couldn't see his face right now. *I just want to forget what happened.*

"It's good to be home," he told them cheerfully. "All I want is to go back to normal life with my troop."

Thorn fell silent, and at last Fearless glanced back, in time to catch his friend exchanging another look of unease with Mud.

"What? What is it?"

"Fearless, we, uh . . ." Thorn seemed unusually tongue-tied; Mud just cleared his throat and averted his eyes. Puzzled, Fearless glanced around at the baboons in the trees, and it finally struck him: *No one else came to welcome me. They called the alarm when I arrived, but now? The troop looks quiet.*

They didn't only look subdued, either; some of the baboons were glaring at him with outright hostility. Some turned away as he approached; others—the members of the troop who'd always been friendliest to him—looked too embarrassed to speak to him.

"Thorn," he growled, "what's going on?"

"Nothing," began Mud unconvincingly. "It's just that . . ." His voice trailed off.

"Fearless, there's something we've got to tell—"

But before Thorn could finish, Nut came bounding through a clump of ferns, a broad grin on his muzzle. "Hey, Big Talk! Have you heard the news yet?"

"What news?" Fearless stared at Nut. Thorn and Mud stood on either side of him, looking angry and protective.

"Shut up, Nut!" snapped Thorn. "It's not right for you to tell him!"

Nut opened his jaws mockingly and seemed about to say more, but at that moment Stinger came hurrying across the clearing, his face drawn. He placed a large forepaw on Fearless's neck.

"Fearless! I'm so sorry."

"Sorry for what?" Fearless had a sick feeling in his stomach.

Stinger chittered his teeth in distress. "Fearless, you can't stay here. You're going to have to leave. I'm so very sorry."

"Leave?"

Fearless's throat dried. For an instant he had the wild notion that Stinger meant he should leave this clearing—go to his own sleeping area, maybe, or the Council Glade—but the misery on the baboon's face shattered that faint hope.

"You mean, leave Tall Trees?" Fearless growled. "Leave Brightforest Troop?"

"Oh, Fearless," said Thorn, turning to him and rubbing his shoulder. "It happened while you were away."

"Grub organized a vote," Stinger told him grimly. "About whether you should stay in the troop or go. Many baboons wanted you to stay," he said hurriedly. "But . . ."

"But more wanted me to go." Fearless curled his muzzle. His shock drained away, replaced by sharp bitterness.

"You will *always* belong with Brightforest Troop," said Stinger, his eyes fierce with emotion. "I believe that."

"And so do we," said Thorn, nodding at Mud. "We're furious. About the result—and about Grub holding the vote at all, when you weren't here to defend yourself."

"We couldn't stop him," said Mud in a small voice.

"Of course you couldn't." Fearless dipped his head to nuzzle him. "Don't worry, Mud. It's not your fault."

"I don't want you to go," the little baboon wailed. "None of us do."

"I don't want to leave," sighed Fearless. "But it looks like I don't have a choice."

"Listen to me. You'll be fine." Stinger reached out to lay a paw on his muzzle. "I honestly didn't think you'd survive a confrontation with the hyenas—but here you are, Fearless. You're strong and resourceful—it'll be all right."

"But where is he supposed to *go*?" asked Thorn angrily.

"Don't worry," Fearless told him. "Honestly, Thorn. I've got some good news. While I was out there, out on the plains, guess who I met? My sister, Valor!"

"You did?" exclaimed Thorn. "She's alive? That's great!"

"Yes, and the other lionesses of Gallantpride." Fearless decided not to mention the part where they'd saved him from certain death at the jaws of a hyena pack. "But the pride's in trouble. Titan's a terrible leader. So I'm going back to my pride to help them."

Stinger scratched his broad shoulders thoughtfully. The sunlight streaming through the leaves picked out the silver thread of his scar. "Well, Cub of the Stars. When you were tiny, and I rescued you from that tree, you told me you were going to take your pride back. It would certainly be wonderful if you did it one day."

"I remember that." Fearless smiled. "And one day I'll make good on it. I'll beat Titan, and I *will* take back my pride."

Thorn flung himself forward and hugged Fearless's chest tightly. "I know you will."

Fearless, feeling choked, bent to lick his friend's furry head. "I'd better go—before Grub comes to throw me out."

Thorn looked miserable as the other two hugged Fearless. "I'll come with you. As far as the watering hole."

Fearless nuzzled him. "I'd like that."

It helped, having Thorn at his side as he walked out of Tall Trees for the last time. Fearless's heart didn't feel as heavy as he'd expected. Of course he ached with sadness, but only at leaving behind Thorn and Mud and some of the others. *I wouldn't have lasted long with Grub as Crownleaf anyway. Better this happened sooner than later.*

"I don't care what Grub says," announced Thorn as they left the forest behind. He clambered onto Fearless's back, and the two of them set off across the savannah at an easy stroll. "And I don't care what Nut thinks, or any of the others. We'll always be friends, you and I."

"Of course," rumbled Fearless.

"If you ever need help, promise you'll come and find me." Thorn paused, making Fearless halt and turn to look into his eyes. "Promise?"

"Yes." Fearless nodded. "And the same goes for you, Thorn. I'll be there if you need me."

They traveled on in silence for a while, Thorn gently grooming Fearless's neck. Fearless felt soothed, and quite sanguine about his sudden exile. It hurt that the troop didn't want him, but perhaps he'd been meant to meet Valor when he did. Seeing his sister had changed something inside him. *Would I have been happy,* he wondered, *if I'd stayed with the Brightforest Troop forever?*

Maybe it really was time for him to be a lion.

Still, when the watering hole came into sight at the horizon, Fearless felt an intense twinge of sadness; soon he'd be parting from Thorn, and they'd each move on to live separate lives.

He stopped to stare ahead. *Watering hole* didn't really do this place justice, he decided. It was a silver lake, fringed with date palms and crotons and scrub acacias; there were several bays, bare of vegetation, that were pockmarked with animal tracks. He could make out well-worn paths through the scrub, and scars and smooth patches on bark where animals had rubbed themselves. The water itself was an enticing vision, rippling and glittering as they drew closer. Though the rains had softened the grassland's arid yellow, the greenness of the lake's stumpy trees and bushes stood out, vivid and lush with fresh foliage.

Fearless came to a halt at the water's edge. Thorn's paws grew still against his neck fur, and they watched the play of silver light in entranced silence.

It's beautiful, thought Fearless sadly. *I guess it's a good place to say good-bye.*

But the two friends had stood there for only a few moments when they were disturbed by a rumbling sound. It drifted from far across the plains, and it was growing louder. Thorn furrowed his brow, twisting to peer at the horizon. Fearless drew himself taller, tensing his muscles, narrowing his eyes at rising clouds of billowing dust.

"What is it?" he wondered.

"Sky and stone," breathed Thorn. "It's the herds, Fearless. It's the grass-eaters."

Now the approaching animals were visible, hordes of them

teeming across the horizon. Fearless could make out the black and white of zebras, the milling dun and gray of wildebeests and kudu, and the bright gold of gazelles.

"The great migration, isn't it?" exclaimed Fearless. "Mud told me all about it."

Thorn nodded, a grin on his broad face. "It's the grass-eater herds, returning for the rains. What a sight!"

Fearless stared, awed by the sheer number of creatures that trampled across the savannah toward them. "Look, there are giraffes!" he growled, pleased to recognize the elegantly striding animals. "But what—great stars, Thorn! What are *those*?"

He stared at the enormous creatures that marched behind the herds, far bigger than anything he had ever seen. The giraffes might be taller, but these creatures were altogether massive, their gray bodies huge, their ears broad, their legs thick and powerful. The ground shook with the force of their tread as they approached.

"Elephants!" whispered Thorn. "Those are elephants, Fearless. And one of them . . . one of them must be the Great Mother."

"The Great Mother?" Fearless blinked. "The leader you told me about?"

"Yes. The Great Mother of Bravelands." Thorn's voice was hushed with respect. "She summons the Great Gathering every year, and the other tribes of the plains come to her to ask advice, or plead for help, or let her judge disputes. It happens on the first day of the first new moon after the rains start, and every creature comes—grass-eater, flesh-eater, or rot-eater."

He shot Fearless a rueful look. "Well, every creature but the lions."

"Why not the lions?" Fearless still couldn't tear his gaze from the elephants.

"Because you lot don't think you need any creature's advice." Thorn laughed. "Lions don't recognize or respect the Great Mother, any more than you do the Great Spirit. You're funny that way."

Fearless took no notice of his friend's gentle teasing. He felt that he would never again see a sight as astonishing or captivating as the movement of the great herds, and he didn't want to miss a moment of it. In silence, the two friends stood and watched as the herds marched closer. Zebras, wildebeests, gazelles: their numbers were uncountable. Fearless's heart swelled within him. *I'm so glad I saw this with Thorn. Every creature of Bravelands. All of them, together.*

The fur on the back of Fearless's neck prickled. Despite the hordes, despite the noise and the thunder and the vast clouds of dust, his attention was drawn inexorably back to one creature only: those magnificent, awe-inspiring elephants.

CHAPTER 13

Now that they were so close to the watering hole, Sky's thirst returned with a vengeance. She could no longer ignore the sandy dryness of her parched throat, and her trunk felt as if it might shrivel up altogether. She picked up her pace, her breath rasping hard, the delicious scent of the fresh water seeming to fill her whole skull.

"Oh, it's beautiful!" cried Moon beside her. His little trunk was raised high as he tried to catch the luxuriant scents.

"Yes," murmured Sky.

The vast stretch of water sparkled beneath the sun, its flakes of light dazzling. Even the colors of the bushes felt cool against her aching eyes. But Sky just could not shake the sense of dread that had clung to her since that horrifying vision on the Plain of Our Ancestors.

She started as water splattered her ear; Moon had squirted

a trunkful at her, and he was already sucking up more. Shaking herself, Sky tried to enjoy his antics and the obvious delight of the other animals gathered at the water's edge. Two giraffes, their legs splayed, had dipped their long necks to drink, and Moon, distracted from his game, was gaping at them with fascination. There were gazelles, too, and bushbuck, and many zebras; those who had drunk their fill were moving away to make space for a seemingly endless horde. Even a leopard slunk down through the bushes to lap at the water, and not a single one of the grass-eaters flinched.

Sky couldn't see any lions, though, or baboons. Perhaps her vision had been symbolic? She scanned the line of creatures. Could the leopard be the danger? Or a less obvious animal, like a wildebeest? A group of rhinos was staring at Sky and her herd resentfully. *I wouldn't be surprised if they wanted to hurt us. You can tell how much they hate elephants.*

But apart from the glowering rhinos, every animal seemed peaceful and happy; no fights broke out despite the numbers who had gathered. Grass-eaters exchanged polite greetings with flesh-eaters; zebras and wildebeests who had squabbled on the trek now stood together, chatting amiably. Sky could make out fragments of their conversations, and none of their words sounded suspicious or alarming.

Everyone is excited about the Great Gathering. Every creature is looking forward to it. It's hard to imagine anything bad happening in this place.

Yet still Sky could not shake that awful foreboding. Every sudden movement made her jump and blink.

She gasped and started as a dark shadow blundered

between the two giraffes, then shook her head, smiling. It was only Moon.

But he might start to annoy those giraffes!

Sky trotted over to her little cousin and reached out her trunk, trying to guide him away from the tall, slender creatures. "I'm sorry," she told them hastily. "I'll get him out of your way—come on, Moon. No more squirting!"

One of the giraffes laughed. "Oh, we don't mind the little one. He's having fun. So long as he doesn't knock us over!"

"I hope not!" exclaimed Sky. "Moon, you must be careful—"

Sky's words dried in her throat and her blood ran suddenly cold in her veins. Beyond the two giraffes, up on the crest of a steep sandbank, stood a maneless lion, calmly watching the watering hole.

Sitting on the lion's back was a baboon.

All the images from her vision flooded back into Sky's mind. *A lion, roaring in pain. A baboon, baring its fangs in a snarl. The watering hole, running red with thick blood.*

"Moon!" she trumpeted. "We have to go, now!"

"Aw, Sky—"

"Now!" Nudging him with her trunk, she harried him back toward the elephants. He resisted, protesting with squeals, and almost tripped over his own trunk. As Sky pushed him, she stumbled against one of the giraffes. It tottered, swaying, and gave a bray of alarm.

Horrified, gabbling an apology, Sky didn't wait for a scolding, but drove Moon back at a rapid trot to their family.

"Sky, what is it?" Great Mother raised her head and flapped her ears with concern as the two young elephants stumbled into the midst of the herd. "What's wrong?"

"Great Mother!" It came out in a sob. "My vision, it's come true. We have to leave!"

"Leave the watering hole?" said Comet, one of Sky's aunts. Her long-lashed eyes were wide. "Why, don't be silly, young Sky!"

"Great Mother, *please*! Look, I'll show you—over there!" Sky spun and pointed with her trunk at the steep bank of sandy earth.

It was empty. A few gazelles grazed beneath it, but the lion and the baboon were gone.

"They were there! Just now! The lion and the baboon, the ones I saw in my vision . . ."

Great Mother touched her trunk gently to Sky's. "I believe you, little one," she murmured. "But remember: elephants can see only the past, not the future. What you saw must have been a terrible thing, a dreadful ancestral memory—one that happened generations ago."

Sky was trembling against the matriarch's legs. "But Great Mother, it was so clear. And these ones—they looked just like . . ." *They didn't look evil, though. The baboon's face, it wasn't like the one in my vision.* "Well, they were different from the animals I dreamed, I suppose, but the baboon was sitting on the lion and—"

"Little one, you must be so tired after the trek." Great Mother stroked her head.

"Yes," agreed Star. "You poor thing, no wonder you're fragile. Even Moon had it easier, since he still had my milk."

"I'll go and get you some leaves," offered Rain. "You rest for a little while, Sky. That'll make you feel better."

Sky gave a feeble nod, too tired and scared to argue anymore. *I'll never convince them. They'll never leave the watering hole because of this.*

But I know something awful is going to happen. I know it!

For the rest of the afternoon, Sky did as she was told and lay resting, stretched out in the shade of an acacia tree. It did help, she realized: at least she got some energy back, and she managed to feel a little less frantic.

She was still determined, though. *I know I'm right. My aunts, Great Mother—they're so kind, and they care for me, but this time they're wrong.*

Night was falling when Sky got to her feet again and stood, swaying slightly, watching the peaceful watering hole. Most of the herds had wandered away from its edge, and many—her family included—had lain down to rest, or were dozing on their feet. Crickets and frogs began to pipe in the bushes, and the darkening dusk was soon full of their soothing song.

Sky wasn't tired anymore; she had no intention of sleeping. She paced around the watering hole, alert for anything unusual, any small sign that would show her where the danger lay.

Because there is danger. I'm sure of it.

Not all the animals were asleep. A knot of rhinos were gathered at the water's edge, muttering and grumbling to one another. Sky edged closer to them; they looked even huger than the one that had shouted at her and Moon. *Big enough to fight an elephant. I'd better be careful.*

The rhinos' tough hides gleamed palely in the starlight; their heads were square and heavy, their expressions resentful and hostile. She caught bits of their conversation as she crept closer.

". . . tried talking to Rockslide, but will he listen? No."

"Rockslide's whole crash is as stupid and lazy as he is. They believe everything's just fine the way it is."

". . . sometimes think we're the only ones who understand the unfairness . . ."

". . . not as if they don't see what's wrong. Rockslide's crash just doesn't care."

". . . likes an easy life, that's his trouble. If it was up to me . . ."

Sky craned in, listening hard. Their conversation about this idle, peace-loving rhino called Rockslide was giving her an idea. . . .

"Well, I'm not going to put up with it," grunted the biggest rhino. "He just doesn't get it! I'm sick of the way those elephants treat us! Rhinos have always been far too passive. It's time for us to come together and stand up for ourselves!"

Summoning her courage, Sky cleared her throat. When that didn't get their attention, she gave a huffing, polite cough. Four heavy square heads turned to her, glaring in angry surprise.

"*What?*" snapped one.

"Horn and hoof, it's an elephant youngster!"

Another leaned menacingly toward Sky. "Were you listening in? Were you?"

"Get rid of it, Stronghide!"

Sky swallowed hard, holding her ground despite her trembling legs. "I just want to ask you something," she squeaked. "Please?"

The one called Stronghide lowered his horn and grunted angrily, "Get out of here!"

Sky shivered. Stronghide was the biggest, and the heavy wrinkles in his stony skin did not hide the power of his muscles. Every instinct was screaming at Sky to run away.

She shut her eyes tight, then opened them again. "You don't like elephants, I know—"

"No, we don't," bellowed Stronghide. "So clear off!"

"I ... I ..." Sky tried to steady her voice. "I don't want to be here, at this watering hole. I want the elephants to leave too! Maybe you can ... maybe you can help? You could make our herd leave!"

"What?" Stronghide shook his horn and gave a deep-throated grunt of fury. "How dare you! How dare you—*an elephant*—ask us for help! What have you ever done for us?" As he stamped toward her, Sky flinched back. "All you've ever done is keep the role of Great Mother for yourselves!"

"The nerve of it!" spat another rhino.

"How dare she, indeed!"

Sky swallowed hard. *They really do hate us.*

"Does Great Mother ever ask us what we want?" demanded Stronghide. "No! Her herd has the best of everything—elephants always do, because they make sure of it. Your Great Mother is corrupt. She doesn't care about any other animal, and the sooner she's gone the better! Then we'll see a proper leader, a proper Great Parent—a rhinoceros!"

Sky had had enough. "That's not true!" she squealed. "Great Mother isn't a bad leader and she does care! You wait until the Great Gathering—you'll see!"

Stronghide strode heavily toward her. He thumped the ground with a large, heavy forefoot. "Are you calling us liars?"

"An elephant," rumbled another rhino, "calling *us* liars!"

As one, they lowered their horns. Sky tensed, her blood running cold as water. *What are they—*

The rhinos lunged and charged. Squealing, Sky stumbled around and ran.

Behind her she could hear the thunder of the rhinos' great hooves, drawing closer. She gasped, terrified, and pounded faster. Raising her trunk, she trumpeted a breathless alarm.

This might work out for the best, it occurred to her through her cold terror. *If I can just reach safety—if they don't trample me—they might chase off the herd by accident!*

She glanced over her shoulder to see the rhinos, far too close—then looked forward again and gasped. Great Mother loomed ahead, her ears flapping forward, her trunk raised. The huge matriarch stamped a foot and bellowed in fury.

Immediately the other elephants were awake and alert,

tramping into line at Great Mother's side, facing down the rhinos. Squealing hoarsely with relief, Sky hurtled between Rain and Star, and they closed in to protect her. Moon stood there behind them, shivering with shock.

"What's happening, Sky?"

"Not now, Moon! Stay back!" Sky turned toward the protective line of her aunts. Just beyond the elephants, the rhinoceroses had trotted to a halt, and now they stood with their horns lowered, grunting in rage and pawing the ground.

"We've had enough of your arrogance!" That was Stronghide; Sky recognized his voice. "Leave, now!"

"Leave?" Great Mother's voice resounded around the watering hole; she sounded even more frightening than the rhinos, Sky thought with relief. "We will not leave, Stronghide! Bring your grievances to the Great Gathering, as every other creature does!"

"We will get no justice from an elephant!" yelled Stronghide.

"Yes," trumpeted Great Mother, her voice hard. "You will, whether you are prepared to accept it or not. But charge us now, and all you will receive is a bloody fight. You may cause some of us harm, but it will be far worse for you and your crash. Is it worth it, Stronghide?"

In the silence that followed, Sky could hardly breathe. The only sound was the scrape of huge hooves against the ground; even the nighttime insects had fallen quiet. *This is my fault. If any of my aunts are hurt—or Great Mother—it'll be because of me.* She gave a muffled whimper of distress.

Then she heard Stronghide's gravelly grunt again.

"We will not forget this insult," he told Great Mother. "*You*—you will regret it!"

When the rhino and his crash had slouched into the night, Great Mother turned at once to Sky, stroking her head with her trunk, checking her legs and flanks for any injuries. "Sky, did they hurt you? My dear one, are you all right?"

If anything, her anxious care made Sky feel even worse. *I brought it on myself, Great Mother.* "No, no, I'm fine. Really, Great Mother. I'm sorry."

"Rhinoceroses are often dangerous, little Sky—and Stronghide's crash in particular. He's a clever rhino, and a very aggressive one. You must stay away from him if you can."

Sky nodded vigorously. "Oh, I will, Great Mother. I promise." She leaned her head gratefully into her grandmother's leg.

It was a stupid idea. I shouldn't have done something so reckless. I'll never ask rhinos for help again.

Still, her dilemma had not gone away, and those awful moments with the rhinos hadn't wiped out the greater terror of her vision. If anything, her task seemed more impossibly dreadful than ever.

I still need to make the herd leave the watering hole.

This time, I have to succeed.

CHAPTER 14

The peaceful, shady air of Tall Trees was shattered by the screeching and hollering of fifty or more angry baboons. Thorn raced alongside the other Highleaves and Middleleaves, crashing and leaping through the undergrowth, his heart beating wildly with the thrill of impending battle. Through the blur of vegetation he could make out the running shapes of monkeys above; their shrill chattering cries clashed with the screams of the baboons until the whole forest echoed with the noise.

Berry was at his side, her face as grimly determined as his own. "We can't let them colonize Tall Trees!"

"We won't," growled Thorn. "Why are they even trying?"

Berry sprang for a low branch and bounded to another, with Thorn right behind her. "My father says they've been pushed out of their own land by all those grass-eaters. It's the Great Gathering—it's disrupted their territory."

"Well, they don't have to invade ours!" barked Thorn. "They didn't do this last year, did they? They wouldn't have dared come here if Fearless was still—"

"Watch out!" Berry swung to a halt, staring at the horde of monkeys charging along the branches toward them. "I've fought this kind before. They might be smaller than us, but they can climb higher. They're fierce and quick—and their teeth and claws are sharper than a baboon's!"

"They're noisier than us too," grumbled Thorn, remembering how the shrieks of the invading monkeys had woken the troop that morning. The monkey scouts who'd breached the camp itself had been seen off, but now a huge throng of the attackers was gathered at the edge of Tall Trees. Judging by the racket they were making, Thorn reckoned they must number at least two hundred—many more than the baboons.

"Stay close to me," warned Berry, touching his shoulder.

"Attack!" came Grub Crownleaf's howl from behind them all. His command was barely audible over the shrieks of both monkeys and baboons, but it was enough.

Thorn sprang forward, baring his fangs. The monkeys weren't very much smaller than him—some looked bigger than Mud—and they rushed to meet the attacking baboons in a swarm of screeching, hollering, greenish-brown bodies. Their black faces were fringed with white fuzz, their mouths open to reveal long, pointed fangs. One of them skidded to a halt in front of Thorn, shaking a branch aggressively. Thorn rose up on his hind legs, peeling back his lips in a scream of threat.

"Our turn to rule Tall Trees!" shrieked the invader. "Our turn!"

Berry leaped at the monkey, but his friends were right behind, and they flung themselves at her.

Thorn joined the assault, snapping and screeching as the monkeys piled onto him and Berry. She'd been right; they were ferocious. Claws raked through Thorn's fur, catching and ripping his skin, and he felt the sharp stab of teeth in his shoulder and flank.

Three of them grappled with him, their weight dragging him sideways, and as they all tumbled to the ground together, the monkeys kept clawing and biting. Thorn rolled over as he landed on the forest floor, kicking them away with his hind claws in time to see Berry start tearing at his attackers.

I'm glad Lowleaves aren't allowed to be fighters. Mud could never have coped with these brutes, no matter how badly he wanted to help.

From the corner of his eye he saw Nut flee into the trees, pursued by a band of invaders. Other baboons were scrapping frantically with whole gangs. One lanky monkey landed heavily on Thorn's back, snarling and tearing, but Berry dragged it off.

"Careful!" she yelled. "Up there!"

Above them, five monkeys were poised to leap down in ambush. Yanking Berry out of the way, Thorn rolled aside into the bushes. The monkeys crashed down in the spot where they'd been, barked in angry frustration, then darted off to attack another, more exposed group of baboons.

Panting, Thorn gave Berry a quick hug. "Are you all right?"

"I'm fine," she said through gritted fangs. "Determined, aren't they?"

"Let's go and get them." Thorn grinned. Springing up, they both raced back toward the struggle. One unwary invader was focused on pursuing Nut, and Thorn prepared to spring at him from the side.

"Wait!" Berry paused and gripped his arm. "Grub's directing us—look!"

Thorn snatched a branch, cutting short his headlong rush. It was his first troop battle since he'd become a Middleleaf, and he was glad for Berry's guidance.

"All together!" Grub was screaming. "Group! Hold back— Mango, Berry, hold!—now *attack!*"

A coordinated rush of baboons was exactly the strategy they'd needed, Thorn realized as he hurtled into battle alongside his troop. The flow of the fighting suddenly turned, as the larger baboons began to dominate the desperate monkeys. Yammering with disappointment, the monkeys extricated themselves one by one and fled from the fight. Brightforest Troop's fighters, hooting triumphantly, chased them until they were well clear of the trees.

Thorn, in hot pursuit of a young monkey, at last slowed and came to a halt, slapping the ground. He let out a screech of victory. All around him, the other Brightforest baboons were jumping and whooping. Berry, at his side, turned to him with eyes that glowed with excitement.

"You did well, Thorn—you're a natural fighter!"

"It was—*fun!*" He gave a yelp of laughter. "I really enjoyed it—once we started winning, anyway."

"Oh, you were enjoying it before then. I was watching you!" Berry sat back on her haunches, her large brown eyes shining. "You're a great defender of the troop already, Thorn."

He felt a warm sensation course through his blood, but he had no time for a quiet moment alone with her. Stinger was pacing toward them, picking out scraps of leaf and twig from his fur. His face was twisted with contempt.

"Green monkeys!" he exclaimed. "Hmph. I've eaten more than one of those, in days gone by. And they wanted to move into Tall Trees! I wish we'd caught one of them; I've worked up quite an appetite."

Berry laughed as Thorn's eyes widened. "I bet they don't taste as good as scorpions, Father."

"Indeed." Stinger scratched at his back and tugged another twig from his fur. Around them, the other Highleaves and Middleleaves were gathering, looking pleased with themselves. "I reckon we should post better lookouts in the future. In case this happens again."

Behind him, Grub Crownleaf growled, "That's a matter for Council meetings, Stinger. Highleaves do not discuss such things in front of the lower ranks." He shot an unpleasant look at Thorn.

Still exhilarated from the battle, Thorn ignored it. *We did a good job here, but the monkeys wouldn't even have attacked if Grub hadn't made Fearless leave!*

"No," he muttered under his breath, "it wouldn't do to have the lower orders listen in. We don't tolerate outsiders in this troop, do we?"

"What was that?" demanded Grub. He spun to face Berry. "What did he say?"

"Nothing, Grub!" said Berry quickly. "Thorn was just agreeing with you. Weren't you, Thorn?" She gave Thorn a sharp look.

"Huh." Grub drew himself up. "Well, I'm going to make a formal complaint about that incursion. I'm going to tell the Great Gathering exactly what happened, and I'll make sure Great Mother knows that it's never to happen again!" With his tail high, he strutted off back toward the center of the forest.

Thorn watched him go. "I think Great Mother has enough on her mind," he growled. "She's got plenty of animals to keep in order without our Crownleaf pestering her. And it's Grub's fault anyway, having that stupid vote—if Fearless was still here, the monkeys wouldn't have dared to come near Tall Trees!"

Stinger didn't reply at once. He tilted his head and furrowed his brow.

"Well, it's true Great Mother has much on her mind," he said at last with a shrug, "but the Great Spirit chose her for a reason. She's supposed to *guide* all of us." He breathed heavily through his nose. "I suppose everyone makes mistakes, though. Great Mother led the grass-eaters to the watering hole and pushed the monkeys out of their territory."

"She didn't do that deliberately," protested Thorn, surprised that Stinger would defend Grub. "And if the monkeys had smelled lion here, they'd have gone somewhere else!"

"Well, that seems likely," agreed Stinger. "But that's not the only thing that's gone wrong lately. Look what happened to Fearless's pride—and look what happened to Bark Crownleaf. Remember, Great Mother is old now, so it's little wonder she doesn't seem to be controlling things very well, is it?" He gave a grunting laugh. "There's never been a baboon Great Parent. Maybe it's time that changed!"

"Oh, Father," said Berry fondly, "I can't see that happening anytime soon."

"Maybe not." Stinger laughed. "Anyway, whatever Grub says, I think we should post more lookouts. The Great Gathering isn't over yet." He surveyed the baboons who were still gathered around, getting their breath back. "Grass and Fly," he said to the other members of his retinue, "you two go to that tall kigelia tree on the sunset side. Make sure you stay on high alert—if the monkeys attack again it'll most likely be from there. Stone, Mist . . ." He gave directions to each baboon, and Thorn noticed that no one questioned his right to do it; no baboon argued. Of course Grass and Fly obeyed him instantly, but with the others too Stinger had a natural, easy authority. It gave Thorn—and, he guessed, everyone else—a strong sense of security.

"Nut and Berry, you go to the southern border," Stinger went on.

Thorn's fur sprang up, but he bit down on his frustration.

He kept his jaws firmly shut as Nut shot him a look of vicious smugness. *I can't argue with Stinger—but I wish Nut would wipe that smirk off his face.*

"I'm sorry, Thorn," whispered Berry, but she could do nothing but bound off alongside Nut.

Of course I can't do sentry duty with Berry; we're not the same status and we never will be. But it still rankled horribly.

"That should cover it," remarked Stinger thoughtfully, as he peeled bark from a twig. There were only four baboons left in the little clearing. "It would be best if the rest of you go hunting. Those monkeys have completely disrupted our day. You can all go and find some food."

Still nursing an ache of unhappiness, Thorn turned to pad away with the others, but Stinger called him back. "Thorn, wait a moment. Now that you're in my retinue, I've got a special task for you."

Thorn's throat felt tight with resentment, but he managed to grate out politely, "What is it, Stinger? Where do you want me to go?"

The older baboon grinned in a friendly way as Thorn tilted his head. "I haven't had time to do any hunting myself today, and now I've had to organize the sentries. And I need to go back and check on the Deeproots and the Lowleaves, and make sure things are getting done in the middle of all this excitement." He picked absently at the notch of the scar on his muzzle. "Could you do me a favor?"

Thorn nodded submissively. "Of course, Stinger." *Besides,*

even if I had the right to sulk, there's no point. I have to impress Stinger as much as I can, at every chance I get.

Stinger leaned closer. "I've got a hankering for scorpions," he murmured. "No one else is as good at finding them as you are, Thorn—well, apart from me, obviously." He grinned again. "Could you find me one? Or maybe two?"

"I'll find as many as you like!" Thorn was pleased that the task was a fun one—and that it would make the older baboon particularly pleased.

"If you can trap them and keep them alive, that would be lovely." Stinger licked his lips wistfully. "I like them when they're fresh."

"Of course. It'll be my pleasure."

"Thank you, Thorn." Stinger leaned in to pick a scrap of leaf from Thorn's fur. "I don't know what I'd do without you, youngster."

And that's exactly what I want him to think, thought Thorn cheerfully as he scampered off through the trees. *Even if I'm not a Highleaf, Stinger might get to like me enough. . . . Then one day he might ask Grub for special permission for me and Berry to be paired! Now, where is Mud . . . ?*

Mud, it turned out, was lounging with Bird Lowleaf in a fork in a fever tree, enjoying an idle mutual grooming session as they kept lookout. He looked a little bored, and his eyes brightened as Thorn ran up to him and scrambled onto a nearby branch.

"Hello, Bird. Listen, Mud, I need you!"

"What's up?" Mud looked delighted.

As Bird chittered a farewell and climbed down the tree, Thorn turned to his friend and explained what had happened and the task he'd been given. "Can you help, Mud? Stinger wants his scorpions fresh, and you're so good with traps and tools."

"Of course! I know how much you want to impress Berry's father." Mud slapped Thorn's back. "Come on. I'll show you what we can do!"

Eagerly Thorn bounded after him. Mud stopped near the mango tree and scuffled about in the mossy undergrowth. "Ah!" He tugged out a thick piece of branch and picked off straggling bits of fern.

The branch was clean of bark, smooth and well-worn, and there were three long claw scratches on its mottled yellow surface. And it was hollow, Thorn realized—when Mud shook it, a couple of dried-up insect legs and a wing fluttered to the ground.

"Mother uses this to keep live beetles inside. See? Let me find the stones she uses. . . . Here we are!" Mud crouched to pick up a broad, flat pebble that was almost perfectly round. "There are two, see? You seal one end with this one. And the second stone fits the other end. It took her ages to make it, but it's really useful. The beetles can't get out, but they stay alive. And so will the scorpions."

"That's wonderful!" Thorn hopped up and down with excitement. "I knew you'd have a solution, Mud; you always do." He furrowed his brow, thinking, *Scorpions like to hide under* rocks. *There are a lot of loose rocks in the secret ravine. . . .* "Now follow me!"

The two young baboons loped out of the forest, carrying the hollow branch between them. "Where are we going?" asked Mud.

Thorn grinned. "The ravine—remember it? Where the gazelles graze."

"Ah, yes. Do you still know the way?"

"I do indeed." Thorn's heart warmed as he remembered the happy, secret times he'd spent there with Berry. He pointed to a small rocky hill. "See that kopje? You have to go between the rocks and climb up, and you can see the way into the ravine from the top. Remember?"

"I do now!" Mud scrambled up behind his friend. "You're brilliant, Thorn!"

Dragging the hollow branch, they scrambled up the kopje, and at the top squeezed between two sides of a split rock into a narrow gorge. Together they slithered down until it opened out into a gentler, grassy slope. Gazelles were clustered at the foot of a steep incline, hidden from the view of flesh-eaters on the plain; they raised their heads and swiveled their ears; then, clearly deciding the baboons were no threat, they returned to their peaceful grazing.

Thorn led Mud around the edge of the valley toward a scattered patch of dry stones and boulders. "Here we are," he said, eyes gleaming.

Mud nodded. "Looks like a good place for scorpions."

Hoping his instincts had been right, Thorn seized a stone

and rolled it onto its side. A scorpion darted out, scuttling for new cover, but Thorn snatched it by its tail and dangled it triumphantly. "First try!"

Mud held out the log for him to drop it in. "Beginner's luck!"

The next six stones yielded nothing, but just as Thorn was starting to think Mud was right about the first find being fortunate, his friend exposed another panicked scorpion. After that, they seemed to find one beneath every second stone. The two baboons hooted in delight as they dropped scorpion after scorpion into the Starleaf's ingenious trap.

Thorn paused and stretched his aching shoulders. "I wonder what Fearless is doing."

"One day soon we'll see him again and he'll tell us," said Mud confidently. "I'm sure he's fine."

Something flashed in the corner of Thorn's eye; he dived on another scorpion. "I don't doubt it. I miss him, though."

"This is going well. We've got lots." Mud peered into their log. "I'm more worried about Berry than Fearless right now. Imagine having to do sentry duty with Nut."

"I expect he's being charming," said Thorn bitterly. "He'd love to be paired with her, just to annoy me. And I'm really worried that Nut will tell Grub about me and Berry. Or worse, tell Stinger."

"Don't worry." Mud patted his shoulder. "Stinger likes you, Thorn. He didn't choose Nut to be in his retinue, did he? He chose you. And don't worry about Berry; she's far too smart to be taken in by Nut. She likes him about as much as we do."

"I guess so." Thorn sighed. "I wish Stinger had been voted Crownleaf. Things would be so much better than they are under Grub. How are we doing? Let me see the log."

Mud held it toward him, and Thorn peered in. His eyes took a moment to adjust after the brightness of the sun, and for an instant he could see only vague, chaotic movement. But when he finally made out the mass of scorpions in the dark log, he couldn't repress a shudder. They seethed and writhed, snapping their pincers in fury, crawling over one another, and lashing out blindly with their stingers.

"That's enough," he said quickly, clapping the round stone firmly onto the end of the trap. "Even Stinger will take a while to eat all those."

"I never really understood the appeal myself." Mud wrinkled his muzzle, then grinned. "Let's take them back to him. I've seen enough scorpions to last me for quite a while."

CHAPTER 15

The long savannah grass rippled in the breeze; Fearless could smell approaching rain on the cool air. He was thirsty, and the damp, rich scent reminded him enticingly that the watering hole wasn't far away, but he held his motionless crouch. Tantalizingly near to him, a herd of zebras moved across the plain, cropping peacefully at the plentiful grass. He was so close he could hear the crunch and grind of their jaws.

Fearless wasn't the only flesh-eater watching them. He had noticed three others, stalking low and sleek in the grass, so far unseen by the zebras. The strange, slender predators crept on delicate paws, patient and cautious, pausing now and again to go entirely still. They were cats, too, but Fearless knew they weren't lions; they were maneless, skinny, and long-limbed, with spotted fur and dark trails on their faces, as if black water had been squeezed from their eyes. Fearless was fascinated, but unafraid.

And he was hungry again.

He licked his jaws, his mouth watering already. So far, the zebras were blissfully unaware of all four of the hopeful predators.

He wasn't at all sure he could bring one down. *But if I can't, those other cats certainly can't either. They're far too skinny and delicate.*

He blinked in surprise as one of them sprang forward, sprinting toward the herd, its companions behind it in an instant. The zebras bolted. The three cats spread out, homing in on one of the outlying zebras with ruthless precision. But it wasn't their clever teamwork that made Fearless stare in awe.

They're so fast!

They had become little more than flashes of light in the grass, a blur of yellow movement. They were far faster than the rhinos, faster than any baboons or lion he had ever seen. As they hurtled after their target, the rest of the zebras scattered with screaming whinnies of alarm.

The herd stampeded, bolting across the grassland, but one of the swift cats slinked at a sharp angle between them and the lone zebra, cutting it off from its friends. In a wild panic it darted first one way, then another, but the cats were closing in.

The desperate zebra ducked its head and twisted, then galloped headlong in Fearless's direction, straight between two of the fleet-footed oncoming predators. *Nice try*, Fearless thought, but the cats had reversed their charge with astonishing agility and were racing after their prey again.

No, wait! Fearless straightened a little higher in the grass, watching the hunt with keen curiosity. All three cats were slowing. Had they given up?

This is my chance!

Fearless crept forward, then broke into a trot, cutting across the path of the terrified zebra. Keeping his shoulders low, he tensed himself to run—

A tawny shape rose from the grass ahead, and Fearless froze, one paw raised. His eyes widened as another lion swung its great maned head toward him.

If it's one of Titan's cronies, I'm dead!

He lowered his trembling paw and tried to back away.

"Stay still." The rumbling growl was so low, Fearless wasn't sure he'd heard right.

But he stayed motionless anyway. *Valor said Titan would kill me on sight. If this lion is one of his—*

"Hold *still*. Don't scare the zebra." Again that soft voice, barely louder than the rustling breeze.

Fearless followed the older lion's gaze. His amber stare was fixed on the zebra.

"The cheetahs have worn it out for us," murmured the strange lion, as the zebra cantered closer. There was relief as well as weariness on the grass-eater's striped face; the cats called *cheetahs* had slowed to a disappointed trot, far behind, their flanks rising and falling in panting breaths. The older lion lowered himself closer to the ground, half closing his eyes. "Don't move, youngster. Wait . . . wait . . . waiiiit . . . and GO!"

The command was so sharp, so authoritative, Fearless obeyed by pure instinct. He hurled himself at the zebra; its eyes widened and its nostrils flared in renewed horror. It doubled back and tried to escape, but the older lion was already moving, bounding straight toward it. Its hooves scrabbled in desperation as it sought another way out, but Fearless bunched his haunches and sprang.

Hooking a powerful paw across its neck, he let his weight drag the zebra down, then fastened his jaws around its raised throat. It was still trying to gallop, its legs flailing, but it had fallen now, its jaws wide in a scream. Fearless held on, sinking his teeth over its windpipe as it struggled and kicked. On the other side of the animal he was aware of the bigger lion, his jaws now also gripping the zebra's neck.

The zebra gave a last jerk, shuddered, and went limp. For a long moment Fearless held on tight, his breath rasping against the animal's fur. Then he released it, his mouth bloody, and shook himself.

He stared at his kill. *My first zebra!* Elation rippled through him, leaving him with a hot glow of pride.

"Well done, youngster." The older lion paced around the zebra's corpse to sniff at him.

Before Fearless could growl a reply, he saw the cheetahs bounding over the grassland toward them. Their black-streaked faces were furious, and as they slowed to a trot and approached the lions, their muscles were taut with aggression.

"This again?" yelped the leader. "We're sick of lions stealing our kills!"

"Too bad," growled the older lion, squaring up to them with an expression of disdain. "That's life in Bravelands, after all."

"What are you talking about?" Fearless bared his fangs, hunching his shoulders as he faced the cheetahs. "We made the kill, not you."

"Every time we change our hunting grounds, Titanpride follows us!" snarled the leader.

"That's right." The big lion drew himself up arrogantly and glared down his muzzle at the cheetahs. "And we're keeping this kill, too." He paced forward, snarling.

A jolt of fright ran through Fearless. So this lion was from Titanpride after all. He was big—as big as Gallant had been, Fearless thought, with a tangled mane of black shot through with gold. The muscles of his shoulders rippled as he moved. On the left side of his face, below his orange eyes, was a ragged scar. The cheetahs clearly realized that they had no choice but to obey him: turning their long, bushy-tipped tails, they fled, chittering angry, impotent insults.

"Lumbering hairy fatheads," squealed one.

"Thick sluggish brutes," agreed another in a high snarl.

Barely making a ripple in the long grass as it enveloped them, the cheetahs vanished. Fearless wondered if he should follow their example. He eyed the big lion beside him, his elation fast dissolving into fear. *He's huge and he's strong; much older than me.*

As the big lion licked experimentally at the zebra blood, Fearless began to edge away, slinking surreptitiously backward into the grass. *Better to lose my first zebra, and live to catch another one day* . . .

"Where are you going, Fearless?"

Fearless froze. *He knows who I am! This is bad, this is bad.* . . .

"How . . . how do you know my name?"

"Oh, I'd know you anywhere," said the lion. He lifted his head to gaze into Fearless's eyes. "That scent. Straight from your father."

Fearless's throat was bone-dry. *My father? This lion must be one of Titan's companions, from the day Gallant was murdered.* He licked his jaws and tried to swallow. "Why aren't you trying to kill me, then?"

"Oh, I was lying to the cheetahs. I'm not from Titanpride." The big lion drew back his muzzle in a wicked grin. "My name's Loyal, and I'd sooner eat my own tail than submit to that stupid bully Titan. I'm—I was a friend of your father's."

The tension and fear drained out of Fearless so fast, he felt dizzy. His legs were a little shaky as he padded back to the zebra; he hoped Loyal wouldn't notice. "You were Gallant's friend?"

"Indeed I was, Fearless Gallantpride."

Loyal's words sent a shiver of conflicting emotion through Fearless. *I haven't been called that name in so long. It feels good, and yet* . . . *wrong. As if I don't deserve it.*

"Well, you look hungry," Loyal said into the uncomfortable silence, "and I can't eat this entire zebra."

Fearless needed no further invitation. He crouched beside the zebra and began to tear into its flesh, gulping down a great mouthful.

"Wait, wait!" Loyal nudged him so hard, he rocked sideways. "Not here. If we stick around, Titanpride will find us—or the hyena pack will. Then you can say good-bye to our zebra. We'll take it to my den."

Embarrassed, and still chewing, Fearless leaped to his paws. *I don't know what lions do. I don't know how I'm supposed to behave.* "Sorry." He sank his jaws into the zebra's shoulder and helped Loyal drag it along the bumpy ground.

"I'm glad I met you." Loyal let go of the zebra after some distance and caught his breath. He studied Fearless intently again, making the younger lion feel very small.

"I'm glad too," Fearless stammered.

"I've been hoping I'd run into you, young Fearless. I know Swift and Valor are still with Titanpride, and I hoped you'd survived the takeover too. I've kept my eyes open for you for a long time, but I never caught a single glimpse of your tail." There was regret in Loyal's voice. "Perhaps I should have looked harder."

"I think I saw you once," said Fearless slowly; there was something familiar about this lion, and now he thought he knew what it was. When Loyal's tail twitched, he saw that it had been broken at some point and was now crooked. "I was patrolling for Brightforest Troop, and I saw a lion by himself on the horizon. He looked a lot like you."

"That was probably me, yes." Loyal rested a paw on the zebra's flank. He narrowed his eyes. "Brightforest Troop? I heard a rumor of a lion among the baboons. But I thought it was a myth!"

"I've been . . . living with them," confessed Fearless, squirming a little inside. "They found me and took me in, and they were good to me." Noticing the astonishment on Loyal's face, he added hurriedly, "But those days are over. I'm going to go back to my mother and Valor. They need me."

"That's not a great idea," murmured Loyal, glancing pensively away across the plains.

"I could take this zebra to them," Fearless said, with a sudden spark of inspiration. "I could take it to Titanpride as a gift! That's what the baboons did when they wanted to show loyalty: took food to the leader."

"That wouldn't work," said Loyal bluntly. "Titan won't ever let you join his pride. He'd just kill you."

"Oh," said Fearless, disappointed.

"Sky and stone," muttered Loyal. "You've got an *awful* lot to learn about lions."

He sank his jaws into the zebra again, and Fearless followed suit, ashamed at his ignorance. *My unlion-ness*, he realized, dismally. There was silence for a while, as they dragged the carcass toward a rocky outcrop on the slope of a kopje.

Fearless could feel his nerves jangling as they approached the rocks. "Is your pride there? At the den?" he asked.

"Pride? I don't have a pride anymore." Loyal shrugged and

huffed. "I hunt alone. Well, I have until now." Thoughtfully he studied Fearless. "You're welcome to stay with me, if you like. Two lions always make for a more fruitful hunt."

Fearless felt a rush of happiness so unexpected, he wanted to leap on Loyal and bowl him over. "Yes! Yes, I'd like that. Thank you!"

"Good." Loyal gazed proudly at a tumble of boulders, shining white in the sun. "Welcome to my den!"

It took one more surge of effort to drag the zebra up the rocks. When they let the carcass fall, on a flat patch of sandy earth dotted with stubby, dried-out plants, Fearless paused and stared around.

Beyond the flat, another shelf of rock rose up steeply against the dazzling blue sky. Not far up the precipitous flank of the kopje, half hidden by a jutting blade of stone, Fearless could see the dark slash of a den entrance. Loyal's pungent scent marks were everywhere on the rock, and matted clumps of brown and gold fur were caught on the edge of boulders where the big lion had scratched himself. Scattered around the den mouth and on the sandy flat, bleached even whiter than the stones, lay the bones and skulls of long-dead grass-eaters.

This is the true home of a true lion, thought Fearless, his heart swelling.

"This place is wonderful," he breathed.

"I'm glad you like it," growled Loyal in amusement. "It's been home to me for a while."

"It's beautiful," declared Fearless. "Thank you for asking me to stay with you, Loyal. It means a lot." He cleared his throat, feeling suddenly both ashamed and bashful. "Maybe, Loyal, if you would . . . ? You can teach me to live like a lion."

Loyal's brow kinked up. "I will do my best. But first—let's eat!"

CHAPTER 16

The rain Fearless had scented had come and gone; the ground outside Loyal's den felt soft and damp beneath his paws. The energy of his first big kill still lingered, buzzing in his blood like a swarm of mosquitoes. *Father said I could be a great hunter one day. It looks as if he was right!*

He'd known instinctively what to do with the zebra. His mother had never had a chance to teach him, but perhaps Swift had somehow gifted him her talents anyway. *It's in my heritage, in my blood and bones. I can still learn to be the best hunter in Bravelands. I'm going to make up for lost time.*

He looked back into the cave where Loyal was still dozing, his black and gold head resting on his enormous paws.

"Loyal," Fearless called, "I'm off to practice hunting. I'll be back soon!"

Loyal was immediately alert. He got to his feet, shaking out his mane. "Remember what I taught you—get as close as you can before you attack. Watch out for those cheetahs. And stay clear of buffalo—they're too dangerous. You might catch a calf if you're careful, but I don't think you're ready for that yet."

"Okay."

"And if you smell hyenas, run."

Fearless laughed. "You don't need to remind me about that one. See you when I've caught something!" He bounded down the slope that led away from the den, weaving past boulders and the bones of the zebra they'd picked clean yesterday, and sprang onto the grass that stretched out below. A startled lizard darted beneath a bush.

"Fearless, listen to me!"

He looked up. Loyal had jumped onto one of the boulders, the sun catching the pale skin of the scar below his eye. His crooked tail swished back and forth.

"One last piece of advice. Don't go near the plains that lie west of the kigelia forest," Loyal rumbled. "That's where Titanpride is."

Fearless nodded and set off. Prey animals were likely to be gathered near the watering hole, he reasoned, so he headed in that direction. He picked up his paws, enjoying the sun on his fur, wondering what he'd catch; but when he saw the distant smudge he knew was the kigelia forest, he found himself veering toward it and had to force himself to stop. *Somewhere on the other side of those trees is my mother.*

He couldn't help it. He had to see her again, just to make sure she was all right.

That won't do any harm, will it? Loyal will understand.

Quickening his pace, he made his way toward the trees. Their branches were heavy with strange long fruit, almost as large as he was, and the birds feasting on them screeched as he passed. He emerged on the other side onto shimmering plains. The zebra herd he'd seen yesterday had moved on—which was hardly surprising after the three-way ambush they'd suffered—but a herd of buffalo was grazing, with young calves at foot.

And between Fearless and the buffalo, indistinct tawny-golden shapes were visible, half hidden in the long grass.

Titanpride!

In the center of the lazing pride lay a huge male, his black mane instantly identifiable. Titan yawned, his savage yellow fangs glinting in the sun. The hairs on the nape of Fearless's neck sprang up, and hatred warmed his blood. Cautiously, he moved closer, placing each paw with aching slowness.

Lounging against Titan's flank was a big lioness; there was a smirking smugness about her face. A tiny cub wriggled against her flank and she bent to lick his head. *She must be Artful. The one who blinded my mother. And that's Ruthless, her cub. Her son with Titan.*

Loyal had told him about the cub. Fearless couldn't believe he had a name already. *He's barely newborn, and Artful and Titan have already decided what he's going to be like. Typical arrogance!*

Anger flooded through Fearless. Artful looked so plump and content; the glances she cast the other lionesses were full of superior disdain. He could not keep watching her—at least, not without throwing caution to the savannah sky and charging at her—so he turned his focus to the rest of the pride, trying to pick out his mother and Valor.

Valor told me Titanpride moves around a lot. I guess they've come here to follow the cheetahs and steal their prey. Fearless let himself feel contempt for such a lazy, treacherous hunting style, then remembered it was exactly what he and Loyal had done. *But we have no pride to hunt with us. Loyal and I have to do whatever it takes to eat. Titanpride is strong, and they could catch their own prey!*

Shaking his head, he studied Titanpride once more. He recognized a familiar lion with a damaged ear, basking alone on the periphery of the pride. *I remember his name: Cunning. He's one of the lions who killed my father. He's the one who chased me when I was a tiny cub, the one who tried to kill me.* Fearless drew his lips back in a silent snarl and let his eyes drift to the other lions. Surely Valor was here somewhere?

Then he saw her. She too lay on the edge of the pride, not far from Regal and Agile, but Fearless didn't recognize the lioness who lay at her side. Valor's paw was hooked over the lioness's shoulders and she was grooming her intently, running a tongue over her neck. Fearless crept a little closer, peering through the grass.

He gasped, and his heart stuttered and leaped. *Mother!*

No wonder he hadn't recognized her at once. Swift looked so much older; she was thin, and her coat was coarse and dull. Her eyes were closed in bliss as Valor gently groomed her head and neck; Fearless couldn't see the scars that must be there, but he longed to bound over to the two of them, to witness for himself what Artful had done, and to comfort his mother.

And to kill Artful and Titan, he thought, clenching his jaws in rage.

But I can't. Not yet.

Cunning rose to his paws and stretched, then sniffed the air, his tail twitching. Regal and Agile followed his cue, stirring and half rising. Fearless held his breath. *Do they know I'm here?*

But Cunning slumped back down onto his belly, licking his jaws and making himself comfortable. The lionesses did not relax; they stood up properly, stretching and loosening their limbs, and roused the others. Honor nuzzled Valor, who butted her mother gently in farewell, and all the lionesses except Swift and Artful padded away through the grass in the direction of the buffalo herd.

Artful watched them go, that haughty expression still fixed on her face. She pawed Ruthless lightly, rolling him over. *Playing some game with her spoiled cub while the others work,* thought Fearless. *While my sister is forced to hunt for two.*

Left alone at the edge of the pride, it wasn't long before Swift rose, too, and began to pick her way hesitantly away through the grass. She snuffled at the ground before cautiously placing each paw; once or twice she stopped to turn over a stone with her claws, or rake through the grass. Sniffing for insects or small rodents, Fearless guessed. *My mother, who was once the finest hunter in Gallantpride.*

He gazed at her, his heart swollen with grief and regret. *Farther, Mother. Go farther from Titan. This way. Please . . .*

Perhaps she'd sensed him; she kept padding on, her progress agonizingly slow but steady. Fearless could bear the waiting no longer. He took a deep breath and slunk after her, his belly low to the ground, following her toward a clump of thornbushes.

Still a little distance away, Swift padded into the cool undergrowth, her tail swishing slowly back and forth. Tree shadows shifted on her fur as she hesitated, then halted. She lifted her muzzle and sniffed the air, her whiskers trembling.

"Fearless?" Her voice was cracked with doubt. "Fearless? Is that you?"

"Mother!" Throwing caution to the savannah air, Fearless bounded into the scrub and flung himself toward her, licking and rubbing her face. Her taste and smell were just the same. Swift staggered a little under his emotional greeting, swaying and righting herself before giving a small, grunting cry of disbelief and joy. She licked him back, nuzzling his face and neck, mewling and growling his name.

"Fearless, it's really you!" She dipped her head, letting him lash her ears with his rough tongue. "Valor told me she'd spoken to you, but I could hardly bring myself to believe it!"

Out of breath, Fearless swallowed and drew back to gaze at his mother. Now that he could study her properly, he felt the sting of dismay. It had not been a trick of the glaring sunlight, as he'd hoped: Swift's bones were visible through her dull, thinning coat. Her eyes were fixed on his face, but it was clear they saw nothing. One eyeball was missing altogether, leaving only the socket; the other was horribly scarred, an unseeing mass of opaque whiteness.

Sorrow and rage filled his blood. "Mother, what she did to you—what they both did—I swear I'll avenge this!"

"No, Fearless, no!" Swift blundered forward, tucking his head beneath her chin, pressing her chest tightly against him. "You mustn't. I manage. Valor and the other lionesses look after me. You mustn't worry, and you mustn't *think* of revenge! You have no mane yet, my son. You can't fight Titan!"

"I won't fight him, then," snarled Fearless, though every muscle and nerve in his body ached to do just that. He pulled back to look at her. "I'll take you and Valor away. We'll make our own new pride. We'll be together, far from that brute and his vicious mate."

Swift was trembling; she barely seemed to hear him. "Listen to me, my Swiftcub, my Fearless. You mustn't stay here. You have to go now, before Titan finds you!"

"Titan already has." The grunting, menacing roar came from behind Fearless and echoed through the bushes. "And you're going nowhere. Never again."

His heart clenching cold in his chest, Fearless turned. At the edge of the bushes, silhouetted against the blazing white sunlight, stood Titan. On either side of him were the brutish cronies Fearless remembered so well: the torn-eared Cunning and a lion with huge, powerful shoulders. Cunning smirked and gave a snarl of threat.

Fearless began to back away, only to feel the rake of claws across his rump. He started and looked over his shoulder to see two more young male lions behind him. They paced forward, driving him and Swift out of the bushes and into the sunlight of the plain. Now he and his mother were surrounded, and Titan peeled back his muzzle in a vicious grin.

"Fearless Gallantpride," he huffed maliciously. "So, you've come back. I don't believe your father was ever quite *that* stupid."

Fearless growled, shifting protectively closer to his mother.

"And you, Swift," Titan sneered, turning his dark, glittering gaze on the blind lioness. "You thought it was a good idea to shelter Gallant's last cub, did you?"

"No!" roared Fearless. "She didn't. This is the first time she's seen me since—since you broke the Code and murdered my father!"

"Titan, please," begged Swift, pushing blindly past Fearless. "Please spare him. He only wanted to talk to me."

"Shut up, both of you," snapped Titan. "I've had enough of you, Swift Titanpride. It's not as if you can hunt."

"Whose fault is that?" snarled Fearless.

Titan ignored him. "You're a drain on the pride, Swift. I have been patient and kind with you, but you repay that by harboring an enemy and defying me? This is unforgivable!" He stalked toward her slowly, death in his eyes.

Fearless shouldered his mother gently aside and stood in front of her, facing Titan. He lowered his shoulders and tensed his muscles, snarling in defiance.

"Fearless, no!" cried Swift desperately.

"Fine," snarled Titan. "You first, Fearless. Then her."

Fearless extended his claws, raking them into the ground, and gave a furious roar. *This time I won't run. This time I'll stand and fight. Even if it's the last thing I do.*

Titan drew himself up to lunge, his savage jaws wide for the kill—

—and halted mid-strike. He twisted his head. Flicked an ear. There was a new and different roaring coming from the plain behind him: a shout of terror and desperation.

"Artful?" he growled uncertainly.

"*Titan!*" Her desperate cry echoed across the grassland.

Fearless, confused and trembling, could only stare. The circle of Titanpride lions had all turned to gape in stupefaction at the plain.

There was quick, deadly movement in the rippling grass. Three lithe spotted bodies were sprinting toward Artful and Ruthless, their long legs a blur of motion, their tails balanced elegantly behind them. They looked beautiful, and graceful, and deadly.

The cheetahs!

With a roar of fury, Titan bounded back toward his mate and her cub. Cunning and the others, snapping out of their frozen shock, raced after him; Fearless darted forward to watch them go, his heart pounding. *I should be dead by now. What's happening? What are the cheetahs doing?*

The lions were running at full speed now, but compared to the cheetahs, Fearless realized, they looked sluggish and clumsy. They were still a good distance away, and the cheetahs had already surrounded Artful and Ruthless; two of them darted in, snapping at the big lioness and dodging her defensive swipes.

Fearless understood their strategy immediately, and he gasped. Artful was entirely distracted by the lunge-and-retreat attacks on her; meanwhile, the third cheetah had sprinted in behind her haunches. It seized something from the grass, spun in a single graceful twist, and raced away. Now its pace wasn't quite so quick, because it was carrying a burden. From its jaws dangled a helpless, small shape, whose terrified, mewling cries were audible even to Fearless.

"What's happening?" cried Swift. "Fearless, what is it?"

"Artful's cub. The cheetahs have taken Ruthless!" Fearless sprang forward and took a few loping paces after Titan. Glancing back once, checking that Swift was following, he bounded farther, desperate to see what would happen to the little cub.

Even Titan, far ahead of his cronies, was nowhere near the fleeing cheetahs. *It's no use*, realized Fearless. He'd seen how fast the cheetahs could run. *He'll never catch them.*

"Fearless, be careful!" Swift was still behind him, blundering as fast as she could through the grass. Remembering suddenly that running after Titan was a bad idea, Fearless trotted to a halt by Titanpride's resting place.

As the lead cheetah raced away, Ruthless still gripped in its jaws, one of the others skidded to a halt and turned for a moment, tauntingly flicking its tail.

"You want your cub to live?" he mocked Titan in a high-pitched grunt. "Stay away from our prey!"

Titan's roars were terrible to hear, but however hard and fast he thundered across the ground, he drew no nearer to the cheetahs. Artful was right behind him now, outstripping even the young male lions, but none of them had a chance. The cheetahs vanished into the long grass, the ripples of their movement faded, and a dreadful silence settled across the plains.

"Fearless, go!" urged Swift. She trotted up behind him, clumsily, her steps uncertain. "Run! This is your chance!"

Titan had already turned, the cheetahs lost, and now he was loping back toward Fearless and Swift with hatred in his glowing eyes.

"No, Mother." Fearless shook his head and swallowed hard. "I can't leave you alone with Titanpride." He waited, his throat dry as dust, his body protectively blocking Swift from Titan's approach.

For the moment, though, Titan seemed to have other killings on his mind. "I'll tear those skinny cheetahs to pieces!" he snarled.

"We should go after them right now," growled one of the young males. "They'll run out of energy soon enough."

"Don't be so stupid, Fervent!" snapped Artful, padding between them. "You attack them, and they'll kill Ruthless."

"How would we find them anyway?" Cunning glared after the cheetahs. "They're good at hiding, those sly wretches."

Not one of the lions looked as angry as Titan, thought Fearless. The huge alpha lion stood rigid, his claws protracted, his whole body trembling with fury.

"The cheetahs stole my son." Titan's voice was a terrifyingly quiet snarl. "They have taken away the future of Titanpride." The snarl rose to a strangled, hate-filled roar. "And all because of *Gallant's brat!*"

He turned so swiftly, Fearless staggered back in shock.

Titan loomed over him, his jaws wide, his fangs bared and glinting.

"Titan, wait . . ." he began.

"You distracted us," snarled Titan. "You drew me away from my son and left him vulnerable. This is all your fault. And now you're going to *pay*."

Fearless didn't see the strike coming. There was only the motion of a massive muscled body, springing toward him. Before he could even take a breath, the crushing weight of a full-grown lion hit him.

A clawed paw slammed the side of his head, flinging him into the air. As Bravelands upended, spinning and tumbling around him, Fearless's world became a red blur of shock and pain.

CHAPTER 17

His vision swimming with pain and terror, Fearless tried to drag himself out of reach of Titan's bloodied claws. He felt the second strike before he saw it: a massive blow to the side of his neck, bowling him over again. Digging his claws into the ground, gasping in desperation, he struggled onto his belly. *I can't escape him.* He pressed his body hard to the ground, trying to make himself small. *He's going to kill me now.*

"Titan, please!" His mother's hoarse cry sounded distant in Fearless's ringing ears. "Please, no! What are you doing? Stop!"

"Get back, Eyeless Lion!" That was Cunning's hard voice. Fearless heard him swiping at Swift, then her yelping pleas and cries of pain.

They'll kill her too. Not just me. I have to think.

The trouble was, he could barely form a single thought, let alone a plan. He rolled instinctively as Titan's claws slashed again, and he managed to coil his haunches beneath him and shove himself just out of reach.

"Titan!" he bellowed through the pain. "Titan, I can get Ruthless back!"

"Liar!" Titan bounded on top of him, making Fearless grunt at the pressure of his tremendous weight. The huge lion opened his jaws and raised a paw spiked with long, bloody claws.

"I can!" gasped Fearless, through his struggles for breath. "I'm your only hope of getting your cub back!"

"*Liar!*" roared Titan again. Fearless saw the madness in his eyes. *He won't stop until I'm dead.*

"*Titan.*" A lioness's roar of protest echoed in Fearless's ears. "*Enough!*"

That's not my mother's voice. Fearless blinked, gasping, as Titan froze, paw still raised for the kill. Slaver dripping from his jaws, the massive lion turned his head to glare at his mate.

"What is it?" he barked.

Artful paced forward, her eyes glinting with cold fury. "Let the Swiftcub speak," she snarled. "He says he can save Ruthless."

"I can," gasped Fearless, shuddering with pain as silence fell. "I was raised by the baboons of Brightforest Troop. I know all kinds of tricks. Baboons are always stealing things."

"His words are dung," growled Titan, fury flashing in his

eyes. "He'll say anything to save his worthless hide. He cannot do this."

"Yes. Yes, I can," panted Fearless in desperation. "Artful, listen to me!"

Artful didn't give him the dignity of a reply. Instead she turned to her mate, her eyes glinting but her head bowed with respect. "If there's the smallest chance, Titan, you must let him try. We need our cub back. Who knows—maybe the cheetahs will tear him to shreds and save you the trouble? And if he survives them, but he fails to find Ruthless—" She swung her head to glare at Fearless. "Then we can kill him anyway."

A low rumbling swelled in Titan's throat. "Fine," he growled. "Let him try. I may kill him either way, but this is his chance to atone for what he has done." With a contemptuous flick of his tail, he turned away, sheathing his claws. "Prove yourself, son of Gallant. Bring me my cub by nightfall tomorrow. If you fail to return, *with Ruthless alive and well*, I will kill your useless mother. And then I will track you down and kill you too."

Fearless raised himself up on his forepaws. His head ached and reeled, and his hide stung with the pain of Titan's claws, but he wasn't going to die. *Not right now, anyway.*

"Titan," he growled. "If I bring back Ruthless—and I will—you have to promise to let my mother live. Peacefully. With Titanpride."

Titan spun back, his jaws widening in disbelief. "You are in no position to make demands!" he roared.

"No," admitted Fearless, his breath rasping, "but that's what I want. Promise me."

"All you'll get is your life—and maybe not even that!"

"Titan!" Artful intervened again, her eyes glittering. "So long as we have Ruthless, what do we care about a useless lioness like Swift? Let her stay. She'll waste away soon enough."

Fearless staggered to his paws, swaying. A dark ember of rage ate at his belly, but he knew he had to repress it. *I'm too small. I'm exhausted. I'm beaten.*

For now.

"Titan." Swift's voice made Fearless look up in surprise. "Artful may have taken my eyes, but there are things I can still see. I know how these things should be done, and I know how the agreement is made solemn and binding. You must both swear an oath."

Titan was for a long moment absolutely still. The glare he gave Swift was deadly, and his muzzle curled, but he said nothing.

"Very well," growled Artful when it became clear Titan wasn't going to speak.

"I don't understand." Fearless looked from Artful to Titan, and back to his mother. "How is that done?"

Swift padded close and touched her whiskers to his. "You and Titan must scratch each other on the throat and swear that you will hold to the bargain you have made."

Fearless narrowed his eyes and gave Titan a suspicious glance. "Can I trust him to keep to his word?"

"Yes," she told him with surprising firmness. "A lion who does not honor a sworn oath is no lion at all! Such vows are binding to *all* lions." Swift's expression became contemptuous as she flicked her ears at Titan. "Even to lions who ignore the sacred Code."

"Watch your words, Swift Titanpride," snarled Titan. "And I have not agreed to swear an oath! Why should I give my word to this brat of Gallant who caused me to lose my cub and heir?"

"Titan!" Artful's voice was as cold and relentless as a mountain stream. "What does this lion matter to either of us? Swear the oath, if it will get Ruthless back!"

Titan watched her for a long moment, his muzzle twitching with indecisive fury. Then he nodded once. Turning, he paced up to Fearless and stared into his eyes.

"Very well. The oath will be binding for both of us. Raise your head."

Fearless paused, unable to bring his head up and expose his throat. *He could kill me in an instant.*

"You must, my cub," said Swift gently. "Do not fear."

Fearless forced himself not to flinch and did as his mother said. Titan raised a paw. *I won't even blink.*

Titan drew back his paw and lashed out. For a moment, Fearless felt nothing. Only when Titan's paw was back on the ground did he at last feel the sharp burn across his throat and a trickle of warmth.

Gazing into Titan's eyes, he wondered if he'd been killed

after all. But there was no gush of hot blood. The wound was shallow.

Artful watched intently as Titan tilted back his own head. The big lion looked down his muzzle, keeping his contemptuous stare on Fearless.

Fearless's mouth felt dry. Titan's sheer disdain made his blood cold with dread. He remembered the day his father had died.

For years, I've longed for my revenge. And here it is, presented before me. I could do it now.

His body tingled with anticipation, and his blood roared in his veins.

The truth is, I'm afraid even to scratch him.

His muscles were knotted with tension. Taking an abrupt pace forward, he lifted his paw, protracted his claws, and raked one across Titan's throat.

Titan didn't blink. He went on looking at Fearless for a long, scornful moment, then turned away.

It's like he can read my mind.

Fearless glanced down at his claw. There was a tiny smear of Titan's blood on the very tip. *I've drawn blood from him for the first time.*

And one day, I'll do more than that. One day, I will kill him.

He lifted his head and stared at the black-maned lion.

That is my oath to myself, Titan.

Swift padded slowly and hesitantly to his side, then pressed her face to his neck. Turning his head, he licked her gently.

"Good-bye, Mother," he murmured. "Be safe. I'll be back before nightfall tomorrow."

"Farewell, my Swiftcub." She rubbed her head against his. "I know you'll return, and I know you'll succeed. One day you will be a great lion, Fearless. You have a destiny to fulfill, and this is not the end of it—for you, or for the pride."

As he drew away from her and set out on his journey back to Loyal's den, Fearless wished he was as certain as Swift was of his future.

The sky was dimming, the silhouettes of the acacias blurring into the shadows of the savannah. A bronze moon hung above the horizon, bigger and clearer with every darkening moment. Crickets chirruped in the grass, gathering energy and volume for the song of the night. It seemed an eternity, Fearless thought, since he'd set off in high and confident spirits to practice his new hunting skills.

Loyal's tawny shape loomed out of a patch of thorn scrub. "Fearless! You've been gone a long time."

He halted, his tail twitching. "Hello, Loyal." He was glad to see the older lion, but he couldn't help sounding morose. "It's been a long day."

Loyal gave an apprehensive growl. "I've a feeling you have a lot to tell me, and not all of it good."

"Not all of it was bad," Fearless said, licking his jaws. "I saw my mother again."

Loyal's eyes widened. "You went to Titanpride? Even after I warned you?"

"Yes. I couldn't help it." Taking a deep breath, Fearless told his friend what had happened, from the moment he had seen the buffalo herd across the plain to the oath he had been forced to take to save his life. They walked side by side toward Loyal's den in the rocky outcrop of the kopje, and the older lion did not interrupt once as Fearless went over the day's events.

"So," he concluded with a sigh, "I think I'm in big trouble now."

If he'd expected sympathy from his friend, Fearless realized, he'd been hunting the wrong prey. "Trouble?" grunted Loyal. "That's putting it kindly, you young fool!"

"I didn't mean for this to happen," Fearless protested lamely.

"Obviously, but it happened anyway. Didn't I tell you not to go near Titanpride?" Loyal gave a snarl of frustration. "But that's not the worst of it. What were you thinking? You've sworn an oath you can't possibly keep!"

"I didn't have a choice—"

"Oaths are sacred!" roared Loyal, jumping up onto the first rock ridge to glare down at him. "There's no way you can break it, or renege on it—you keep it or you die! Do you understand?"

Fearless halted to glower angrily up at him. "Of course I do! Titan would have killed my mother as well as me. I told you, I didn't have a choice!"

For a moment there was a tense silence between the two lions. Loyal's crooked tail lashed back and forth, and he curled his muzzle, clearly fighting the desire to insult Fearless some more. But at last he huffed out a frustrated sigh.

"Very well. Since there's nothing to be done, you'll just have to go through with this." Turning his rump, he stalked toward the mouth of his den, and Fearless leaped up onto the rocks to follow him.

"I'll think of something," he told Loyal, trying to sound confident.

"You'd better," grunted Loyal. "And of course, I'll help you however I can. Idiot."

His tone was almost fond, despite everything. Relieved, Fearless loped to his side. "I do have one advantage, Loyal. I've got something on my side that Titan will never understand."

"Oh yes?" said Loyal dryly. "What's that?"

Fearless grinned and licked his friend's ear.

"Baboons!"

Tall Trees loomed before him in the dawn, like a giant beast sprawled over the plains. A ghostly mist lay around the forest's edges, and the early gray light gleamed on the thick lichens and creepers that shielded the trees from prying eyes. Fearless couldn't help thinking it already felt a lot less like home. For the first time, it looked not welcoming, but forbidding.

Fearless crouched in the untidy grass just out of scenting distance and waited. *I used to be their defender*, he thought, *but if I sauntered in there now, it's quite possible the troop would attack me.*

One by one, the baboons were waking up. He heard rustling in the branches, the soft hoots of mothers, and the hungry squeals of their babies. Two sentries on the outskirts exchanged chittering conversation. He thought he could even make out Stinger's distinctive grunting yawn as the big baboon woke and stretched.

As the sky paled, one or two shadows were visible, moving through the foliage on the edge of the forest. Bird Lowleaf bounded between date palm trunks, then vanished through a curtain of lichen.

Fearless rose up a little higher in the grass, peering hopefully into the lush green depths of the trees. Just when he thought he might give up hope, a familiar shape loped out of a fern thicket and took a few bounding paces across the grass.

Belly to the ground, Fearless slunk toward the baboon. "Thorn!" he rumbled.

Startled, the young baboon spun around, rising defensively onto his hind legs. But when he caught sight of Fearless, his bare-fanged snarl melted into a delighted grin.

"Fearless!" Thorn bounded to him on all fours, then flung his long arms around his neck. "It's good to see you!"

Fearless nuzzled his friend, his heart warm with delight. "And you! I've missed you."

Thorn gave him another tight hug and then drew back, narrowing his eyes to study him thoughtfully. "What are you doing here? Not that I'm not thrilled to see you, but—"

"You guessed it," said Fearless gloomily. "I'm in trouble."

"Already?" Thorn gave him a mischievous nudge. "Tell me all about it, then."

Fearless did. The story sounded even more stupid on its

second telling, and he felt himself grow hot with shame as he reached the moment when Titan had scarred his throat. "But I scratched him back," he added hastily. "It's a ritual, that's all."

Thorn frowned, parting Fearless's fur with his clever fingers to examine the scratch. "It's not deep," he confirmed. "But it must have nipped your tail to just let him do it. I'm glad you did the same to him."

"Oh, Thorn," said Fearless desperately, "I had to make the deal, but I don't know how I'm going to keep my side of it. How am I going to persuade those cheetahs to give me the cub?"

Thorn scratched his chin pensively. He plucked a tick off his chest and ate it.

"There might be a way . . ." he said at last.

Fearless perked up, feeling hope kindle inside him at last. "You have an idea? I knew you would, Thorn. I knew it!"

Thorn shook his head slowly. "Don't get too excited," he warned. "But you said the cheetahs took the cub because Titan stole their prey, right?"

Fearless nodded swiftly.

"Well," Thorn went on, "I know a place where there is lots of prey just waiting to be eaten. It's a secret place, but if we offer to swap that secret for Titan's cub, the cheetahs just might go for it."

"That . . . that sounds really promising." Fearless licked his jaws. "It's a good idea, Thorn. Worth a try. But how will we even find the cheetahs to offer them the deal?"

"That's where we're going to need help." Thorn placed a paw on his friend's neck. "But there's help nearby at this time of year. If we want to meet with the cheetahs, there's someone we can ask to arrange it."

Fearless sucked in a breath of realization. "The Great Mother."

"The Great Mother," Thorn confirmed with a nod. "If any creature can help us, she can."

CHAPTER 18

The eerie mist that had lain over the watering hole had dissipated, and the morning sun sparkled on its gently rippling surface. Beside Sky, a family of warthogs trotted down to the edge of the water, squealing and grunting with pleasure as they dipped their tusked snouts to drink. Moon was pestering them, blowing dust at their rumps and tweaking their stubby tails, but although Sky was supposed to be minding him, she could hardly focus on anything but Great Mother. A cold feeling of dread filled her body. *I don't want to be here! None of us should be!*

A vulture glided and flapped down to land before the matriarch, hopping forward to place a spindly leg bone in front of her huge feet. There was a small heap of bones by now; Great Mother was picking each one up, caressing it with the sensitive tip of her trunk, murmuring to herself as she studied and considered each death. As she laid one fractured bone aside and picked up the next, the vulture launched itself skyward with a beat of its great wings, making room for the next to soar down with its offering.

What will Great Mother see in the bones? wondered Sky.

I hope it's something to make her want to leave the watering hole.

Moon, clearly bored of making a nuisance of himself with the warthogs, trotted to Sky's side and tapped her flank with his trunk. "Sky, what is Great Mother doing?"

"Examining these bones," explained Sky. "The vultures bring them from carcasses of the dead, if they think the death might have broken the Code."

Moon snorted as if he found that hard to believe. "How would they know?"

"They can taste it," Sky told him. "I don't know how, but it's always been that way. So they bring a bone to Great Mother, and she reads it to find out what happened."

"And then what does she do?" persisted Moon. "Does she go and punish the animal that killed it?"

Sky shook her head, blowing a little impatiently. *I want to watch Great Mother, but he's so full of questions!* "Of course not, Moon. But it lets Great Mother see what has been happening all over Bravelands. And she tries to settle quarrels and bring justice if she can."

"Oh," said Moon. He swung his trunk, looking a little bored. "Well, I'm going to play again."

"Try not to go near those warthogs!" warned Sky. "They looked a bit annoyed before—"

As she nodded at them, she realized that they were staring the other way, grunting and huffing. "Who's that coming?" one warthog rumbled.

"Let's see," another said, shouldering her friend out of the way. "So very curious," squealed a third. "Move, move. I want to look."

Warthogs, thought Sky. *Always so nosy!* But she couldn't help following their gazes to the beaten track below a red rock ridge. Something was coming toward the watering hole, an odd-shaped creature silhouetted in the morning sun. Sky narrowed her eyes, taking a breath, and peered closer. Then she went still, her blood chilling inside her.

It wasn't one animal; it was two. A baboon walked beside a young lion, its head close to the big cat's shoulder. The lion's fur was pale gold, catching the sun's light so that he almost shimmered.

The baboon isn't riding the lion, Sky told herself as panic rose in her throat. *It's walking on all fours and its face isn't evil.*

"Great Mother!" she squealed in alarm, trotting up to the old elephant. Rain was with the matriarch now, telling her in a soft, unconcerned voice about the new arrivals; next to them, Comet and Twilight listened with mild interest.

". . . lion and a baboon, Great Mother. They arrived together. . . ." Rain paused, and the four grown ones turned curiously as Sky stumbled up to them.

"What is it, Sky?" Great Mother flapped her ears forward.

"Those animals—the ones I saw, the ones from my vision. They're back!"

"I know," said Great Mother gently. "Rain was just explaining. They don't look dangerous, my dear."

"But, Great Mother—"

The old elephant caressed Sky's head with her trunk. "I understand you're worried, Sky—but if they are the creatures from your vision, it will help me greatly to talk to them. I may be able to interpret what your dream meant."

"No, Great Mother," begged Sky. "They're dangerous! Make them go away!"

Comet and Twilight exchanged glances with Rain; some of the other grown ones were gathering around, too, murmuring in concern. "Sky might have a point, Great Mother," said Twilight. "Lions do not believe in the Great Spirit. So what is this one doing here? Surely he can't have come to see you."

"That's what we're going to find out," Great Mother told them firmly. "But a single lion cannot hurt me, so please, cease your worrying." She turned to face the newcomers as they padded hesitantly up to the elephant herd.

For a moment there was a heavy silence; the lion and the baboon looked at each other with trepidation. *Maybe Great Mother is right*, Sky tried to reassure herself. *A lion wouldn't dare try anything with so many elephants around.* Great Mother took a step forward, her huge foot stirring up white dust.

"Come," she called to the odd pair. "You wish to talk to me?"

The baboon's eyes widened in awe as he moved forward; his tail twitched and he blinked slowly, dipping his head as if overwhelmed. The lion, Sky noticed, seemed much more sure of himself: he strutted forward, so confident and proud it was almost possible to imagine a golden mane swathing his neck.

As they came closer, though, she couldn't help noticing that his forelegs were trembling.

This makes no sense! thought Sky, her brain aching with confusion. *They don't look threatening at all. How can these be the creatures from my vision?*

The lion cleared his throat, a little pompously. "I am Fearless," he declared, "once of Gallantpride, and now Cub of the Stars."

Great Mother inclined her head graciously. "A lion has never asked for my advice before," she rumbled, with gentle amusement. "It makes a pleasant change."

The young lion looked slightly embarrassed, but he cleared his throat and went on. "And this is Thorn Middleleaf of Brightforest Troop." As the baboon bowed, looking terrified, the lion licked his jaws, seeming much less confident. "We know, Great Mother, that we should wait for the day of the Great Gathering. But we . . . we need your help now."

"It's a matter of . . . urgency," stammered the young baboon.

Great Mother studied them both, then nodded. "Tell me, what is it that concerns you?"

"There's a group of cheetahs on the plain," said the lion. He twitched his tail. "They have stolen the cub of Titan, the head of Titanpride."

"Ah. This thing they have done is wrong," murmured Great Mother, swinging her trunk slowly back and forth. She tilted her head at the young lion. "But why do you come to me for help, Cub of the Stars?"

He glanced at his baboon friend, looking suddenly rather overwhelmed. "We . . ."

Thorn Middleleaf coughed politely, but kept his eyes averted. "We have . . . something we can offer the cheetahs. In the cub's place."

"We'd like to strike a bargain with them," added the lion. "But, you see—we need to find the cheetahs. Before we can— well—make the offer. Great Mother, would you ask them to meet with us?"

The old elephant gazed at him. "It is a noble thing, young Fearless, for a Gallantpride lion to help Titan. I know what happened to Gallant."

There was a long moment of heavy stillness. The lion swallowed and stared at Great Mother with new respect. "I am Gallant's son," he told her hoarsely.

"I see," murmured Great Mother—rather as if, Sky decided, she had known it already.

Under the matriarch's steady gaze, the Cub of the Stars let his head drop. "I'm not doing this to help Titan," he admitted. "If I don't return the cub to his pride, Titan will kill my mother. She's blind, you see, and she can't hunt. . . ." His voice trailed off.

Sky felt an unexpected twinge of sympathy for the Cub of the Stars. *His poor mother. How awful to be a blind lion.*

"And I'm here," babbled the baboon into the silence, "because I'm Fearless's friend."

With a thoughtful nod to the odd pair, Great Mother turned away from them, then beckoned Sky with a flick of her trunk. Sky trotted after her in surprise.

When she was a little way from the lion, the baboon and the other elephants, Great Mother stopped and lowered her head to Sky. "What do you make of them, my dear?" she murmured.

Awkwardly, Sky stirred the dust with her feet. "They're . . . not what I expected, Great Mother. They don't seem scary. Not at all." She swallowed hard. "The ones in my vision were so different—vicious and terrifying. Thorn Middleleaf and the Cub of the Stars don't seem like that at all. But I can't help thinking—"

"Go on, Sky." Great Mother touched Sky's ear with her trunk.

"I still think what I saw is *important*," blurted Sky. "When I look at them, when I think about my vision, it feels . . . heavy. A weight inside me. And my gut tingles. It means *something*. Am I being silly?"

"No," said Great Mother sternly. "Not at all, my dear. Every vision means something, and every vision is important; sometimes we simply have to work harder to interpret it. We will work out what yours means, young one. And you and I will do that together."

"Oh, thank you." Sky felt quite weak with relief. "Thank you, Great Mother."

"Now," rumbled the old matriarch, "I need to give the lion

and the baboon their answer. What do you think? Should I help them?"

Remembering the lion's agonized words, Sky nodded. "Yes, I think you should."

"Then we are of one mind." Great Mother's eyes twinkled as she turned and led Sky back to the meeting place.

The lion and the baboon stiffened, exchanging a glance; they then dipped their heads in respect. Great Mother lifted her trunk and gestured at a tree on the plain, beyond the rocky ridge. "The Lightning Tree: do you see it?"

They both raised their heads and looked. "The one split into three?" asked the baboon eagerly.

"That's it. I will ask the cheetahs to meet you there at dusk."

"Thank you, Great Mother! That's . . . I'm grateful, and . . ." The baboon shot a slightly anxious look at his friend; the lion frowned and nodded. Both still seemed a little on edge, their paws and tails twitching.

Great Mother watched them thoughtfully. "And I shall be there too, to make sure all goes well. Does that satisfy you?"

They both nodded, looking relieved. "Thank you, Great Mother!" hooted Thorn Middleleaf.

"Yes. Thank you!" The young lion lowered his forequarters in a bow. "We won't disturb you any longer, Great Mother. We're so grateful for your help."

The two animals backed off a couple of paces before turning to leave. As they did, Thorn Middleleaf caught sight of the pile of bones the vultures had brought, and he gave it a curious second glance. Sky saw his eyes narrow; he furrowed his brow.

Then he gave a shocked cry and bounded over to the heap. "Fearless!"

"What is it, Thorn?" The lion loped to his side.

What do they think they're doing?

The baboon was delving gently into the pile of bones. He set aside a small rib, and with more effort, a thick fractured leg bone that might have come from a buffalo. Then he blinked and drew a breath, staring at what had lain below them. Sliding his hands very carefully around something, as if he was cradling a tiny baboon baby, he drew a skull from the heap. He turned to show it to the Cub of the Stars.

Sky stared too: it was the skull of a baboon, picked clean by the vultures. But one fang had been snapped off, leaving only a jagged stump.

The lion gave a rasping grunt of shock. "Bark Crownleaf!"

Thorn Middleleaf nodded, his expression stunned. "Great Mother—this baboon was head of our troop."

Sky took a tentative step forward—though she stayed safely in Great Mother's huge shadow—and peered closely at the baboon skull. Its jaws were open, its single long fang clearly displayed. Something about the skull's expression was disturbing—she could almost hear its scream of shock and rage—and a shiver rippled along her spine.

"I am sorry to hear that," Great Mother told the baboon softly. "The bones in this pile belong to creatures whose deaths may have broken the Code."

Thorn Middleleaf stroked the skull's smooth top. "With respect, Great Mother, I don't think that's possible in this case. Bark Crownleaf died fighting a hyena—she was protecting the troop. That doesn't break the Code."

"Well," murmured Great Mother, pacing forward to touch the skull, "I can read bones to tell how an animal died. You know this, don't you? But you don't need me to tell you about this remnant." Gently she took hold of the skull with the tip of her trunk and turned it in the baboon's paws. "There."

The young baboon stared at the back of the skull for a moment, as if he could not quite believe what he was seeing. Then he sucked in a high-pitched breath.

Sky crept forward, too curious to resist.

It was not smooth and round as it should have been; there was an ugly, shattered hole in the back of it.

The lion gasped at the same moment Sky did. "Her head was smashed!" he exclaimed hoarsely.

Thorn Middleleaf's head snapped up, and he hooted in angry grief. "A hyena couldn't do this!"

"No," agreed Great Mother sadly.

"What happened, Great Mother? What more can you tell us? Bark's killer . . . they must have come from behind. . . ." The young baboon's voice cracked.

"A moment, young Thorn." Closing her eyes, Great Mother ran her trunk across the skull. Her eyes squeezed tighter, and she flinched just a little. Long heartbeats passed in silence; the animals around her all seemed to hold their breath.

Concerned, Sky raised her trunk to touch her grandmother's shoulder, but the old elephant finally opened her eyes.

"Death was brought to Bark Crownleaf by one she trusted," said Great Mother. "Could that have been a hyena?"

The baboon was silent for a long time, his jaws grinding as he seemed to struggle with what he had been told.

"Th-thank you, Great Mother," he stammered at last. "I . . . we have to leave but . . . thank you."

For a moment, he seemed unable to move. He leaned briefly on the lion's flank, as though he needed support, and the Cub of the Stars dipped his head to nuzzle him comfortingly.

At last, though, the baboon drew himself up, clenching his jaw. The two odd friends turned and trudged away, muttering to each other as they went. Though Sky couldn't make out their words, she recognized the tones of confusion and grief.

The rest of the elephant herd dispersed almost at once, gossiping about the strange visitors as they browsed the bushes, but Sky stared after the lion and the baboon, her mind in turmoil. Her grandmother still stood nearby, quiet and pensive. Sky edged closer to her.

"Great Mother . . ." She cleared her throat. "Great Mother, may I come to the meeting with the cheetahs?"

The old elephant looked down, cocking her ragged ears forward in surprise. But she nodded slowly.

"I think that's a good idea. Yes, you may come. It is clear

this pair must be connected to your vision." She rolled the baboon skull lightly on the ground. "Sky, I think we've found your visions are unusual. You see things in the bones that are hidden from other elephants. Will you try to read this skull for me?"

"A bone of another animal?" Sky pinned back her ears in doubt.

"Let us say I'm curious," rumbled her grandmother. "Perhaps you can read it, perhaps not. But shall we find out?"

"I'll try." Tentatively Sky approached it and extended her trunk toward the skull. Then she hesitated. "Will I see how she died?" she murmured.

"Don't be afraid of it, young one. The bone cannot hurt you." Great Mother blew a soft breath against Sky's neck. "Your vision came from your mother's bones, so learning to read other remnants might help you understand that vision better. And it might well help me, too."

Carefully Sky mimicked her grandmother's technique, which she had witnessed so often, running the tip of her trunk delicately across the shattered skull. *Great Mother is right. This isn't frightening. It's almost soothing. . . .*

Her eyes drooped, and she swayed slightly. The foliage of the watering hole blurred and melted into green and ocher ripples, and sleepy warmth enfolded her.

And then, with an abruptness that turned her own bones cold, something flashed into her vision.

A baboon's eyes, bloodshot with hate and vicious cunning. Jaws gaped wide, and long savage fangs glinted in the brutal white sunlight. And it screeched—

Snapping out of her trance, Sky stumbled and cried out in fear. There was no baboon here; only the calm, sparkling lake, and the idly grazing herds, and the concerned face of Great Mother, bending down to her.

"Sky! My dear, what did you see?"

"A baboon! Grandmother, I saw it again—but I don't think it was Thorn Middleleaf. This one is evil!"

But there was no fear in Great Mother's kind eyes. She looked proud as she curled her trunk around Sky's.

"You have the gift, young Sky. You do not simply receive messages from the bones; you read the very heart of them."

"What was it?" Sky was shaking, and despite the heat of the sun, a chill lingered in her blood. "What did I see?"

"The baboon you saw in the bones, Sky?" Great Mother gave a deep sigh. "That was the murderer of Bark Crownleaf."

CHAPTER 19

"Good luck, my friend," said Thorn, pressing his forehead against Fearless's chest. "If anyone can get the cub back from the cheetahs, it's you."

His heart ached, his head reeled with unanswerable questions about Bark Crownleaf's killer, and he wanted nothing more than to stay in the comforting company of his friend. But he could see that Fearless's mind was elsewhere.

"I hope you're right." Fearless licked Thorn's head. He was staring in the direction of the three-branched Lightning Tree.

Much as he wanted to scramble onto Fearless's back and stay with him, wandering the savannah until night fell, he could only watch his friend turn and pad away. When the lion was out of sight, Thorn took a deep breath, clenched his jaws, and bounded for the gully where Berry had found Bark Crownleaf's body.

As he paused on the edge of the ditch, he swallowed hard. He scrambled down, clutching at vines and scrubby thorn-bushes to slow his descent. He didn't want to fall straight down and possibly disturb the remains that lay there.

Grass and tendrils of flowering balsam were already beginning to creep over the skeletons. Carefully Thorn picked and tugged away the encroaching vegetation to expose the bodies; of course, both had been scoured clean by insects and rot-eaters. Bark's skeleton, though, was more disturbing than the hyena's; her spine ended abruptly at the neck, the skull taken by the vultures to the Great Mother. Thorn shivered.

Frowning, he inspected the ground nearby, pulling aside creepers. It was hard to tell if there had been a struggle here, and whether it had been only between Bark and the hyena. It wasn't possible to read anything in the terrain, he decided.

He turned to the hyena's bones. They had been tugged apart by the scavenging birds and beasts. Rib bones were scattered in a haphazard tumble, and Thorn pulled them impatiently aside. Though they were scored with teeth marks, they were unlikely to tell him anything. But beneath those, tangled in the grass, lay the beast's skull.

With a grunt of determination, Thorn gripped it and pulled it free of the vegetation. An unexpected shiver rippled through him as he gazed into its empty eye sockets. Slowly, he turned the skull over.

For a moment he simply stared at it, his heart thudding

slowly. He'd half expected this, but he'd still dreaded being right.

The hyena's skull, too, had been smashed. A section at the back was cracked, with a small hole in the center.

None of us examined the bodies, he thought. *But how could we have suspected? How could we have known to look for evidence of bad deeds?*

It would take something hard and heavy to smash two skulls.

His blood pounding in his veins, Thorn rummaged in the undergrowth, yanking dead branches aside, flinging chunks of earth and rotted leaves out of his way. In the depths of a thick clump of lantana, he finally found what he didn't know he was looking for.

For a moment he went still. Then he pulled the rock out of the shadows—a wedge-shaped fragment, pointed at one end, and the perfect size to fit into a fist.

It certainly felt heavy and sharp enough to do damage even to the toughest old bones. A pang of grief twisted Thorn's gut as he thought of poor Bark, trusting and unawares. *Great Mother said our Crownleaf was betrayed. Surely that has to mean a baboon did this? And not many other creatures could grasp a rock and smash it down. . . .*

But the real evidence was the crust of blood that had dried in every crack and crevice of the stone. Thorn scraped at it with a claw, shivering, then wiped his paw frantically on the lantana leaves.

So a baboon killed Bark and the hyena. With this stone. But after it killed them—

A shudder ran through his bones. Bark's fang had been snapped clean off. The killer must have done that, just so he or she could sink it into the hyena's corpse.

And there's only one culprit I can think of. There's only one of us who could have been so ruthless. The individual who stood to gain the most when he became Crownleaf.

Grub.

Dizzy, he scrambled back up to the lip of the gully. His whole body felt heavy and clumsy as he made his way back to the center of Tall Trees. His heart ached inside him, but his head was numb, and his paws felt as if they didn't belong to him.

Within the camp, there was lively bustle; as Thorn padded in, it felt odd and wrong to him that life was going on in this normal, cheerful way. Stinger hailed him from the forked branch of a cassia tree.

"Thorn! Where have you been?" Stinger rose up on his hind legs, gripping a branch for balance, and peered at him. "Never mind. There's a Council meeting shortly, and we're gathering the best food from our stores for the members. Can you help, please?"

It wasn't really a request, thought Thorn dully, but he was glad of a distraction while he tried to wrap his mind around the awful discoveries of the day. He took his place in the group of working baboons; in a daze he sorted through berries and nuts and tender leaves, picking them out and placing them aside for other young baboons to carry to the Council Glade. As Grub strutted past on his way to the Crown Stone,

Thorn stared at him, feeling sick.

What happens now? I don't know what to do!

Nut grabbed a handful of leaves from Thorn's discard pile. "Why are you putting these aside? They're perfect." He flung them with a flourish into the pile meant for the Council Glade and gave a chitter of disgust. "*Why* do we have to work with stupid Middleleaves?"

Thorn barely heard him. *I can't just let this go. I have to say something. But when? And who can I tell?*

"Thorn." He felt a paw on his back. "Are you all right?"

Startled, he turned to see Stinger's concerned face. "Er . . . yes, I'm fine."

"You don't look it. You've been in a trance since you arrived." The older baboon drew him aside, behind a colorful thicket of orange and red croton plants. "What's wrong?"

Miserably, Thorn licked his jaws and gazed at Stinger. *He's a senior Highleaf*, he thought. *And I trust him.*

"I went to see Great Mother today," he blurted. "And something happened. . . ."

Stinger watched Thorn's face intently as he listened to his frantic tale. As word followed terrible word, the older baboon's expression darkened, and he drew back his lips in horror as Thorn described his search of the skeletons in the ditch.

"And Stinger," finished Thorn miserably, "I think Grub did it. Remember how eagerly he came forward to be leader? I think Grub killed Bark Crownleaf."

Stinger subsided onto his haunches, then peered over

Thorn's shoulders nervously. "It's true he was . . . enthusiastic," he rasped. He stared at his own paws. "I . . . put it out of
my head. I didn't want to think anything so terrible had happened."

"So do you think I'm right?" asked Thorn desperately.

"I do not know." Stinger laid a paw on his trembling arm.
"But I trust your instincts, Thorn. You've always been a clever
baboon. And . . . I did have my own suspicions. I just didn't
want to think too hard." His amber eyes looked sunken and
shadowed.

"Would Grub really break the Code just to make himself
leader?" whispered Thorn.

"I hope not." Stinger raked at his shoulder fur with his
claws.

"We have to tell the troop!" Thorn said desperately. "We
can't keep this to ourselves. Even if Grub is innocent somehow, the troop has to hear about what I found."

"I hope he *is* innocent," Stinger said, his voice agonized. "If
he's guilty, one day we'll find out for sure. But Thorn, we can't
say anything just now. We have no proof! Grub could turn
this against *us*. I assume you've left the evidence?"

"The skeletons are still in the ditch—but Great Mother
has got Bark's skull." Thorn chittered his teeth, torn between
anger and indecision. "What should we do?"

"I think it's wise to keep our counsel for now," Stinger told
him. His intelligent face was grave. "Remember, I lost the
vote to become Crownleaf to Grub. If we say anything now,
he could accuse me of just wanting him gone."

"I . . . maybe you're right. Yes, I see that."

"If Grub did this awful thing, we'll find a way to expose him. But in the meantime, Thorn, it's important to be careful. Grub is Crownleaf now, and who knows what he's capable of? We have to keep our eyes open."

"Then I hope no one has noticed us talking about it," said Thorn with a stab of fear.

"You're right," said Stinger grimly. "Come on. It's time we were at the Council."

It was so hard to keep a normal, relaxed expression as Thorn took his place behind Stinger in the Council Glade. Sunlight filtered weakly through the creepers and lichens that draped the surrounding trees; behind each of the fourteen Council Highleaves, their retinues sat in greenish shadow, eyes glowing. To Thorn, for the first time, the dimness of the glade felt sinister, as though something menacing lurked behind the creepers. And he could barely bring himself to look at Grub, perched so self-importantly on the Crown Stone. Looking at his haughty posture, it was all too easy to imagine him being a murderer.

The Council, it seemed, had returned to the concern Thorn had heard them discuss many times before. "If we move the troop now," Mango was saying gruffly, "we miss half the fertile season in Tall Trees."

"But the monkeys might well try another attack," pointed out Twig. "What if we can't fight them off next time? I say we find new territory before they come back."

"But where would we go?" asked Beetle tremulously. "We

may face more threats at our new home."

"Well," said Stinger—a little too brightly, thought Thorn— "I think a change would do the troop good. We've been rooted here for too long."

"I'm not so sure," grumbled the Crownleaf. "There's been a lot of upheaval lately. We need some stability, and moving is always chaos. I don't want young baboons starting to treat their elders with disrespect, or thinking they can pair with lower statuses. That's where instability leads: to that kind of uproar and nonsense."

Thorn swallowed hard at Grub's talk of interstatus pairings.

"Youngsters, didn't you hear me?" Grub was glowering around the retinues. "I said, bring in the food! This is hungry work."

Snapping his focus back to the job at hand, Thorn sprang down from his rock behind Stinger and bounded to the collection of the finest food, piled in a small neighboring clearing. It wasn't all nuts and berries; there were a few mice and hares, too, and a dik-dik. *That should obviously go to Grub, as Crownleaf.* Thorn reached for the tiny gazelle.

His paw was slapped away. Nut glared at him with his small, mean eyes and snatched up the dik-dik.

"I'm a Highleaf," he hissed. "You're a Middleleaf, remember? *I'll* serve the Crownleaf."

Thorn bared his fangs, but right now he couldn't bring himself to care about Nut's stupid antics. *If only you knew what I do*, he thought bitterly. Grabbing up an armful of mangoes, he followed Nut back to the main glade.

Nut was already at the Crown Stone, obsequiously offering the dik-dik to Grub, who snatched it without taking a breath. Clearly Grub was into his stride on the subject of the disrespectful youngsters of the troop.

"And another thing," he was saying, "there's a bit too much insolence to the elders for my liking. Why, just the other day"—he tore a strip of meat from the dik-dik's haunch and crammed it into his mouth—"a Lowleaf refused to hand over his mango to me. *Me*, the leader of the troop!" He sank his teeth into the dik-dik and chomped another mouthful. "Well, I soon set him straight. And let me tell you, moving around will give these youngsters even more ideas above their status. Suddenly they think being young and quick gives them the right to question orders." He gulped and ripped another mouthful. "And they are very rarely right about anything. Not that that matters, anyway. It's the principle that's important. Tradition. *Respect*. But in the arrogance of youth, they—" He stopped suddenly, coughing.

Beetle obligingly slapped his back. Grub coughed again and cleared his throat, then nodded irritably. "Thank you, Beetle. Yes, yes, I'm fine. Now, as I was saying regarding pairings—"

Another coughing fit racked him. Other Council members exchanged concerned glances.

"You needn't look at me like that, Twig Highleaf. I'm not choking to death, though I'm sure you wouldn't mind if I *were*, because—"

This time, when his body convulsed, his violent cough

sprayed bits of dik-dik flesh across the Crown Stone. With a vacant, startled look, he stared down at the blood-flecked spittle.

"He's foaming!" cried Mango.

"Nonsense," spluttered Grub. He stood up on all fours, wiped an arm across his mouth, and stared uncomprehendingly at the dribbles of gray foam that stuck to his fur. "I'm absolutely—"

With a strangled gasp, he clutched his throat. A few Council members dashed forward, including Stinger with Thorn behind him; others simply stared, frozen in shock, as Grub toppled from the Crown Stone. Even those who had run to him backed off, chittering and whooping in distress, as his body began to convulse. More foam and blood spurted from the corners of his mouth, and his eyes rolled wildly back in his head.

Thorn shrieked in horror. It was clear Grub was trying to speak, but all that came from his throat was a gurgling rattle. He stiffened, his form bizarrely rigid and twisted, and then, as silence fell, he went limp.

For a moment, not even the birds sang.

Then, "He's *dead*!" screamed Mango.

The whole Council Glade erupted. Baboons jumped up and down, shrieked, pummeled the ground, and shook branches. The rest of the troop came hurtling and leaping to the glade, eager to see what the fuss was about; when they realized what had happened, they added their panicked distress to the already echoing clamor.

"The Crownleaf is dead!"

"Murder!"

"Disaster!"

"Treachery!"

Thorn stood in motionless shock, breathing hard.

Berry and Mud dashed to his side. "Are you all right? Thorn!" Berry shook his arm.

"Thorn, say something!" Mud hugged him.

"I'm fine," he rasped. His limbs were shaking.

Bark was murdered. And now Grub's dead. How has this happened?

Thorn stared at Nut, who was standing closest to Grub's corpse; the young baboon was gaping at the horrible sight. Nut's usually tiny eyes were so wide, the whites showed all around them.

"Two leaders dead!" hollered Twig over the uproar. "And one so soon after the other!"

"What does it mean?" yelped River Middleleaf. "Somebody ask the Starleaf. *Quick!*"

"The Great Spirit is sending us a message," howled Beetle.

"The troop is *doomed!*" bellowed Branch, her voice carrying clear across the glade. That set off a new jabbering and screeching among the baboons.

"Quiet! Keep calm! Quiet!" Stinger was the only baboon trying to control the panic, but his words were lost in the tumult. As Thorn watched, the older baboon's face set firm with determination, and he bounded up onto the Crown Stone. Rising to his hind paws, he hollered again.

"Quiet!"

Now, one by one, the troop began to turn to him, stunned. The screams and hoots faded, and they all stared at the baboon who stood on the very stone Grub had occupied only moments ago.

Thorn felt the hairs rise on his arms and his back, as a sense of relief flooded him. Stinger looked every inch the leader, motionless and silent, his commanding gaze steady on the frantic troop.

When every baboon was quiet, and they were all watching him in awe, Stinger nodded once.

"This turn of events is dreadful." His voice was calm, but intense. "What has happened is terrible enough, without baboons panicking and throwing accusations."

River crept forward, breathing heavily. "You're right, Stinger. Yes." Stretching his nose toward the dik-dik corpse, he flared his nostrils nervously. "It smells bad, though. Rank."

"Perhaps it was rotten." Mango was trembling. "If it had been dead a long time, it might have gone bad."

River shook his head slowly, his eyes still huge with shock. "It doesn't smell like that kind of bad, Mango."

"And it was fresh!" hollered Twig, bounding forward. "I caught it myself this morning! It was young and healthy, I swear it!"

"So what happened to it between this morning and now?" Mango put her paws over her mouth. "Did someone . . . *tamper* with it?"

For a long moment, there was an awful silence as the

meaning of it all sank in. Then Stinger dropped to all fours and sprang down from the Crown Stone. He stood beside it, holding them all with his gaze, and laid his paw against its smooth surface.

"No baboon has the right to stand on this stone," he declared, his voice resonant, calm, and powerful. "No baboon but Grub Crownleaf. And it seems clear that someone here has broken the Code and *murdered him.*" He shot a quick glance at Thorn, and in his eyes Thorn saw restrained panic. *He's trying to be strong, but he's worried.*

No baboon spoke. The stillness of the glade was oppressive.

"We will discover the culprit," growled Stinger. "This crime against Brightforest Troop will not go unpunished."

Twig stood up. "Grub was poisoned. I think that much is clear."

"True," said Stinger, nodding. "Who gave the dik-dik to Grub?"

Silence fell once more. Thorn couldn't help but let his gaze drift to Nut. The young baboon was still wild-eyed, and now he was panting audibly. He clenched and unclenched his paws and glanced crazily around the glade, as if searching for a way out. *I've never seen any creature look so guilty*, realized Thorn with a sickening lurch in his gut.

Then he sprang away.

Nut did not make it far before several baboons brought him down. Thorn saw fists pummeling and heard Nut's cries of terror.

"It wasn't me!" he shrieked. "Let go of me!"

"Enough!" shouted Stinger. "Stand him up."

The baboons gripped Nut's fur and dragged him back to the Crown Stone.

Nut was bleeding from his side where someone had torn at his fur, but he didn't fight.

"Why did you run?" asked Stinger, cocking his head.

Nut didn't answer. His chest was still rising and falling, and his eyes darted across the clearing.

"He served Grub!" shouted one of the baboons, yanking Nut's arm. "Admit it—you poisoned our leader."

"No . . . it's not like that," said Nut, shaking his head.

"You didn't serve him?" asked Stinger sarcastically.

Nut's head hunched low between his shoulders. "Yes, Stinger, I gave it to him." His voice was high and harsh. "I served it to Grub but I didn't know, I didn't know it was poisoned!" He was babbling now, almost incoherent. "I had nothing to do with this. I wasn't the only one serving! Thorn Middleleaf, he was serving too!" Raising his head, he tried to shove through the crowd toward Thorn. "Thorn, tell them! You know I didn't do this!"

Stinger turned grimly toward Thorn. "Tell us, Thorn Middleleaf. Tell the troop exactly what you saw."

Thorn swallowed hard. He could feel the eyes of the whole troop on him, but mostly he felt the gazes of Berry and Mud, watching him, willing him to come up with a rational reason for Grub's death.

He cleared his throat. "I picked up the dik-dik—I knew

it should go to Grub—but Nut grabbed it. Said he was a Highleaf, and that he should serve Grub. So I let him."

A ripple of dark murmurs went round the glade. Stinger turned to Nut once more.

"Why," he asked, "did you want so badly to serve Grub's food?"

Nut's mouth opened and closed, but no sound came out.

Stinger leaned closer to him, his fangs bared. "Were you worried someone else might eat the poisoned dik-dik? Were you making sure your plan worked?" As Nut backed away, terror in his eyes, Stinger bellowed: *"And why did you run?"*

"I . . . I was scared," babbled Nut. "I saw how it looked, but I just wanted to serve the Crownleaf, that's all, I swear, I . . ." His voice faltered and dried. His whole body shook with fear—and with what looked horribly like guilt.

"Starleaf!" called Stinger, his voice ringing clear around the glade.

Mud's mother came forward, her face furrowed with anxiety. As she made her way to Stinger's side, Mud leaned forward to whisper in Thorn's ear.

"I never liked Nut, but I didn't think he could ever do something like this. Did you?"

"No," Thorn replied slowly, "but Stinger's right. Why did he run?"

The Starleaf dipped her head solemnly toward the empty Crown Stone.

"Starleaf," pleaded Stinger, his tone suddenly far softer. There was real pain in his eyes. "We need guidance."

The Starleaf's head sagged; Thorn thought she looked terribly tired and strained, her brindled fur dull. Beside him, Mud gave a whimper of concern.

"Stinger Highleaf, the stars do not tell of guilt or innocence," she intoned. The Starleaf shook her head sadly. "But I can say that the rains are unpredictable this year, and that storm clouds cover the stars just when they are not expected. Winds struck the ground yesterday and spun the savannah earth into the whirling funnels we call dust devils. All I can say is that the Great Spirit must be warning us that uncertainty faces the troop now."

Stinger's face was bleak. He closed his eyes for a long moment, then blinked them open.

"Your words are wise, Starleaf, and I thank you for them." He turned to Nut. "The charges are grave against you, Highleaf. The evidence is damning."

"But I didn't do it!" shrieked Nut.

"Liar!" someone cried.

Stinger held up a hand. "It is not for me to be your judge," he said. "None of us can know for sure. But action must be taken and order *must* be restored. Just as our Starleaf puts her trust not in a single omen, or the movement of a single star, but in their multitude, so we should put our trust in many voices. I propose a vote, among the wisest of our number. Highleaves of the Council, set aside your grief for one more duty. I ask you to raise your arms if, in your judgment, Nut is guilty. Only a majority will decide his fate."

Thorn held his breath, as the Council baboons looked to

one another. Some hands shot up, others lifted slowly, and as they did the horror dawned on Nut's features. Soon there were fourteen arms raised. Stinger, Thorn noticed, didn't even take part.

He doesn't need to. It's overwhelming!

Nut went limp in his captors' hands, and the Council Highleaves exploded into screeching, hooting tumult.

"Murderer! He should die for this!"

"Assassin! Strike him down before he kills again!"

"No mercy! *Kill Nut Highleaf.*"

Cold horror flooded Thorn as he watched the baboons jump and shriek and demand Nut's blood. *I shouldn't care!* he thought fiercely. *He's a nasty, vicious brute and I hate him and he killed our Crownleaf, but—*

"No!" he yelled. He forced himself through the mob, tugging on arms, hooting desperately into furious faces. "No, we can't do this—it's wrong!"

"Wait!" Stinger was hollering. "Quiet, all of you!" He leaped back onto the Crown Stone. *"Be silent."*

The bloodthirsty screeching faded to an angry muttering.

"Thorn Middleleaf is right," cried Stinger, giving Thorn a reassuring nod. "He speaks the truth: to kill Nut now would be to break the Code as terribly as he did himself. We must show mercy. We *will* show mercy."

"What about justice?" hooted an angry voice from the back.

"There will be justice, Notch," said Stinger grimly. "Nut will be exiled from Brightforest Troop, never to return."

"No!" yelped Nut as every baboon turned to glare at him.

"No, Stinger, please—I'm innocent—"

Three huge baboons sprang forward. Bug, Stone, and Sand, Grub's most loyal cohorts, raced toward Nut, lips peeled back to show their fangs.

Nut turned tail and fled from the glade.

That was the cue for the rest of the troop to turn on him. As one, they screeched and yammered, sprinting after the fleeing Nut. Thorn stood frozen. He could not bring himself to join the harrying of Nut.

"He's guilty," whispered Mud miserably. He arrived at Thorn's side with Berry.

"I don't doubt it," murmured Berry, stroking Thorn's arm comfortingly. "This is horrible to watch, Thorn, but it's justice."

Justice or not, Thorn was glad that his friends had stayed behind with him. The three of them were the only baboons left in the Council Glade as the menacing shrieks and yells and the crash of branches faded into the distance, along with the fleeing howls of the exiled killer.

No, he realized. *It's not just the three of us. Stinger didn't join the mob either.*

His eyes dipped in profound sadness, Stinger Highleaf sat hunched on the Crown Stone.

CHAPTER 20

The Lightning Tree was unmistakable. It stood out stark and grim, even against the looming darkness of a bank of storm cloud. Dampness glistened on its burned bark; its crown had been split into three giant charred splinters, jutting out at freakish angles. A pale lizard scuttled around its trunk and vanished as the two lions approached.

"I still think you've been foolishly reckless," growled Loyal. "Elephants don't normally take kindly to lions marching right up to them."

"It was the only way I could think of to contact the cheetahs," admitted Fearless. "And you know, Great Mother isn't like that. She's *different*."

"She's an elephant with four huge feet, any one of which could crush your skull," huffed Loyal. "Our ancestors stopped following the Great Parent of Bravelands a long time ago,

Fearless, and I reckon they must have had good reason. Lions have managed our own affairs perfectly well since then, without help from some—some *grass-eater* with a swollen sense of her own importance."

"That's not what the baboons think," protested Fearless. "They trust Great Mother to sort out all kinds of problems. Not just for them, for all animals. I think she cares, and I think this is going to work."

"Hmph." Loyal scowled at the Lightning Tree. "You spent far too long with those baboons. They've turned your head."

Fearless stiffened his jaw. "I didn't ask you to come! You're the one who wanted to. If you're going to make a fuss, maybe you should just go."

"Absolutely not." Loyal padded grimly on, not even looking at him. "I'm not leaving you to deal with an enormous elephant and a cheetah gang all by yourself."

Fearless picked up his pace to trot alongside Loyal once more. "Thank you," he growled.

"You're welcome," muttered Loyal. "Idiot."

"Look!" said Fearless, stopping to stare.

Just visible beyond the cloud bank, in the thin strip of pale sky on the horizon, the sun was melting in a blaze of gold. Against its glare, he could see the silhouettes of two elephants, walking toward the tree. Even though he'd seen Great Mother up close only a little earlier, he still felt a tingle of awe in his fur. She trudged toward them, massive and implacable, her tusks gleaming gold in the fiery sunset. The elephant who trotted alongside her was much smaller, and as they drew closer, Fearless recognized her: she'd been standing with Great Mother today, and the old elephant had drawn her aside for a private discussion. *She's young, but she must be important to Great Mother.*

The two lions waited beneath the Lightning Tree as the elephants approached; Fearless noticed that his friend wore an expression of grim resignation. That turned to wariness as Great Mother halted, looming above them.

"Greetings, Cub of the Stars," the old elephant rumbled. "This is Sky, my granddaughter."

"Thank you for coming, Great Mother," said Fearless respectfully. "This is my good friend Loyal."

"A pleasure to meet you," said Great Mother.

"Likewise." Loyal nodded slightly, but without taking his nervous eyes off the matriarch.

"And our timing seems to be perfect," remarked Great Mother. "Here comes Fleet's coalition."

All four animals turned to watch the cheetahs slink low and elegant across the grassland, their black-streaked faces solemn. There were more of them now, Fearless noticed; he counted six as they came closer. All of them dipped their heads to Great Mother as they padded to a halt.

"Thank you," rumbled Great Mother. "I'm grateful you agreed to this meeting, Fleet. I hope we can make peace this evening."

"I hope so too," said the largest of the cheetahs. He sat back on his haunches, flicking his long, black-tipped tail. "But we agreed to a meeting with the young lion. We will not speak to him until the older one leaves."

"That's not going to happen," growled Loyal.

Another of the cheetahs paced daintily forward. "I am Lightning," he purred. "I am the coalition's Star-Runner; I read the omens. And those I have read today give me conflicting signs about this meeting. There will be good outcomes, and bad. We come to you in a spirit of peace, Great Mother, but we will be cautious before we agree to anything."

Fleet gave a mewling growl. "And after the way Titanpride has behaved, we trust lions even less than we did. We are willing to talk with the young one—Fearless Gallantpride—but his friend has to go."

Loyal drew himself up to his full impressive height. Taking a pace forward, he stood protectively in front of Fearless. "That's a coincidence, because I do not trust *you*," he growled. "How can we tell this isn't a trap?"

The big maned lion and the six cheetahs faced one another, lips drawn back from bared fangs. The smaller elephant gave a dismayed gasp.

This meeting is falling apart before it even starts! thought Fearless.

"Loyal, it's all right." He nudged his friend's shoulder. "You can leave me."

"Absolutely not." Loyal didn't take his eyes off Fleet.

"Loyal," rumbled Great Mother, "I am here to make sure nothing goes wrong. Nothing untoward will happen in my presence, I promise you."

"Loyal." Fearless butted his head urgently against the older lion's maned neck. "This is my only chance to save my mother."

"It might be your chance to get stomped. And even if you can put your faith in the elephant, how do you know the cheetahs won't betray her trust?"

"Loyal, *please*. Let me do this alone. I'll be all right."

A low snarl rumbled in Loyal's throat. But at last he said: "Fine. This time." He glared up at Great Mother. "But make sure nothing happens to Fearless. And *you*"—he glared at Fleet—"my friend is to come to no harm, do you understand?"

Fleet curled his lip. "Lions may not respect the Spirit of the Bravelands. But cheetahs keep their word."

Fearless was relieved the impasse had been broken, but he couldn't help feeling a twinge of worry as Loyal padded off across the plain. *I hope I'm not making a big mistake.*

The cheetahs rose and slunk forward, forming a circle around him. They'd looked small next to Loyal—but now that he was facing them alone, Fearless realized the leader, Fleet, was actually a little taller than him. Despite the looming figure of Great Mother, he couldn't help his fur rising with nerves. *Not only that, but I'm seriously outnumbered.*

"Well then," growled Fleet. "What do you have to say, cub?"

Fearless coughed, to clear his throat and steady his voice. "Listen to me. All predators in Bravelands are hungry. I know of a food source—a good, plentiful one—that Titan isn't aware of. I can tell you where it is, and you can catch as much prey as you like without interference from Titanpride." He took a deep breath. "But I'll only tell you if you return Ruthless to me."

Fleet exchanged an incredulous look with Lightning, and all six cheetahs gave chirping, mocking laughs. "And how would you—a little furball—know of this, if Titanpride does not?"

"I'm not in Titanpride!" said Fearless, his hackles rising. "I left when Titan killed my father Gallant! I was brought up by baboons—and it was one of them who told me about this place. You know how smart and cunning baboons are!"

Fleet narrowed his eyes and muttered something to a cheetah on his left. "I've never heard of such a thing," he growled. "A lion raised by baboons?"

"This much is true," said Great Mother. "I cannot vouch for the lion's claims about prey, but that he was raised by baboons is a fact."

Fearless wondered how she could know such a thing, but decided it wasn't wise to interrupt. The cheetahs had drawn aside into a tight cluster by themselves now, mewling and murmuring, their voices skeptical.

Fearless realized he was holding his breath. *This has to work. They have to believe me.*

His hide tingled, and he started a little as he realized the smaller elephant, Sky, had come to stand at his flank.

"I think you spoke well," she whispered to him shyly.

He blinked up at her, too surprised to answer. By the time he had recovered his composure, the cheetahs were stalking back toward them in the darkening evening.

"Very well," mewled Fleet. "You have a deal, lion—so long as no other lions are involved."

The wave of relief was dizzying. Fearless's heart thumped with nervous excitement. "I appreciate your trust—and I promise, there won't be any more lions."

"So?" Fleet tilted his elegant head. "Where is this mysterious source of prey?"

"It's a ravine I know," Fearless told them excitedly. "My friend the baboon found it. It's far from where Titanpride hunts. A herd of gazelles grazes there. There are two narrow entrances—the herd can be surrounded and trapped!"

All the cheetahs were leaning forward now, a hungry, eager look in their eyes.

"Take us there," purred Fleet.

Fearless nodded and turned to Great Mother. "Thank you," he murmured. "This means a great deal to me."

She nodded her massive head. Then she raised her trunk and trumpeted a warning.

"Remember!" Her deep voice rang and echoed, making Fearless's fur rise at the roots. "Both sides *must* keep to their word."

"Of course." Fearless dipped his head to her, then turned to nod to the younger elephant. Sky flapped her ears in delight.

"I knew you'd persuade them," she whispered happily.

He nodded, amused, then turned and led the cheetahs in the direction of the ravine Thorn had shown him. Night had fallen completely now; the savannah was alive with chirruping crickets, the rustle of small creatures in the grass, and the distant, eerie cries of jackals.

It felt uncomfortable walking ahead of the cheetah

coalition. His rump tingled, but Fearless was determined not to betray his nerves by glancing over his shoulder. He knew they were still behind him, though their paws were light and silent; he could hear their murmuring voices now and again.

They'd been going some time, far from safety and the Lightning Tree, when one of them hissed, "Why aren't we just eating the lion? He's little. We could take him."

"Shut up, Bolt," growled Fleet. "We made an agreement."

"And we follow the Great Mother," came Lightning's grave voice. "We're better than lions."

Fearless rolled his eyes in the moonlit darkness. He was tired of hearing other creatures' poor opinion of lions. Why should he be judged by the standards of a lion like Titan? It wasn't fair or just, and—*there!*

Only a few pawsteps ahead, the ground rose up in a tumble of rocks; the hint of a gash of darkest shadow was just visible beyond it. *The secret ravine.* Fearless swallowed the retort he'd been preparing to the cheetahs' bad manners.

"We're here." He kept his growl very low.

"I don't see anything," mewled Bolt.

"That's the point, isn't it?" snapped Fearless. "You'll see it once you're up there. This is the main path down—you can just make it out, where the kopje rises. Near the top you'll see the rocks divide—that's where the path is."

"And the other end?" chirped Bolt. "You said we could trap the herd in an ambush."

"Follow the edge of the ravine southward, and you'll come

to the far entrance. You really can't see the whole valley from up here. It's well hidden, just by the lie of the land."

"Good." Fleet nodded in satisfaction. "The moon is full, but if your ravine is deep, there may not be enough light. Probably we won't hunt until just before dawn is breaking. If the gazelles are here as you promised, we'll bring the cub to the Lightning Tree at sunrise."

It was the unspoken words that made Fearless's throat dry. *What if the gazelles have somehow vanished? What happens to Ruthless then?*

He watched the cheetahs' pale, slender rumps vanish into the darkness. The night closed in around him, its sounds seeming suddenly very loud and unnerving. He jumped as a nighthawk screamed.

Relax, Fearless. This will work. He turned and began to pad back across the grasslands toward the Lightning Tree.

All he had to do was wait.

The sky was paling, a gray dawn that slowly revealed the details of the land: the distant mountains, the gash of a river, the splashes of dark forest, and the lonely, distinctive streaks of acacias. Fearless hadn't slept; he sat on his haunches beneath the Lightning Tree, peering out anxiously across the plain. As Bravelands lightened further, colors began to seep into the landscape: the mountain silhouettes became blue, greenness seeped into forest and tree, and the savannah itself turned pale, ghostly silver.

Dazzling sunlight spilled across the horizon; indistinct shapes moved in the grass. Fearless rose to his paws.

It's them!

The six cheetahs paced toward him, their muzzles drenched in blood. They walked in a loose pointed formation, and in the middle of their group a small tawny shape trotted to keep up.

"Ruthless!" Fearless loped toward the cheetahs.

"You kept your word," mewled Fleet. Turning, he nudged the little cub toward Fearless.

Ruthless looked unharmed, if a little nervous. He sniffed uncertainly at Fearless and came to a halt. "Who are you?"

"I'm a . . . a lion of Titanpride." It stuck in his craw, but it was the only way to convince the cub. Fearless lowered his muzzle. "I rejoined the pride recently. I'm going to take you back to your mother and father."

"Oh!" squeaked Ruthless. "Thanks! The cheetahs were all right, but I miss my mother."

"I expect you do." Fearless nuzzled him gently. "Come on—"

But the cheetahs had gone still, sniffing the air. Bolt gave a low, warning growl.

"There's another lion here!" he snarled furiously.

What? "No, that's not—" Fearless began.

"Yes!" hissed Fleet. "We smell it! I told you, lion—no deal if any other lions showed up!"

"It's a trap!" bleated Lightning, giving short, sharp cries of alarm.

"It isn't, I swear by the Great Mother. My friend Loyal went back to our den! I—"

A great, muscled, tawny shape rose up from the grass at the other side of the tree. The lion was fully maned and badly scarred, and his ear was torn. He paced toward them, muzzle curled in a contemptuous snarl.

"Cunning!" gasped Fearless.

Bolt darted forward before Fearless could even move. He snatched up Ruthless by the scruff of his neck and sprinted back to his friends.

"*Cunning!*" roared Fearless, his frustration erupting into red rage. "You've ruined everything!" *Titan's going to kill my mother and me, and it's his fault!*

"No mangy half-grown prideless lion is going to get the credit for saving Ruthless," snarled Cunning, stalking menacingly forward. "I'll take the cub. Give him to me!"

"Don't, you fool!" bellowed Fearless.

But Cunning ignored him. The huge lion sprang toward the cheetahs, landing with an earth-shaking crunch over Fleet and sinking his jaws into the slender cat's neck.

Maybe he'd expected the rest of the coalition to run; he barely spared them a scornful glance. But he'd clearly misjudged them, Fearless realized: the other five cheetahs gave a united, screeching snarl and flung themselves at the lion.

Fearless saw a moment of shock light the big lion's eyes as he glanced up; then he was buried under a biting, clawing mass of cheetahs. Lithe and fast as snakes, they clung and crawled over his body, ripping and mauling with savage claws and teeth. Cunning gave a bellow of agony, tottering as he tried to rise. A cheetah hung from his throat by its jaws.

Cunning swayed wildly, and the cheetah at his throat lashed its claws at his eyes. Flinching, the lion overbalanced and crashed to the ground, sending up a great cloud of red dust.

It's over, thought Fearless, staring in horror. *He won't get up again.* And he was right: Cunning's paws flailed a few more times, and he gave sharp grunts of pain, but his struggles grew feebler, until at last the great lion went limp.

The cheetahs sprang off his bloodied corpse. Cunning lay lifeless, blood soaking into the earth from a ragged gash in his throat.

Fleet hauled himself to his paws, his face twisted in rage, his neck streaked darkly with his own blood. He shook himself, hissing. Lightning licked carefully at his blood-soaked fur.

"The deal is off," Fleet snarled, as his coalition bleated and hissed their fury around him.

"What? What's happening?" whined Ruthless.

"But that wasn't my fault!" roared Fearless in desperation. "I didn't know Cunning was there!"

"So you say," spat Bolt. He snatched up Ruthless by the scruff and sprinted away with the other five behind him.

"No!" Fearless pounded after them. "No, you can't do this!"

Panic rising hot in his throat, he bounded after the

cheetahs, not even caring when he saw them glance back, slow, and stop. He raced right into the middle of the hostile circle and turned, frantic, finding Fleet's cold amber eyes.

"You can get away now," snarled Fleet. "One chance, lion. *Only kill to survive.* Attack if you like, but we won't be breaking the Code when we kill you."

"Help!" cried Ruthless. "Don't let them take me!"

Fearless panted harshly, his flanks heaving. "Without that cub, I'm dead anyway," he growled bitterly. "I might as well take you all with me."

Bunching his haunches, he opened his jaws and prepared to spring at Fleet's throat.

He hadn't even left the ground when a heavy, muscled body slammed into him. *That's no cheetah!* He gasped as a big, familiar lion rolled him over, knocking him onto his back and pinning him down with huge paws.

"Loyal!" he rasped. "What are you doing?"

"Saving your idiot hide." Drawing back his muzzle and baring his teeth, Loyal turned his head to Fleet. "I'll make sure this youngster keeps the Code," he snarled.

"Let me go—Loyal, *let me go!*"

But Loyal ignored him. Fleet nodded once, then turned and led his coalition at a loping run toward a dense, sprawling woodland of chestnuts, kigelias, and stinkwood trees. Ruthless—the cub who could have saved Fearless's life, and his mother's—vanished into the shadows with them, gripped in Bolt's jaws.

For what seemed like an age, Fearless struggled helplessly. *They're getting away! There's no time!* But the weight and strength of the bigger lion were remorseless; he couldn't shift him.

At last, when he had to accept the cheetahs would be long gone, Fearless gave up and lay limp, panting in despair. Releasing him, Loyal stepped back.

"Loyal! How could you?" Leaping to his paws, Fearless roared in frustration and bared his fangs. "I'll never get Ruthless back now! What if they . . . kill him?"

"They won't," growled Loyal, glaring at him. "You should be thanking me. It was Cunning who messed up your plan— and if I hadn't stayed nearby to keep an eye on you, you'd be dead like him."

Silenced by his friend's pitiless reasoning, Fearless could only stare, sucking breaths into his lungs.

Loyal's gaze softened. "Look, your plan was a good one," he said gruffly. "I see that now. If Cunning hadn't ruined everything, you'd be taking that cub back to Titan and Artful right now."

Fearless blinked slowly, letting his head hang down. "You're right," he panted at last. "You're right. Thank you. I wasn't even thinking straight when I went for the cheetahs. But I didn't know what else to *do.*"

"Don't give up hope." Loyal gave his muzzle a consoling lick. "You have until dusk. Come on, Fearless! You were smart enough to think of your first plan—now think of another. What would your baboon friends do now?"

Fearless stiffened, feeling the tiniest spark of rekindled hope. "The forest. The cheetahs went into the trees."

"And lions may not know the tricks of the forest . . ." said Loyal thoughtfully.

Fearless felt a drop of hope. "But baboons do!"

CHAPTER 21

The Crown Stone stood empty. The Council waited solemnly nearby, but this time, as the troop gathered in the glade, there was little sense of excitement or anticipation. Grub Crownleaf's death had been too awful, thought Thorn: too shocking and too sudden. *His death came so soon after Bark's. It's not right.* And the troop had accepted Bark's death, thinking it had been an honorable one, in defense of the troop.

Not Grub's. His death was cold-blooded murder, and everyone knows it.

He wondered if it was time that they knew the truth about Bark's death too.

But when he glanced at Stinger, the older baboon looked calm and still. There was no hint in his face that he was about to reveal that appalling secret. *He's right,* Thorn told himself reluctantly. *Things are bad enough as it is.*

Besides, Nut had gone, and they'd surely never see him

again. He'd die a lonely death, shunned, in the depths of the forest. Or a flesh-eater would get him.

There were no excited whoops, and if babies yelped or chittered, their mothers shushed them at once. Around him, Thorn heard mutterings of shock, fear, and suspicion. He could see Mud on the other side of the glade; the little baboon hunched miserably next to his mother. Berry, crouched next to Thorn, gave an anxious, mournful hoot as she watched her father. This wasn't just a solemn occasion; it was dark and unhappy.

Beetle shuffled forward. He looked older and more drawn than ever.

"The vote for our new Crownleaf," he said, and cleared his throat. "The vote will take place immediately . . . as tradition demands. . . ." His voice was cracked and hoarse. *He's stunned*, Thorn realized. *He's having trouble saying the traditional words.* "I r-remind the troop that only Highleaf baboons may p-put themselves forward. Any . . . any of you who wish, please speak now, and address Brightforest Troop"—his voice faded— "from the Crown Stone."

For a hideous moment, Thorn thought no baboon was going to step forward. The Highleaves were all glancing at one another, their faces wretched. The glade was hushed except for the whimpers of one tiny baby and the gentle rustling of the leaves in the canopy overhead.

There was movement among the Highleaves, and Thorn saw that Berry was muttering in her father's ear. He shook his head, but she pushed him forward. Stinger looked back, then reluctantly padded forward to stand by the Crown Stone.

"Brightforest Troop," he began, his voice quiet and solemn. "Last time you chose Grub, and he won your trust fairly. I am more saddened than I can say that he never had a chance to achieve his full potential as a leader of baboons."

He paused for a moment, bowing his head. There were a few muffled whimpers of sadness.

Stinger raised his eyes again, but only briefly. "And I know that I could never . . ." He trailed off, as if unsure of himself. But the troop began to hoot.

"Go on, Father," murmured Berry, smiling.

Stinger cleared his throat. "We have suffered great tragedy, but if you can accept it, I wish to put myself forward once again to serve you all."

Thorn felt his heart soar. It wouldn't be right to jump up and down and whoop, but despite the troubled atmosphere, he wanted to. He had to clench his paws to restrain himself. *Stinger would be a wonderful leader; I know that even more now! He's been acting like a leader already—organizing the patrols and the work parties, defending our territory, reassuring all of us.*

Mud whispered to Thorn, "He'd be a great leader."

"Yes," said Thorn.

"We face perhaps our greatest challenge as a troop." Stinger, urged by some of the other baboons, had climbed up onto the Crown Stone and was addressing the troop in an atmosphere of quiet respect. "Bark's death was one of honor, protecting her troop; but Grub's was a deliberate act of malice. The troop needs a strong leader, a determined leader: one who is cunning and intelligent, too. Brightforest Troop, I want to be that leader for you. With your support, with your votes, I will protect our family from all its enemies, both known and unknown." His expression darkened. "No traitor, no murderer should ever gain a foothold in our family again. I will make sure it never, ever happens. So Brightforest Troop *will* be safe; but more than that, it will be *great*. I will face our challenges, I will lead us to a new and better home, and I will strike fear into the hearts of our enemies."

Stinger paused for a few heartbeats, letting his words sink in. Then his voice softened.

"I promised you once before that I would raise this troop to greatness; I respected your decision when you selected another. But now I make that vow to you again." Taking a deep breath, he raised his cry to a stirring crescendo. "Brightforest Troop: let me lead you to a bright and happy future!"

The baboons erupted in whoops, stamping and slapping the ground. The whole glade rang with their cries of relief and delight.

"Stinger! Stinger! Let Stinger rule!"

Thorn's heart was in his mouth. He raised himself up onto his hind paws to look around; surely no other Highleaf could compete with such a speech! *Please, please let Stinger be chosen.*

"Are there any other candidates?" Beetle's tremulous, awkward question sounded out of place among all the whoops of approval.

The old baboon looked almost relieved when no one else came forward—not even the other baboons who had offered themselves last time. Every face was focused on Stinger, and every face shone with admiration.

No one wants to take on such a dangerous position, Thorn realized, *but it isn't just that. They genuinely love him! They want him as Crownleaf!*

Beetle was padding hesitantly forward, still scanning the troop. Even the old baboon looked brighter now. "This is unprecedented!" he declared as the noise of the glade died down. "However, if there are no further candidates, then there is no need to vote. I declare that Seed 'Stinger' Highleaf is—by acclamation—our new Crownleaf!"

In the roaring, whooping clamor that met his announcement, Thorn rushed to Berry. He was about to throw his arms around her, but stopped himself short before he made such a terrible breach of the rules.

Glancing around to make sure no baboon was looking, Thorn reached out his paw to squeeze hers. "I'll look out for him," he whispered urgently. "Nothing will happen to your father on my watch—I promise. But the troop needs him more than ever!"

Slowly, she nodded. "I know he's the right one to lead us," she said, returning the pressure on his paw.

"If anyone can guide the troop through these tough times," he said, "it's your father."

She gazed into his eyes, smiling. *I wish we could stay here like this forever,* he thought wistfully.

He was so wrapped up in Stinger's triumph and the stolen moment with Berry, it took him some time to realize that the tone of the whoops and shrieks had changed. Now the baboons sounded afraid; they were calling the alarm! Chittering, screeching angrily, the troop was retreating higher into the trees. Thorn frowned in confusion and glanced behind him.

Two lions were padding through the forest toward the glade. One of them was instantly recognizable as his friend, but the other, an older maned lion, was a stranger. Thorn blinked. *What's Fearless doing here?*

It was Stinger who calmed the troop, rearing up on his hind legs on the Crown Stone and crying out for quiet. "Brightforest Troop! Don't be scared! This is our friend Fearless—you all know he means us no harm! Grub was wise in many ways, but he was wrong to send the Cub of the Stars away." He nodded to Fearless, who dipped his head in response. "If this other lion Crookedtail is Fearless's friend, he is also ours!"

Warily, the baboons began to descend from the trees, but Stinger strode confidently forward to greet Fearless. It was clear, Thorn realized as the troop began to gather around the two lions, just how much they all trusted Stinger. Happiness swelled in his heart. *Things will be better now.*

The older lion was impressively huge, his gold-streaked mane fully grown. Thorn saw now why Stinger had called him Crookedtail—it was bent like a broken branch. He was staring around at the troop as if he was stunned. That was to be expected, thought Thorn with a grin—but Fearless too looked anxious and unhappy. As Thorn pushed past the other baboons, he saw Mud squeezing through from his side of the glade toward Fearless. Mud was closer than Thorn, but he was still limping from his leg injury, and both of them reached their old friend at the same moment. Together the two young baboons hugged the lion's chest in delight, and he bent his head to nuzzle them.

"Fearless, what are you doing here?" asked Thorn, scratching his neck fondly. "Who's Crookedtail?"

"He's my friend—his name's Loyal. I'll tell you everything," rumbled Fearless. "I promise I will. But there's no time. I need to ask you something, both of you!"

"What?" Thorn swapped an apprehensive glance with Mud. "Ask us anything!"

"Thank you, friends." Fearless gave a shaky sigh of relief. "Because without your help, my mother and I are going to die."

The canopy of the strange woodland was different from Tall Trees, but many of the trees themselves were familiar to Thorn and Mud: the tangled, twisted trunks of strangler figs, the ridged bark of jackalberry trees, the dark leaves and vivid red scars of the stinkwoods. Butterflies darted and fluttered around the two baboons as they crept nimbly and silently through branches and swathes of creepers, keen eyes scanning the forest floor below.

"It's not a very big forest," whispered Mud. "The cheetahs shouldn't be hard to find."

"No," agreed Thorn dryly. "Finding them definitely won't be the hard part."

"Let's stay high, on the thinnest branches," murmured

Mud. "Cheetahs can climb, but they won't risk breaking these and falling."

"I hate the idea that they're somewhere below us," admitted Thorn, peering down through the foliage. "It's making me nervous."

"But we have to help Fearless."

"Of course we do." Thorn tensed his muscles to leap for the next thick yellow-brown branch. "So let's—*aiiiee!*"

The branch flopped down, to dangle and glare at them with opaque, calculating eyes. Mid-spring, Thorn was still off balance. He felt Mud grab his fur and yank him back, just as the thing lunged.

"Snake!" yelped Mud.

Now that he was out of its reach, Thorn parted the dark green stinkwood leaves and peered at the undulating body. The snake was a massive thing, covered in smooth scales patterned in yellow and brown, its thick body half coiled around another branch above them. "Get back, Mud!" he whispered urgently. "Watch its fangs!"

Mud shivered behind him. "It's not venomous, it's a python! They grab you and squeeze you to death—Mother told me about them. Stay away from its tail too!" Nervously he glanced around him. "Where's the rest of it?"

Thorn let his eyes follow the snake's length. It twisted twice around a branch, but its tail was farther away still, wound around the trunk of a stinkwood. The sight of those scaly, thickly muscled loops made Thorn feel sick. *It nearly grabbed me!* "Up there, Mud." Shuddering, he gestured higher up into the canopy. "It was lying in wait. It tried to ambush us!"

The python's body rippled horribly, and it flickered out its forked tongue, letting it quiver in the air. Its head swayed closer to the two friends.

"It's sniffing for us," whispered Mud. "Don't let it get its coils around you!"

The snake gave an angry, sibilant exclamation in Sand-tongue, then slithered forward. It paused, flickering its tongue again.

"Go!" Mud shoved Thorn, who jumped up onto a higher branch, then yanked Mud up behind him just as the python struck. Its jaws gaped wider than Thorn would have believed possible, and he caught a glimpse inside: moist pink flesh, ser-rated teeth made to grab and hold, *and not just one row of them.* They missed Mud's weak leg by a small beetle-length.

The snake cursed again in rasping Sandtongue.

"Let's get out of here," panted Thorn. He sprinted across the branches and into the next tree, glancing back to make sure Mud was behind him. His friend was wide-eyed with fear, but he was leaping away from the snake as fast as his lame leg would allow him. Thorn paused to let him catch up, his heart in his mouth.

"I hope all that racket didn't alert the cheetahs," muttered Thorn as Mud landed beside him and hunkered down.

"I'm sorry, Thorn," growled Mud, crouching beside him. "I'm no use on this kind of mission. It's like the Crocodile River all over again—I'm holding you back."

"Rubbish!" grunted Thorn. "I need your help. If it hadn't

been for you I'd have been busy dodging that snake's teeth while it snuck its entire body around me! *Hey.*" He pointed at the ground far below and dropped his voice to a barely audible whisper. "Look, there!"

Mud peered over his shoulder. In a small, light-patched clearing, a cheetah sat on its haunches, still and alert; from high above, its spotted hide blended into the dappling of sunspots. Only the flicking of its bushy-tipped tail had given it away.

"It's keeping lookout," whispered Mud. "Ruthless must be here."

"I don't know," murmured Thorn. "Look, there are the other cheetahs, beside the bushes." The sleek cats lounged in a patch of sunlight, blinking and yawning and licking their fur. "But I can't see the cub. What do we do now?"

"We should do just what we did when we stole those eggs," said Mud, placing a paw on Thorn's shoulder. "Be patient. Keep watch."

Nodding, Thorn grinned at him. He made himself settle back against the ridged trunk of the jackalberry.

We can't wait as long as we did then, though, Thorn thought. *Fearless hasn't got forever.*

After a while, though, it began to feel like forever. The cheetahs stretched and sprawled; they groomed one another and exchanged bored chatter.

"When are we going to hunt again, Fleet?"

"Don't know. Before sunset."

"Quiet in here, isn't it?"

"Nice and quiet, Bolt. No lions." A chittering laugh. "Well, except for . . . you know."

Thorn felt a hot impatience trickling through his blood. *We can't let Fearless down! Where is that cub?*

"Maybe we should take a chance," he whispered to Mud when he could bear the waiting no longer. "Maybe we should risk climbing down—"

One of the cheetahs stood up and padded languidly over to the tangled, knotted trunk of a strangler fig that stood in the middle of the clearing. The fig had wound its vines around some older tree, choking it to death before establishing itself permanently in its place; now its lower trunk was a twisted network of thick, solid, exposed roots. Fearless narrowed his eyes, studying the cheetah; it was glancing to its left and right, then peering cautiously over its shoulder.

But it never thought to glance skyward.

The cheetah rose onto its hind paws, dug its claws into the wood, and stretched up to peer into a shadowy gap between two thick, woody root-tendrils. Then it backed and hopped down, yawned, and resumed its place in the clearing.

There's something hidden in there. . . .

Thorn and Mud exchanged an excited glance. Together they made their way through the treetops, clambering as quietly as they could from branch to branch. The strangler fig might have grown up in the middle of a clearing, but its crown still tangled with the rest of the woodland canopy; it was easy enough to leap into its topmost branches.

Cautious and silent, the two baboons eased themselves

as far down the twisted trunk as they dared. A few dangling creepers of new roots obscured their view; Mud parted them with his clever fingers and they paused, ears straining. That was when Thorn heard a faint, unhappy whimper from the heart of the tree. It could only be one thing.

We've found Ruthless!

CHAPTER 22

"He's right there, inside the strangler fig tree!" Thorn's eyes glowed with excitement. "We could almost have touched him!" His face fell. "There are six cheetahs guarding him, though."

"Thank you, Thorn!" Fearless felt his hopes rising once more. The two lions and the young baboons stood at the forest's edge, upwind of any creatures within it; tantalizingly, Fearless could make out the earthy scent of the cheetahs, drifting from among the mossy trees. He licked his jaws. "Now we know where Ruthless is." Fearless glanced questioningly at Loyal, hoping the older lion would have the solution that eluded him. "So how do we get him out?"

Loyal huffed thoughtfully. "Cheetahs are fierce fighters and good runners. Even a lion can't outpace them." He sounded a little sulky about that. "A head-on attack won't do it."

"Hmm." Fearless growled softly. "If Loyal and I can keep

the cheetahs busy, maybe you two baboons could grab the cub? Thorn and Mud, what do you think?"

Mud drew back his lips, looking alarmed. "I don't know, Fearless."

"Ruthless doesn't know who we are," pointed out Thorn. "He might struggle. And he might bite. He may be a little lion, but his teeth will be sharp."

Fearless thought hard. "Just mention his father's name—tell him you've been sent by Titan of Titanpride."

"You know, it's not a bad plan," murmured Loyal. "The cheetahs really didn't like me being at that meeting—remember, Fearless? They were worried they'd been caught in a lion trap. Maybe we can make them think that's what's happening. If we approach the fig tree from two directions, they might think it's a sizable ambush."

Thorn looked nervous. "That sounds dangerous."

"Of course it is." Fearless licked his friend's head gently. "But it's our best chance."

"You two will have to be quick," Loyal warned the baboons.

"Yes. If the cheetahs think all of Titanpride has come—and I hope they do—they might decide to make a run for it with Ruthless." Fearless grunted. "We'd never catch up with them if that happened."

"All right." Thorn raised his brows questioningly at Mud, who nodded reluctantly. "We'll be ready. And we'll be fast. Right, Mud?"

"Yes." Mud nodded more enthusiastically. "Really, *really* fast."

"Will you be all right on your bad leg?" asked Thorn. "Are you sure you can do this?"

"I'll be fine." Mud seemed to draw himself up, looking more determined. "Don't even think of leaving me behind!"

Fearless grinned at all three of his friends. "Then—let's go!"

He and Loyal slunk toward the edge of the forest and crept in through the undergrowth, leaving the baboons to clamber high up into the trees. Fearless could feel his nervous heartbeat in his throat. *This is my last chance to save my mother.*

The scents that surrounded him were multiple, rich, and chaotic: lichen, rotting leaves, ant nests and beetles, damp moss, the dung of bushbuck and dik-dik and buffalo. He could make out the cheetahs' strong odor, but it was confused with so many others. *With luck, my own scent will be confusing too. I hope they mistake the two of us for a whole pride of lions.*

Above him, moving shadows caught his eye; he glanced up to see Thorn and Mud crouched in the branches, signaling frantically with their paws. They both peeled back their muzzles and gestured toward a dense patch of lichen-draped trees.

That must be where Ruthless is hidden.

Nodding silently to Loyal, he hauled himself over a rotting log and crept closer. Now he could make out a clearing beyond the hanging moss. Halting with one paw raised, staying absolutely still, he focused his vision on the dance of sunlight and shadow through the trees. In moments he made out the spotted coats of the cheetahs, only a few loping strides away.

Now he could hear their low, chirruping voices. He couldn't

make out the words, but they sounded tense, argumentative, and they kept glancing edgily around at the undergrowth. *Have they smelled us already?*

Fearless craned his head forward, anxious to see without being seen. Beyond a stinkwood tree, its dark scaly bark scored with red gashes, he could make out the strangler fig: the tangled knot of wood was unmistakable. Though the whole tree was draped in gray-green tendrils, Fearless could clearly see those exposed, intertwined roots that formed its lower trunk. *It's clever of the cheetahs. A perfect trap to hold a small lion.*

Two cheetahs got suddenly to their paws, sniffing the air, wrinkling their muzzles.

Come on, Thorn and Mud. You need to get closer to Ruthless before they notice us!

With relief, he spotted two brown furry shapes, clambering carefully down through the fig's branches under cover of its drooping vines. Lower and lower they climbed. . . . They were almost at the knot of thick roots. . . .

Now!

Fearless threw back his head and gave the loudest roar he could muster, the echo resounding through the trees. Its effect was instantaneous: a flock of birds erupted, jabbering, from the canopy, and the cheetahs all leaped to their paws, half crouched, heads low, and muzzles peeled back in defensive snarls. But as Fleet took a single pace in Fearless's direction, another roar rang out from the opposite side of the trees. Bolt and Lightning spun around.

"Titanpride!" hissed Fleet.

The cheetah leader had courage, certainly. Instead of escaping, Fleet bolted straight toward him, with Lightning and another cheetah hard on his heels; Bolt led the others in the opposite direction, charging at Loyal.

Fearless twisted and ran from them, darting and zigzagging through the bushes and over fallen logs. He could hear the cheetahs pursuing him, their paws light and swift and nimble. *I can't outrun them*, he thought grimly. *But I can give Thorn and Mud enough time to grab Ruthless.*

He coiled his haunches and sprang over a half-toppled stinkwood. *That'll slow them down a bit.* From farther away through the trees, he heard Loyal's mocking roar as he taunted his own pursuers. But the cheetahs behind Fearless were persistent; he heard the light drumming of their paws echoing in the undergrowth.

"You!" bleated Fleet, behind him and far too close. "Didn't learn your lesson, did you?"

Fearless didn't waste his breath on an answer. He was maneuvering his convoluted way back toward the strangler fig, keeping half his attention on it, desperate to see what was happening. Blurred at the edge of his vision, he could see the two baboons; Thorn's slightly bigger shape was hanging on the tree's lower vines, reaching with one long arm into a gap between the intertwined roots. Moments later he caught another glimpse: Thorn was hauling out a pale, tawny creature. It hung docilely in the baboon's grasp.

"Loyal!" Fearless barked as his friend's form flashed by, close to him. "We've done it! Let's get out of here!"

Fleet, still racing behind him, mewled with rage. "What have you done? What?" His paws slithered and slowed in the leaf litter. "*No!* Bolt, Lightning, Rapid! They've *taken the cub!*"

Fearless, too, skidded to a halt, panting hard. The cheetahs had abandoned their pursuit and were sprinting through the undergrowth, back toward the strangler fig.

Keep going, he told himself, as he turned and ran again. *I don't think I should wait to find out the cheetahs' reaction. . . .*

Sure enough, as he pounded through the mossy vegetation and barged through thick hanging creepers, he could hear their distant yelps and snarls of fury. For a brief, horrible moment he wondered if he was running in circles and would never find his way out. But finally, as he broke out of green shadows into the dazzling glare of the savannah, he allowed himself a grunt of triumph.

Loyal was already out of the trees, bounding to meet Fearless. "Where are they? Where are the baboons?"

"Here!" shouted two voices, as branches shook above the lions' heads.

Fearless stepped back, peering up into the trees. "Hurry up! The cheetahs might still come after us!"

Thorn and Mud shinned quickly down their chestnut trunk, Thorn still gripping Ruthless under one arm. *Like Stinger did with me!* thought Fearless with a pang of memory. When the baboons were close to the ground, the little cub wriggled abruptly free and sprang the rest of the way, landing with a squeaky grunt.

He flung himself with mews of delight at Fearless and Loyal, scampering around their paws. Fearless crouched to nuzzle the little cub. "Did my father send you?" yelped Ruthless. "That's what the monkey told me!"

"Hey," Thorn yelled after him, "less of the 'monkey.'"

Loyal licked the cub's back. "This was all Fearless's idea, little one. He organized this rescue mission himself!"

Fearless felt almost embarrassed at the pride in the older lion's voice. "With help from my friends here," he pointed out.

"Well, I'll pay you all back one day," mewled Ruthless. "When I'm big, I won't forget this!"

A crackling of leaves and thin branches made Fearless and Loyal turn with bared fangs toward the forest. Shadows flickered quickly in the undergrowth, and the sound of running paws drew closer with alarming speed. The cheetahs broke out of the trees, their streaked faces furious.

"That cub is ours!" snarled Fleet. Ruthless flinched and yelped, scuttling back toward Fearless's paws.

Fearless leaped to defend him, crashing his rump into the cheetah's flank and flinging Fleet into a tumbling roll.

The ease of it sent a thrill of victory surging through Fearless's veins. His blood raced inside him, hot and angry, and suddenly he was filled with a familiar, violent energy. Opening his jaws wide, he stood over Fleet's winded body and bellowed a great roar.

"You got what you wanted," he snarled, as his slaver

dripped onto the cheetah's enraged face. "The gazelle herd in the ravine will keep you fed for seasons! Ruthless is ours now—and *no creature* steals from a lion!"

Between his splayed paws, the agile cheetah got his breath back and twisted. Fearless wasn't expecting more resistance, and his moment of surprise gave Fleet a chance to wriggle to his paws. The swift cat launched himself at Fearless.

With a holler of fury, Fearless met the cheetah in midair, slamming into him again. Both cats dropped to the ground and they rolled over in the dirt, clawing and kicking. Fearless glimpsed the horrified faces of the baboons; he saw Loyal snarling, blocking the other cheetahs as they tried to run to Fleet's aid.

Fleet squirmed, then rolled on top of Fearless, jaws snapping for his throat. Fearless tucked his hind legs between them and kicked hard, scrabbling with his claws at Fleet's belly. One more violent kick and Fleet was dislodged, hitting the ground hard. Fearless sprang up, snarling, and sank his teeth into the stunned cheetah's shoulder. Blood spurted warm onto his tongue and fangs, and his nostrils flared at the scent of it. But the enticing smell that filled his head wasn't all blood: it was fear, too. Fleet was shuddering with terror.

Fearless froze. He glared down at the skinny creature in his jaws, then shook him once and let him fall. Fleet crawled out of reach, shivering and whimpering.

"The cub's yours," he gasped. "You win, lion."

Fearless grunted a triumphant roar as he watched Fleet

limp away with the rest of his coalition, their tails hanging
low in defeat.

He was still glaring after the cheetahs when Thorn and
Mud hurtled to his side, stroking his fur and hooting their
approval.

"You did it!" cried Mud.

"You were amazing!" whooped Thorn.

"You were. Thank you, Fearless." The little rescued cub
trotted over almost shyly. Then he puffed out his chest. "I'm
going to fight cheetahs when I'm big!"

"I wouldn't make a habit of it." Loyal laughed. Shaking his
mane, he turned to Fearless and licked his blood-spattered
ear. Fearless heard the low rumble of the lion's voice.

"Your father would be proud of you, Fearless Gallantpride."

The sun was low in the twilit sky as Fearless strode across
the grassland, the little cub trotting at his side. Loyal had
left them before there was a chance of running into Titan;
Fearless missed his reassuring company, but he was pleasantly
surprised at how confident he felt escorting Ruthless on his
own. *I can protect him. I've proved that.*

Ruthless's eyes were drooping with tiredness, but when
Titanpride came into view, sprawling together in the evening
glow, he perked up immediately and gave a squeak of happiness.

Hearing the sound, Artful rose up on her forepaws, ears
pricked. Titan too raised his great black-maned head. In an

instant they were both on their paws along with the whole pride, loping across the plain toward Fearless and the cub.

"Ruthless!" growled Artful. She bounded almost on top of him, licking him frantically. "Are you hurt? My cub, my cub!"

Pitched sideways by the ferocity of her caresses, Ruthless rolled onto his back, mewling happily. "I'm fine, Mother! Fearless rescued me!"

Fearless glanced beyond her; he could see Valor murmuring to Swift. *She's telling her that I came back, that I brought Ruthless. That we're all safe.* A wave of pure relief flooded through him, and he felt suddenly shattered with exhaustion.

And then a shadow blocked his view of his mother and sister. Fearless repressed a shiver and looked up. Titan stood before him, as huge and menacing as ever. The massive lion peeled his muzzle back from his fangs.

Fearless swallowed hard and bared his own. "I kept my oath," he growled, making himself hold Titan's baleful gaze. "Now you must let my mother live."

"And you," spat Titan, glowering. "Unfortunately. I, Titan, am no oathbreaker." The huge lion's eyes glinted with hatred. "But I do not trust you, Fearless. I don't want you out of my sight, plotting and scheming. So, yes, I will spare you and your mother—but only if you *both* stay with Titanpride."

"What?" Fearless's hackles sprang up. "This wasn't part of the deal—"

He hesitated. Titan's gaze was steady and malevolent on his, but beyond him, Valor stood, her tail twitching. She was blinking at Fearless, her expression filled with warning. *Be careful, Swiftbrother! Be sensible!* He could almost hear her say it.

Turning back to Titan, he licked his jaws, then gave a slow nod. "Very well. We'll stay with Titanpride. Both of us."

Valor closed her eyes briefly, looking relieved. Then she murmured something to Swift, and the old lioness's scarred face lit up with anxious happiness.

"Fearless is staying? Wow!" Ruthless, not looking at all sleepy now, bounded clumsily to his father. "That's great. He's the bravest lion I've ever met!"

The shudder of disgust that crossed Titan's face was worth all the effort of retrieving his cub, Fearless decided with stifled amusement. The big lion swatted Ruthless, only half playfully, and he rolled over with a squeak of delight. Slapping back at his father with his little paws, he rolled around happily as Titan glowered at Fearless.

"I'll be watching you, son of Gallant." The low snarl was the most menacing Fearless had ever heard.

Fearless didn't answer his new leader, but simply inclined his head in as small a motion as he thought he could get away with. Then, turning away, he padded to join Valor and Swift. They greeted him with joyful nuzzles, growls, and licks, and at last they all lay down together, flanks pressed close, basking in the last of the light.

"We were so worried for you," murmured Swift. "My fearless son."

"Not quite fearless," he said wryly, butting her neck. "I had some bad moments. I was *very* scared, actually."

"And you are all the braver for that," she said quietly. "I'm grateful for what you did for me, my Swiftcub. But I wish Titan hadn't made you stay. He means you harm."

"Yes," agreed Valor darkly. "He may be happy to have his cub back, but he'll see your success as a challenge, Fearless. Don't forget that. Be careful."

"Of course." He licked them both with long strokes of his tongue. "I know what Titan thinks of me. But what really matters is that I'm back with you. I missed you both so much."

Contentedly, he nestled closer to his mother and sister. *Maybe—I think—I'm starting to earn my name.*

And one day, he knew, he would keep that other oath, the one he had made as a reckless, lonely, frightened cub.

I will defeat Titan.

I will take back my father's pride.

CHAPTER 23

"I tell you all: these two are very brave, imaginative, and special baboons!"

Stinger addressed Brightforest Troop from the Crown Stone, his voice warm yet commanding. He gestured at Thorn and Mud with one paw, and although the baboons of Brightforest Troop shot admiring glances toward them, they also gazed at Stinger, entranced.

Thorn was rather glad he didn't have the troop's exclusive attention. He was almost embarrassed at the fuss his Crownleaf had lavished on them since their return. Stinger had been so delighted at their tales of the adventure with Fearless and Loyal, he had insisted the two young baboons come to the Council Glade and relate the story to the whole troop.

The other baboons had listened in fascination, gasping and

whooping at some points, and although it had felt awkward telling the tale to such a crowd, Thorn couldn't help being pleased, too. It *was* a good story, he decided with an inward glow. He was especially happy for Mud, who looked thrilled to be the center of attention for once. Thorn noticed with quiet delight that Mud's mother, the Starleaf, looked as if she might burst with pride.

Stinger was still making his speech, and it was clear that the gathered baboons hadn't tired of his voice yet. *A big change from Grub's day*, thought Thorn a little guiltily.

"Thorn Middleleaf and Mud Lowleaf have set a fine example for the troop's future with their resourcefulness and their courage," Stinger declared. "They have spread Brightforest Troop's name and reputation far across Bravelands!"

As he finished with a small bow, the troop yelled and beat the ground. Thorn blinked and dipped his head.

"Hooray for Stinger Crownleaf, leader of baboons!"

"Long life to Thorn Middleleaf and Mud Lowleaf!"

"Bright-for-est! Bright-for-est!"

Berry scampered to his side, her dark eyes brimming with pride. "I loved your story, and, well, I'm glad you came home safe."

"Thank you," Thorn stammered, delighted and embarrassed at the same time.

Berry lowered her voice to a whisper. "Will you meet me in the ravine? I want to hear more about it. I want you to tell the story just for me."

Happiness tingled through him. "Of course. I can't wait!"

"I'll see you soon." With a smile, Berry slipped away to congratulate her father.

Hope swelled in Thorn's heart. Stinger Crownleaf would make the rules now, and Stinger looked beyond the forest, beyond all the old traditions. *He won't be obsessed with the tale of Sunrise and Moonlight*, thought Thorn. *One day, he might allow a real pairing between Berry and me!*

All the same, for the moment Thorn knew he must take the long path to the ravine; there was no point in revealing his relationship with Berry now, when they were so close to a real future together. He made his way in a long, looping route around the forest, heading for his well-used path across the grassland. Just for the fun of it, he snatched at twigs and playfully batted lichen fronds as he ran.

Despite his high and happy mood, something caught his eye as he passed a cluster of date palms. There was a clump of ferns at their base, but something was sticking out of them, something big and solid. He'd almost tripped on it in his heedless haste. Thorn frowned curiously and crouched to tug it out. Its surface was a mottled yellow, scored with three deep claw scars.

The Starleaf's hollow branch. One of the flat stones was missing; Thorn sucked his teeth. *I hope that isn't lost for good. It won't be any use without its stopper.*

Lifting the branch, he upended it; he almost gave a yelp of shock when a cluster of scorpions tumbled out, legs and pincers tangled.

But they were dead; dried up and lifeless. The thump of relief in his chest was quickly followed by confusion. *I thought Stinger wanted them fresh?*

Thorn peered down at the scattered scorpion remains. Stinger ate the bodies and left the tails. But it was only the tails that were missing from these; the rest of the bodies were intact.

Maybe Stinger had pulled off the tails and left them in the log. He shook the branch again, hard. But it was quite empty.

Thorn went absolutely still. Suddenly he felt incapable of moving.

The tails were poisonous.

The venom was in the tails.

The tails are missing.

Thorn's paws felt cold and numb, as if they didn't belong to him; the hollow branch tumbled from his grip into the fern clump. A cold horror spread through his limbs and up his spine.

Grub was poisoned. Could someone have found these scorpions and used their venom?

No, it's not possible. It isn't. I gave these to Stinger; he wouldn't have just left them lying around.

But then why would the tails be missing? Unless Stinger himself . . .

No. Not Stinger, no way.

He wouldn't do such a thing.

Thorn couldn't move, could barely breathe.

Except . . . it's the only explanation that makes sense.

Stinger was his champion, his mentor, his friend. He was going to be the finest leader Brightforest Troop had ever had, Thorn knew it. *How can he possibly be a murderer?*

And yet here were the tailless scorpions. Scorpions that Thorn had caught for Stinger, in the container Thorn had given him.

Thorn felt sick: Nut had been exiled from the troop for the killing. He, Thorn, had been part of that; he'd helped convince the troop to drive him away.

This can't be true.

Yet deep in his numb heart, Thorn knew it was.

Clenching his jaws, he snatched up one of the tailless scorpion corpses. *If I think too long about this, I won't do it. I need to do it now.*

Turning, he bounded back through the forest, the scorpion gripped so tightly in his paw its pincers hurt the soft flesh of his palm. Thorn didn't care. He ran and searched until he found Stinger, crouched on his haunches against a tree as he gave orders to a group of Highleaves.

The young Highleaves were listening intently to their Crownleaf, their expressions full of adoring respect. Thorn felt his brow knotting in a frown. Stinger hadn't even wanted to be Crownleaf, had he? It was Berry who pushed him forward. And Stinger had been the one who refused to condemn Nut without a vote. Why do that, if he himself had been the killer?

When Stinger saw Thorn's expression, he dismissed the other Highleaves. They all nodded and scampered away to fulfill their tasks, leaving their leader alone in the clearing.

Thorn pushed forward through the bushes. He halted, limbs trembling, in front of his Crownleaf.

"What is it, Thorn?" Stinger asked.

Thorn's burning anger cooled a fraction. Could it be that he was wrong?

He opened his hand, showing Stinger what was inside. "I found all of these," he said coldly.

Stinger gazed down at the brittle corpse for a long moment. Then he raised his head to study Thorn. "And?" he asked.

And just from the passionless stare, Thorn knew his suspicions were correct.

"You killed Grub Crownleaf," he said.

Stinger's eyes remained fixed on him. "Yes, Thorn, I did."

For a moment, Thorn had no idea how to respond. What hurt most—worse than any scorpion sting—was his master's betrayal.

"You broke the Code," said Thorn. "And you got me to help you! You made me fetch the poison!"

Stinger was still watching him, absolutely calm. He gave the tiniest shrug.

"The only surprise," Stinger said, "is that it took you so long to figure it out."

A sudden, appalling thought made Thorn's head reel, and he almost staggered. "Did you kill Bark Crownleaf? *Did you kill her too?*"

Stinger picked at one of his fangs with a claw. He licked the notch on his lip. His gaze lingered on Thorn. "I did what I had to do."

Thorn stared. He felt as if something inside his rib cage had broken; he didn't have breath to answer.

"Oh, Thorn Middleleaf." Stinger shook his head ruefully. "Do you see how happy the troop is now? A strong, intelligent leader is good for everyone—but sometimes it takes baboons a little while to realize who that leader should be. Sometimes they make a mistake in their choice, and they have to be guided to make the right decision."

"Guided." Thorn's voice was a barely audible rasp.

"Look at what I will do for Brightforest Troop!" Stinger urged him, his eyes bright and eager. "We will find new and better territory, abundant food and drink. Our strength and influence will expand! You see, don't you, Thorn? Everything I have done, everything I might do in the future: it has all been for the good of Brightforest Troop."

"No. You did it for yourself!"

"For instance: your friend Fearless," Stinger continued, as if Thorn hadn't spoken. "I brought him into the troop, didn't I? I rescued him and made him one of us, and that gave us a lion on our side. Do you think any other baboon would be so innovative, so imaginative, so farsighted?" Cocking his head closer to Thorn, he licked his fangs carefully and murmured, "Do you see how far I will go in my mission to protect Brightforest?"

A shudder ran from the crown of Thorn's head to the tip of his paws. *I know what he's saying.* His voice shook as he muttered, "Y-yes."

"Good," said Stinger cheerfully. "Now, this hasn't been the

most pleasant conversation we've ever had, so let's forget it happened, you and I." Dropping forward onto all fours, he began to pad away, but he twisted to look at Thorn again. "No other baboon needs to know, do they? Not Mud. And *especially* not Berry."

The look in Stinger's eyes as he said his daughter's name turned Thorn's blood cold. For a long time after Stinger vanished into the trees, he stayed motionless, chilled to the bone.

He would kill me if he had to. He's made that clear. Thorn suddenly remembered where he was supposed to be. *Berry.* Shaking himself fiercely, he ran on paws he could barely trust toward the grassland and the ravine, not bothering to take the long way around.

Berry has a right to know! She should be told what her father's really like. Thorn's heart shrank inside him, and his paws faltered. Berry was honest and principled. *She wouldn't stay quiet about this, she'd confront him.* And what would Stinger do then?

Everything in him rebelled at the idea of lying to Berry.

But I'm going to have to. She can't know.

Berry was waiting patiently for him beneath their favorite shelf of rock, the one that overlooked the gazelles' main grazing patch. Above her, the great river of stars glittered in the black night; it was as beautiful as ever, but the moon was no longer full: it was shrinking as if a great python were opening its jaws and swallowing it.

"Thorn!" Berry smiled up at him. "What took you so long? I was starting to think you'd gone off on another cheetah adventure."

He found he couldn't smile back, and the words he wanted to say got caught in his throat. Berry frowned.

"What's wrong, Thorn?"

Tilting his head back, Thorn stared up at the glittering sky. It hurt too much to look at Berry's gentle, concerned face.

He realized then what he had to do. *She won't ever be safe while I have Stinger's secret.*

"I . . . Berry, I think maybe we . . . we shouldn't meet up so often."

"What?" Her smile lingered for long moments; then it faded to a look of hurt that was almost unbearable.

Thorn swallowed. He had no choice but to go on. "We're different ranks," he said; the dryness of his throat made his words sound harsh, but he couldn't help it. "I'm a Middleleaf, and you're a Highleaf. We ought to respect the rules. That's what Sunrise and Moonlight teach us."

Her expression tore at his heart. "I—Thorn, I don't care about that stupid legend! I thought you didn't either!"

"Well, I . . . I do now."

There was a terrible, endless silence. Then Berry sprang to her paws.

"This isn't you I'm talking to, Thorn. It can't be!" Her voice cracked. "Is that all you have to say?"

Thorn couldn't look at her. "It is," he mumbled.

Berry took a deep breath. "Look for me again when you've found the Thorn I remember. I don't want to know this one!"

Thorn watched her go, running and leaping up the narrow rocky path. Every sinew of him ached to run after her, to shout her name and call her back, but he clenched his fists and his jaws until she had vanished over the lip of the ravine. She was running from him so fast, it didn't take long.

Misery swamped him, and he slumped onto his haunches.

And what do you do now, Thorn Middleleaf?

Now?

Well, he had to follow and obey Stinger Crownleaf, even knowing what he knew; he must pretend to admire and respect him. He had to keep Berry and Mud safe and happy, while he lied and lied until they both turned away from him in disgust. He had to keep the most terrible secret he had ever known, letting it eat away at his aching heart.

I can't do it. I can't do this on my own. I need help.

And he knew the only place he could find it.

Tomorrow, the Great Gathering took place at the beautiful, peaceful watering hole. Tomorrow, any creature of the Bravelands, however desperate, could ask for help.

I have to go to Great Mother.

CHAPTER 24

All was quiet on the shores of the silver lake; a waning moon cast its light in a narrow beam across the rippling waters. Nearby in the darkness, as crickets and frogs chirped and croaked, the elephant herd slumbered. Something small rustled in the trees; a rat, thought Sky, or maybe a hare. But she mustn't let the night sounds distract her. Taking a deep breath, she closed her eyes.

Great Mother was right: this gets easier the more I practice. The killer's face is clearer every time. She touched the baboon skull once again, delicately, with the tip of her trunk.

The silver water and the moonlight on the trees blurred together into a pale haze. That face was forming in her vision again; brown-furred and long snouted, its jaws open to display long yellow fangs. Sky squeezed her eyes tighter, concentrating, trying to see it properly.

And there it was! Suddenly, the image was so clear she could make out each gray and brown tuft of hair surrounding its face. She could see its long black snout and the notch of an old wound slashed above its nostrils. The baboon was looking straight at her, its amber eyes glowing with a dangerous intelligence, and as she watched in horror, it opened its jaws wider and gave an earsplitting screech.

Sky backed instinctively away, and the vision seemed to swirl and melt into her last waking dream. She remembered it so clearly: the watering hole, brimming with blood; the trees like claws tearing at the tumultuous sky. *The same baboon. The same one.* And beneath the baboon, the lion it rode, roaring and buckling in anguish.

Sky gasped, blinked, and snatched her trunk away from the skull. The vision vanished. Once again the night was cool and dark and peaceful, the song of crickets soothing in her ears. Not far away, the water rippled and splashed as some creature waded in to drink.

Sky breathed hard, calming herself. *The creatures in my vision are nothing like the lion and the baboon I met with Great Mother.* She remembered the young lion standing up so bravely to the cheetahs, desperate to save his mother's life. She remembered the baboon's face, furrowed with anxiety and grief as he found out about the death of his troop leader.

Perhaps the vision is of their future? But no—she couldn't believe that of them. The baboon Thorn Middleleaf was the furthest from evil she could imagine. And the Cub of the Stars was his friend!

She was so perplexed, it took her a moment to realize that the crickets and the frogs had stopped singing. There was a sudden, eerie calm.

And then the silence exploded into a riotous commotion. Screams, thrashing, splashing, grunts, and roars: Sky stumbled back in shock, peering around in terror, not knowing which way to run—or even if she should.

The other elephants woke at the racket: some shook themselves awake, others who had lain down were rolling onto their knees and shoving themselves to their feet, trunks raised. Ears flapped in fear and confusion, and Rain trumpeted an alarm.

"Great Mother? Something's happening! Great Mother!"

There was only silence. The elephants looked at one another. Sky felt a coil of unease tighten in her gut. "Great Mother?" she rumbled.

"Where is she?" asked Star, bewildered, drawing a sleepy Moon close to her side.

The sounds of conflict erupted again, shattering the night and waking zebras and gazelles. They circled and brayed, and buffalo stamped and bellowed.

"It's coming from along the lake!" blared Twilight. "Come on!"

Sky spun and cantered along the shoreline as fast as she could, blundering her way through shrubs, sending small animals darting away in fright. Except for Star, keeping Moon protectively at her flank, the rest of the Strider family followed right behind Sky; she could hear their massive feet pounding on the earth, but she didn't look back. The moonlight picked out the landscape in silver, but still Sky almost slipped when she careered onto a mudflat that was churned and deeply pitted. She stumbled to a halt, breathing hard.

The ground was torn up, plants and shrubs trampled and crushed. "There's been a fight!" she cried to her aunts in dismay. There was a horrible, cold knot in her stomach. "Where is Great Mother?"

Sky saw the old elephant before her aunts had even caught up with her. A massive, humped shape sprawled in the water, a little way from shore. Tiny waves lapped around it, stained oddly dark.

With a squeal of distress, Sky plunged into the water and lurched toward the ominous form. Behind her, the herd were trumpeting in horror, and she heard the echoing splashes of their feet as they waded frantically after her.

Great Mother lay so still. Sky knew before she reached her side that she was dead.

Sky flung herself against the great matriarch's body, pressing her head to the lifeless flank, stroking the tough hide desperately with her trunk. "Great Mother. Oh, Great Mother, *no.*"

Her aunts surrounded the body, caressing it, rumbling and trumpeting with grief. Sky felt a trunk rub her head gently, trying to comfort her.

"How has this happened?" cried Twilight.

"Look," said Comet grimly. With her trunk she gently touched one of the ugly gashes on Great Mother's flank. Sky could see, too, that one of her tusks had been snapped off.

"She's been murdered!" cried Sky.

There was silence all around her. Every elephant could see that it was true. Comet pulled Sky to her flank, cuddling her close with her huge trunk.

"Why would anyone harm Great Mother?" sobbed Sky. She flinched as a crocodile drifted by, farther out, smirking. Crocodiles didn't follow the Code. "You?" she gasped, knowing full well the creature could not reply.

But Rain shook her head slowly. "I don't think so, Sky. Even a big crocodile would struggle to overcome Great Mother. And they would have . . . they'd have . . ." She swallowed. ". . . Eaten her."

"Who, then? Hippos?" Sky knew how dangerous hippopotamuses could be. "Aunt Comet! Aunt Twilight! Who would *do* this?"

"I don't know." Comet's eyes were dark and moist with grief. "I just don't know who *would* hurt Great Mother."

"What will we do?" wailed Sky desperately.

"There's nothing we can do, young one," murmured Rain, caressing her ear gently. "All we can do is watch over her. We can't help Great Mother now, but there are still dangers in the water." She lifted her trunk fiercely. "No other enemy must come near her."

But Sky's mind was reeling still. *I knew there was danger at the watering hole. And I was right.*

She raised her head as she heard more splashing: Star was approaching now, leading a fearful Moon. The little elephant was trembling at his mother's side, and his eyes were wide with terror. "What happened? Why is Great Mother lying in the water?"

"Oh, Moon." Unable to move, Sky reached out her trunk to draw him close to her. The torn, lifeless body in the water was the most horrific thing she had ever seen, yet she couldn't tear her eyes away from her beloved grandmother.

Star edged close to Moon's other flank once more, so that the little elephant was protected and surrounded. *That's good,* thought Sky numbly. *We can comfort him, even though there's no comfort for any of us.*

"Great Mother has left us, my little one," whispered Star. "She didn't want to, but she has."

Sky lost track of time in her grief and didn't notice the lightening of the sky until finally the sun began to rise. The Strider family stood their ground, silently watching the body, as the colors of Bravelands came alive. And with it, the horror. Around Great Mother's corpse, the silver water was stained dark with blood. Unable to look at the terrible wounds themselves, Sky made herself focus only on the broken stump of Great Mother's tusk, where at least there was no blood. Her breathing echoed loudly in her own ears; she concentrated on the sound of it, barely able to think. *Nothing makes sense anymore.*

"Sky was right," said Twilight, bowing her head with a tormented sigh. "We should never have come to the watering hole."

Sky's aching heart was so heavy inside her, it was hard to move. *My visions were true. The lion and the baboon came. The watering hole turned red with blood: Great Mother's blood.* But slowly, through the grief, a clear thought formed in her head. *Great Mother will tell me what we should do next. She won't abandon us. I know she won't.*

Trembling, she waded through the water toward the great head and the broken tusk. *Show me, Great Mother. Please.*

Sky stretched out her trunk and delicately touched the sad, cracked stump. She closed her eyes and waited for the vision Great Mother would send her.

The water rippled, silver and clear; the breeze rustled twig and fern and leaf. A bee-eater flew from bush to bush in a flash of blue and russet and gold. The colors did not blur; the landscape did not shimmer and turn pale.

And Sky saw no dream, vision.

Nothing at all.

EPILOGUE

High, high above the plains, Windrider soared, resting on the currents, feathers twitching and flaring. Below her, Bravelands stretched to what seemed an eternity; the skies were blue and dazzlingly bright. Not a cloud or a storm or even a whirling dust devil stirred the air.

So the violent wave of shock came from nowhere. Windrider was flung off balance by the unseen force, shuddering through her from wingtip to wingtip. She spun and flailed for terrifying moments before she could balance herself. Glancing back, she saw her whole flock flapping in turmoil, eyes stunned. They, too, had felt the unnerving gust of power.

"My brothers and sisters!" rasped Windrider, braking in the air and beating her wings. "Something terrible has disturbed Bravelands!"

"Did you sense the source?" croaked Blackwing. "We will follow you down."

Windrider banked and swooped, knowing her flock was right behind her. Below her the plains rushed past in a blur of gold and green. Far off in the sky, she could see the distant black dots of more vultures, all converging ominously on the same spot. Windrider's heart twisted with dread.

Windrider skimmed across a ravine, a deep green slash in the grassland where gazelles browsed and grazed. Beyond it, the secretive canopy of a forest sprawled like a great dark flower; baboons raced through the treetops, screeching and pointing as they gazed up at her. On the open plains beyond that, a pride of lions lay basking in sunlight. One of them, a youngster, rose half to his paws, staring at the vultures; she had seen him before, she was sure, but there was no time to wonder.

In moments the watering hole came into view, the great spreading silver lake where the herds of Bravelands gathered. A family of elephants clustered on the bank, huddling close together as if for comfort.

There, in the shallow rippling waters, lay a body she knew with every fiber of her being.

Great Mother.

Grief shivered through Windrider, bitter and sharp. Stretching out her huge black wings, she flapped down to settle on Great Mother's flank. She flinched. *Cold already.*

Her flock swooped and hopped down behind her; then the sky was full of vultures, a chaos of wings that beat and calmed and settled until Great Mother was covered in the birds, their black wings outstretched. When there was no space left on the matriarch's lifeless form, the vultures crowded onto trees and bushes, and onto the muddy bank.

This is one body we will not eat, Windrider knew. *We will protect her.* She lifted up her head and let out a great cry of mourning; the other vulture flocks added their voices to hers until the air resounded with their rasping, croaking tribute.

Windrider paused as the clamor rose around her. She swiveled her head. "Do you smell it, Blackwing? Do you taste it?"

"The scent in the sky?" He nodded once.

"Do you know what it is?" she asked him. "Something we have not tasted for our lifetimes, Blackwing, for though it is slow and constant, it happens so slowly it can't be noticed."

He tilted his head. "And now?"

"Now it comes fast; fast enough to be dangerous. Change, Blackwing. What you smell on the Bravelands sky is—change."

A NEW WARRIORS ADVENTURE HAS BEGUN

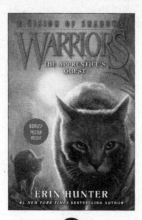

1

2

3

Alderpaw, son of Bramblestar and Squirrelflight,
must embark on a treacherous journey
to save the Clans from a mysterious threat.

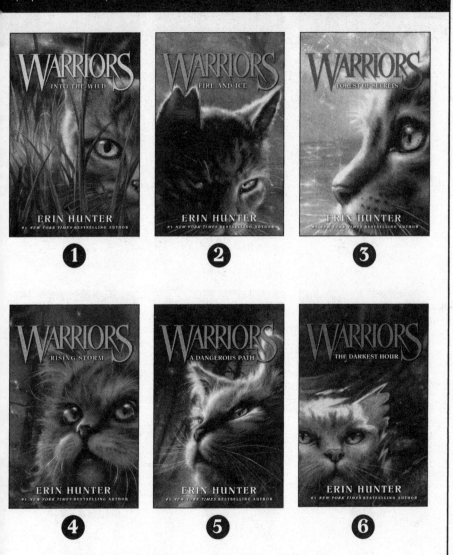

WARRIORS: THE NEW PROPHECY

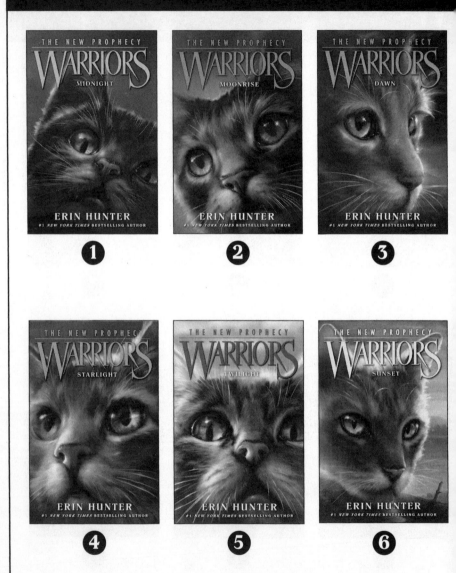

In the second series, follow the next generation of heroic cats as they set off on a quest to save the Clans from destruction.

HARPER
An Imprint of HarperCollinsPublishers

www.warriorcats.com

WARRIORS: POWER OF THREE

POWER OF THREE
WARRIORS
THE SIGHT
ERIN HUNTER
#1 NEW YORK TIMES BESTSELLING AUTHOR

1

POWER OF THREE
WARRIORS
DARK RIVER
ERIN HUNTER
#1 NEW YORK TIMES BESTSELLING AUTHOR

2

POWER OF THREE
WARRIORS
OUTCAST
ERIN HUNTER
#1 NEW YORK TIMES BESTSELLING AUTHOR

3

POWER OF THREE
WARRIORS
ECLIPSE
ERIN HUNTER
#1 NEW YORK TIMES BESTSELLING AUTHOR

4

POWER OF THREE
WARRIORS
LONG SHADOWS
ERIN HUNTER
#1 NEW YORK TIMES BESTSELLING AUTHOR

5

POWER OF THREE
WARRIORS
SUNRISE
ERIN HUNTER
#1 NEW YORK TIMES BESTSELLING AUTHOR

6

In the third series, Firestar's grandchildren begin their training as warrior cats. Prophecy foretells that they will hold more power than any cats before them.

HARPER
An Imprint of HarperCollinsPublishers

www.warriorcats.com

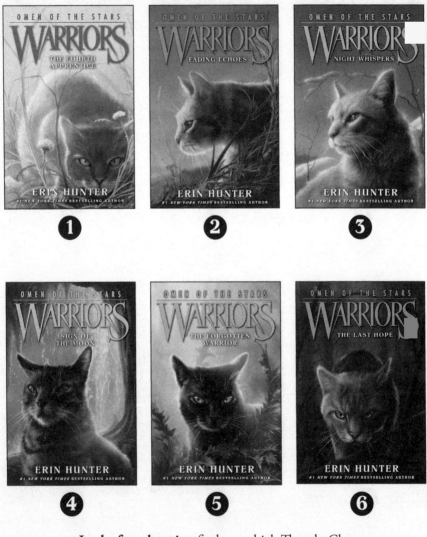

WARRIORS: OMEN OF THE STARS

In the fourth series, find out which ThunderClan apprentice will complete the prophecy.

WARRIORS: DAWN OF THE CLANS

In this prequel series,
discover how the warrior Clans came to be.

HARPER
An Imprint of HarperCollinsPublishers

www.warriorcats.com

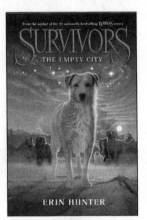

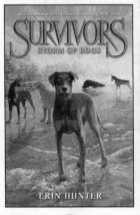

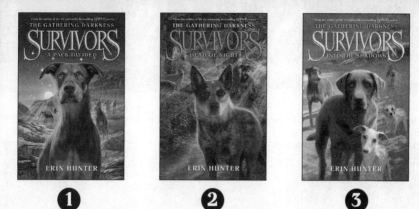

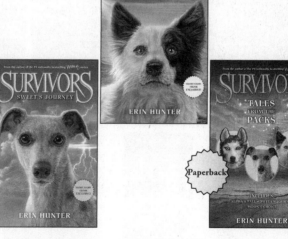